BECKONING
TRAILS

EMILIE LORING

BECKONING
TRAILS

MATTITUCK

Republished 1978 by Special Arrangement
with Little, Brown and Company

Copyright ©1947, 1975 by Robert M. Loring

Library of Congress Cataloging in Publication Data
Loring, Emilie Baker.
  Beckoning trails.

  Reprint of the ed. published by Little, Brown, Boston.
  I. Title.
[PS3.L8938Bc8]   [PS3523.0645]   813'.5'2   76-29708
ISBN 0-88411-351-5

AEONIAN PRESS, INC.
Box 1200
Mattituck, New York 11952

Manufactured in the United States of America

I

"HEAVEN can't be more peaceful," Deborah Randall confided to her reflection in the mirrored wall of a bathroom at Beechcroft, her grandmother's twenty-five-room house in a college town among New England hills.

The looking-glass girl returned her smile. All that was visible of her was a colorless face lighted by shining gray eyes, topped by a short curly mass of blue-black hair which rose from the scented foam of bath crystals in the tub.

"I still can't realize that you are a lady of leisure," she told the girl now looking back at her gravely. After three years as secretary to the head of one of the important government bureaus—for six ten-hour days each week—Nurses' Aide evenings and often Sundays, she had picked up a cold bug and because she was overtired, it, and the fog of depression which had accompanied it, had lingered through July and August and now it was the first of September. Her frightened boss had ordered her on vacation with definite instructions to live out of doors and not to return till the new Congress convened in January, when he would need her desperately.

She drew a deep sigh of relaxation. This was the life. Wonderful to be away from crowds. A knock on the door roused her from the dormouse doze into which she was slipping, a state of suspended animation not to be encouraged in a full bath.

"Who is it?" She yawned and stretched luxuriously.

"Miss Debby, are you plannin' to wear pants at dinner?" inquired Sarah Allen, bred-in-the-bone New Englander who had been housekeeper at Beechcroft for years.

"Pants?" Deborah sat up so suddenly that bubbles in the tub rose like a tidal wave. "Certainly not. Where did you pick up that crazy idea, Sal?"

"I just opened your suitcase, you said your clothes for the evening were in it, that your trunks would be comin' along later, and there was a white coat and pants. I thought perhaps because you'd come from Washington where I hear there's queer goin's on," she sniffed disdain, "you might have taken to wearin'—"

Without waiting for the end of the sentence, dripping with

moisture, sparkling with iridescence, Debby did a mermaid rising from foam. Tying the sash of her white toweling bathrobe she entered the bedroom with its mayflower pink walls and Wedgwood blue hangings and furnishings. Sarah Allen straightened her tall, angular, black silk-clad figure which had been bent over a suitcase on a rack at the foot of the bed. She pushed up the steel-bowed spectacles which had slipped down on the sharp ridge of her nose.

"My sakes, you smell sweet, Debby, like the white lilac hedge in spring."

"Like a whole hedge of white lilacs? My word, I must have overdone the bath crystals. Sal? Sal, do you realize that I'm free, free? My heart is so light it's skipping from mountaintop to mountaintop."

"You'd better slide down them mountains quick, Debby, you're all keyed up! 'Tain't natural. You'll go to pieces."

"Me, go to pieces with three months' vacation ahead? Sal, you're crazy."

"Maybe I am, but, you better quiet down. You look awful pretty with your hair curled all over your head like that." The nasal voice was warm with affection. "Just like the black-haired kid that come to visit your grandmother the year after she married millionaire Roger Stewart who owned this place. My sakes, but you were a tomboy, your clothes always torn an'—"

"Soft-pedal my sinful past, Sal. Concentrate on this bag. It isn't mine." She frowned down at the cowhide case which on the outside was like hers, but inside revealed white trousers folded over a strap in the cover and a matching dinner jacket below instead of the lime-green and turquoise sheer evening frock she had interred tenderly in tissue paper. "Who brought up this?"

"The new houseboy. He ain't more'n sixteen. Only person I could find for the job. It's about all my life is worth to get help for the inside of this great place, to say nothin' of the outside. As for the faculty wives, they haven't had hired help for four years. Beats me why anyone wants two hundred acres, a wooded island on the lake with a log cabin, four small houses, greenhouses, three barns and the livestock that goes with the last."

"Perhaps Molly B. doesn't. You can't get rid of big places these days. No one wants the care."

"Madam Roger Stewart may not, but Molly Burton, author, likes it fine. She claims she works better here. Perhaps she does, she writes real good. Did you know she'd hired Stella Dane for her secretary?"

"The little girl with whom I played when I visited here?"

2

"That's her. The Wild Danes, folks called 'em. They were supposed to be awful rich, kept a racin' stable. They aren't so wild now. Stella and two sons is all that's left. I've heard their big house is mortgaged from roof to cellar and that Judge Lander holds the mortgage."

"I'm sorry for Stella. I never really liked her. I thought she was a double-crosser, but it must have been terribly hard to see that beautiful home slipping away."

"She's got a good job now typin'. I have a feelin' that in Molly Burton's next book there'll be a dead body floatin' face down in the swimmin' pool front of the game house. She had a map of the grounds pinned up on the wall of her workroom all winter, an' that pool marked with a red X."

"A dead body in the swimming pool. You do have the most cheerful ideas, Sal. From now on I shall slink past with my eyes closed. Hunt up the houseboy. Tell him to find out in which room he left a bag like this, get it and bring it here."

"I will, but I have a feelin' he isn't bright as a button, that he won't remember. Six guests besides you arrived within the last two hours. 'Tain't no wonder he got the bags mixed."

"Six arrivals within an hour. My word, must I go the rounds knocking on doors to find my clothes? That means that Molly B.—Madam Stewart to you—has finished her latest whodunit. She never has guests when the WOMAN AT WORK sign is out, till the manuscript is in the hands of the magazine editor or her publisher. Who's here?" As she asked the question her fingers burrowed into the bag in the hope of finding a clue to the owner. Was a man at this moment investigating hers for the same reason?

No wonder the thought set her pulses quick-stepping. Suppose he found her loose-leaf diary? Suppose he opened it? Suppose he read even portions of it? Between the black covers were recorded her experiences and reactions during the three most critical years of her life; estimates of the men and women under and with whom she had worked—some of the men were making current history; scraps of inter-bureau politics; confidential opinions of her boss which if given publicity might mean out for him. The diary had been her refuge in years of disillusionment, homesickness and heartache, in short it was her soul laid bare. She rated this attack of screamies for not locking the bag after she had opened it on the train.

"Sophy Brandt is here, of course." Sniff, sniff. Sarah was answering the question she had forgotten she had asked. "Because she was your grandmother's roommate at college she's always here when there's guests, everlastin'ly knittin'. I have a feelin' she knows that that, and card playin', shows

3

off her beautiful hands and rings. I guess she's glad of the invite, she ain't got much to live on. My stars, how she does mimic the townspeople an' everyone else for that matter. She's got a cruel tongue."

"I wonder why she doesn't visit one of her two married sons occasionally?"

"I guess her daughters-in-law can't stand her round everlastin'ly talkin' about how old and useless she is till a man near her age appears, then she's all smiles an' blushes. You'd never catch Madam Stewart bein' kittenish. Beats me how two women so near an age can be so different."

"Molly B. has her work, Sal. I've observed that the man or woman with a big interest in life never is age-conscious. They are too busy to count passing years."

"I guess you're right, I know I don't have time. Judge Lander, your grandmother's lawyer, is here—someone's been stealin' her writin' for radio. Usually he has the guest suite in the game house, but the painters ain't quite through there —it's bein' redecorated, so he's in the left wing."

"It's a beautiful apartment. I don't wonder Prexy likes to have guests of the college put up there. Who else is here?"

"Professor Burke Romney, the new man for the Science Center, he's so sad and sorry-lookin' he ought to be in the movies. As if that wasn't enough, your cousin Sam Farr, he's Dean of Students now, an' his wife moved in today while their house on the campus is bein' freshened up. Why they couldn't stay at the Inn beats me—"

Deborah lost the rest of the sentence as her fingers touched something hard. She carefully lifted a fold of white coat, dropped it quickly to cover an ivory-handled revolver. Curious thing to carry on a country house visit. It gave her the shivers. She closed the suitcase. Time was flying and her diary was in strange hands.

"Find the houseboy quick, Sal. Whoever owns this bag, if he has mine, must be on the verge of a nervous breakdown for fear he will have to appear at dinner in a lime and blue sheer. Hurry. It is almost time for sherry in the hall."

"You'd better be ready to put on that dress when I find it." Sarah seized the handle of the suitcase. She paused at the door. " 'Tain't fair for you not to be prepared, Debby. I've been talkin' and talkin' gettin' up courage to tell you. Clive Warner showed up this afternoon, he's out of the Army, he was a captain, flyin' a plane, to take his old teachin' job. He's goin' to stay in this house."

"Here? Who invited him?"

"Don't shoot, I didn't. He had no place to live, him and a few hundred others, every boardin' house and roomin'

4

house is engaged to overflowin', with three hundred more students comin' than were here last year, some of 'em bringing a wife and kid, so your grandmother took him in."

"Is his wife with him?"

"Not in this house and if anyone would know I oughtta. Now I've got that off my mind I'll go find your bag."

While she showered and dressed Deborah thought of Clive Warner. She had left college in the middle of her junior year to marry him; it was being done then, he was a soldier going into danger. One week before the wedding he had married a girl he had met at camp. She thought of the battle she had waged with herself, whether to return to college and face the battery of questions, or enlist as a WAC and escape them. She had gone to college, had held her head high, had packed her heart in a deep-freeze unit, graduated with honors and immediately had taken a war job in Washington.

As she brushed her hair before the mirror to a satin sheen, she thought of many of his ways she had instinctively distrusted at nineteen; now at twenty-three she recognized them as glaring faults. Except that since his desertion she hadn't trusted any man's protestations of love, the aching, stinging wound to her pride had healed, only the scar tissue remained. She knew now that she had been caught up in the warwedding hysteria. Suppose Clive had her diary? She wouldn't put it past him to read it and use—

"Got the right one this time, Debby." Sarah's entrance followed a knock. She opened a suitcase and spread a lime and turquoise frock with a gleaming silver sequin belt on the bed. "Where was it, Sal?"

"You sound all choked up. Your voice is husky. Drat that boss keepin' you workin' with a cold."

"He didn't keep me working. I wouldn't leave till I had finished a certain job. Who had my suitcase?"

"I didn't stop to ask where the boy found it. He's so fresh I didn't dare find fault for fear he'd up and quit—this country being the land of the free and the home of the brave—I asked Ingrid Johnson to find the owner of the bag with the pants. You'd never think she was a hired companion. She seems more like Madam Stewart's sister. She ought to after the years she's lived with her. Here's your green slip and silver sandals."

"Does my bag look as if it had been mussed?"

"No child, everything's smooth as you packed it, looks like. You shouldn't have put this heavy book in with this swell dress, though."

Deborah picked up the loose-leaf book. It was heavy. Why not when it held a record of the three most important years of her life? Suppose this house burned when she was not here? Her precious diary might go up in smoke! The possibility sent a little shiver along her veins.

"Has Molly B. gone down to the hall, Sal?"

"No. She won't be goin' for fifteen minutes. Somehow it don't seem respectful for you to call your grandmother Molly B., Debby."

"She loves it. I'll run down to see her for a minute."

She strapped the silver sandals, belted a turquoise satin house robe over her lime green slip and with the bulky book under her arm stepped into a cool and softly lighted gallery from which opened countless doors. She stood motionless as she thought of the gay house parties, of the men and girls who had trooped down the beautiful spiral staircase. She blinked back tears. Many of them never would come again.

"It's your job to get those papers."

The fierce whisper drifted from the plant-filled, unlighted bay at the head of the stairs. An indistinct murmur was followed by an impatient whisper, not so restrained this time.

"If you don't, you know the consequences to you."

Deborah's heart skipped a beat and thudded on. In the hope of achieving invisibility she flattened herself against the door of the room she had left. Had she really heard the voice or had Sal's suggestion of a body floating face down in the swimming pool given her the mystery-jitters? She held her breath. Listened. A door in the left wing closed softly. Immediately from the same direction floated a man's voice singing:

> From the desert I come to thee
> On my Arab shod with fire.

Who had a radio in that part of the house? She glanced toward the bay. No movement there. There must have been two persons talking. Had they left together? Suppose whoever it was suspected she had overheard? What would happen to her? The shivers again. Curious how every little while her heart, maybe it was her stomach, seemed to drop to her sandals.

Softly she opened the door against which she had been leaning and closed it with a bang. If she were seen now it would appear as if she had just left her room. Humming, "From the desert I come to thee," heart thumping, fearing that she might be grabbed as she passed the bay, she raced down the stairs. Halfway she collided with someone charging up. The impact drove her teeth into her underlip and plumped her back on a stair.

"I'm sorry. I'm terribly sorry," a voice apologized.

6

She looked up into a face bronzed as tanned leather, with hollows beneath the high cheekbones, a straight nose, a large, generous mouth, keen eyes dark as the hair above a broad forehead; the man was a pushover for a romantic lead. The sudden change of his expression to surprised warmth, as if he recognized someone he knew and liked, sent a responsive glow along her veins.

"Is this your usual method of ascending stairs in a strange house," she inquired, "or is it a hangover from Sword and Dagger technique?"

"Leatherneck, division of amphibious warfare, in case you're interested. Is plunging headlong your usual method of going down? Hey, wait a minute. Your lip is bleeding. Boy, am I responsible for that?" He produced a white handkerchief and gently dabbed her mouth. "Don't tell me I have your blood on my conscience."

"Not guilty. It was my fault. Apparently my chin sagged in surprise when I saw you coming and the collision snapped it up. Thanks for the first aid. Now that everything is under control suppose we move on." She noted his broad shoulders, lean waist and hips in gray tropical worsted, the tiny blue ribbon with scarlet bars in the lapel of his coat.

"I am Deborah Randall, Debby to those I like. That bit of world-shaking information out of the way I will remind you that sherry will be served in the hall in fifteen minutes—or less, and that our hostess expects her guests to punch the timeclock on the minute."

"Says you." The stern lines in his face belied the boyishness of his laugh. "You don't look as if you'd be ready to report in fifteen minutes—to say nothing of less—but, perhaps negligee at the sherry hour is the custom of women guests here. I wouldn't know."

"Evidently this is your first visit to Beechcroft. Though an atomic bomb threatens we dress for dinner, Marine. Better be quick and change or it may be your last. Perhaps, though, you won't care if it is?"

"I care, I have just discovered, terrifically. I'll be seeing you." He took the stairs two at a time.

She stood at the door of Molly B.'s living room in the right wing and watched him till he disappeared. Who was he? Professor Burke Romney who had come to teach at the Science Center? No, he couldn't be called "sad and sorry" looking. Could his have been the voice which had declared: "It is your job to get those papers"?

Not unless he had dashed down the left wing stairs, through the hall and up the front, and he wouldn't have had time for that before he crashed into her—or would he? He was a fast mover. Had it been his suitcase that had held the ivory-handled revolver? Even so, he didn't look like a man who would threaten fiercely:

"If you don't, you know the consequences to you."

Someone had said it. She hadn't been dreaming. Who could it be?

II

INGRID JOHNSON opened the door in response to her knock. She was the Junoesque type, tall, with blond hair, classic nose and full red lips, eyes blue as her short dinner frock and as brilliant at the moment as the diamond fringes at her ears. Definitely, handsomely, Norwegian. A welcoming smile widened her large mouth.

"You, at last, Debby. It is good to see you. But, you are not dressed for dinner. Did you not get your bag about which Sarah was in such a dither?"

"She ran it to earth. I'll be ready on time. I have something important to say to Molly B. Beat it, will you, Ingrid?"

"Certainly I will beat it—and quick. Like this." She laughed, closed the girl in and herself out.

Deborah was impressed anew by the spaciousness of the room she entered. Walls and trim and velvet rug were pinky beige. Matching damask hangings framed windows that opened on white lacy-grilled balconies to admit the pungent scent of pine and balsam and the more delicate fragrance from the pink and violet petunias in the balcony boxes, to reveal a glint of blue lake through tall trees and a purple line of hills beyond. An Inness sunset hung above the carved cream and beige marble mantel, the only picture on the walls, the bouffant skirt of a Royal Doulton figurine reflected in the mirrored top of a small table repeated the rich flame color of the painted sky. There were deep chairs covered with damask in soft green and beige and faded rose, and an occasional gay chintz, an Empire sofa and a marquetry desk that were museum pieces. Tables held softly shaded lamps and bowls of flowers. There was a wall of books and a crystal aquarium in which the sunset colors were flashed by swimming, diving goldfish, a tall mirror screen shut off a doorway at one end of the room.

"Had you forgotten what it looked like, Deb?" The amused question brought her eyes to the woman smiling at her from a chair beside a lamp.

"Having shared a small apartment with two girls for the last three years, this room impresses me as being nothing

9

short of palatial, Molly B. That screen is new. It adds a *Through the Looking-glass* touch."

She thoughtfully regarded her grandmother. The tangerine shade of her square-neck, stiff-lace, short dinner frock contributed a faint glow to her gardenia-smooth skin, accentuated the platinum sheen of the waves of her parted hair and the darkness of her laughing eyes, a restrained touch of lipstick brought out the curve of her sensitive mouth. A necklace of diamond links matched the bracelet on her left wrist.

"I was thinking also that you are a dish"—she perched on the arm of a wing chair—"that you look even younger than when I saw you two months ago in Washington and goodness knows you looked young enough then, you the grandmother of a great big girl like me."

"Why shouldn't I look young? Age is a state of mind— and health. Our contract group has just given Sophy Brandt a party to celebrate her sixty-fifth birthday. I fought it tooth and nail. If they start to celebrate mine I'll wring their collective necks good and plenty."

"You've got something there. Why tag a woman like you with the number of her years who earns more with her brain per annum than the salary of the President of the United States?"

"And more shame to the government that underpays and then taxes him, say I. What happened to your mouth to smear the lipstick? It looks as if it had been kissed and kissed hard. Don't tell me that Clive Warner dared—"

"Why all the excitement? Suppose he did? You invited him to stay here, I understand, and you knew he was a heel."

"Guilty on the first count, though not entirely responsible. He has come to teach applied physics at the Science Center, the subject he was teaching when he went into the service. In very poor taste for him to apply for the job—there is more than the return of the native behind it, my mystery scout warns me; but, with the influx of GIs the majority of whom appear to be hell bent for the study of engineering science and allied subjects—charge that up to the atomic bomb— every instructor we can corral is needed."

"Even so, why invite him here after his walkout on me?"

"He couldn't find a place to live, all dormitories, fraternities, sororities, boarding and lodging houses are full up. Prexy, blandly ignoring past events, asked me to take him in till he found a place. As my husband, Roger Stewart, was head of the board of trustees and made the Science Center possible, I am considered a sort of godmother to the college. I didn't want to do it, but, the world is full of people who are doing things they don't want to do. Why should I be an exception? I was sure that Clive Warner means nothing in your life or I wouldn't have taken him in if he had had to bunk on a bench on the campus."

"Don't worry about the effect on me. I was in luck. No men in my life wanted. I'm all set to be a career woman. The war rather put that expression out of date, didn't it? Is Clive's wife here?"

"Hadn't you heard? He and Odile are divorced. While he was fighting in the Pacific theater she was lonely. As soon as matters could be legally arranged she married the man twenty years older with whom she had been running around. That's the story. What happened to your mouth?" Deborah described the encounter on the stairs.

"Who is he? Another teacher?"

"No. He is Timothy Grant, the son of Roger Stewart's daughter, Cobina, and now co-heir with me to the Stewart estate."

"I had forgotten there was a son. He was always away at school when I visited you."

"He is a scientific engineer like his grandfather. Purposeful, is my word for him. He knows what he wants and is going after it, won't stop till he gets it. Good-looking, isn't he?"

"Super. Wasn't there some sort of family row between father and daughter?"

"Yes. 'Coby,' they called her, had a furious temper. She wouldn't come to Beechcroft after her father and I were married. When she married Grant, who was Dean of the college, Roger gave her that charming old house on the campus. After her husband's death she closed it and made her headquarters in New York. Although it has been terribly needed she has refused to rent or sell it."

"I remember it, lovely, velvety, pinkish brick with four tall white pillars, southern fashion, an adorable garden from which there is a gorgeous view of the hill-rimmed lake."

"That's the one. She shared equally with me in her father's large fortune and ownership of the laboratories from which that fortune had come, but this estate was left to me unconditionally. She was furious, contended that it should have come to her for her son. She resented her father's marriage."

"Why? Nothing grubby about your family background and as Molly Burton you had become internationally known as a successful writer of whodunits."

"And how I worked to get there." She closed her eyes and leaned her head against the tall back of the chair. "I was a student at a coed college, just eighteen, when Bill Randall, my professor in English, and I fell in love. We married. Your father came along. Then, as another child was

11

on the way, Bill became helpless. We had nothing saved. I lost the new baby. Our living, the care and support of an invalid and small boy were entirely up to me. I had grown up in a family of writers, whatever work I did had to be something I could do at home. Bill encouraged me to try fiction; at first he could help me. I worked nights when the house was quiet. I *had* to make good. I was lucky. My first novel made a slight stir."

"I wouldn't call ten printings 'slight.' "

"Heavenly day, how I worked after that. Before my husband died I was able to provide professional care for him. I had counted on our son, your father, as a confidant and comfort as I grew older, then five years ago he and your mother slipped away together." She blinked long lashes.

"Why am I telling you all this which you have heard a dozen times before? Good heavens, I haven't reached the thrice-told-tale age, have I? Talking of my marriage to Roger Stewart brought the memory of what had gone before sweeping back. I admired him, his money meant nothing, I was earning plenty myself, but, we enjoyed the same things, he was enormously proud of what I had accomplished. We were great companions, and Debby, in the last analysis, the good companion is what counts most in marriage."

"That's right. I suppose Coby was jealous of you."

"That may have started it. She and her father had a furious quarrel and he swore he never would see her again. She refused to allow Tim to visit here; that hurt Roger cruelly, he had counted on the boy's following his profession and, in time, heading the Science Center. When Judge Lander, his legal adviser, though many years younger, routed out a scandal in which Cobina Grant figured, her goose was cooked to a crisp. She came to the Inn during Roger's last illness and begged to see him. He refused. I tried to change his mind but he would close his eyes and say, 'No. Don't *talk* about it.' His physician forbade the mention of her name."

"What has brought the son here now?"

"His mother died a year ago. Recently he returned after four years in the amphibious service—he was a major. He wrote from Washington that now that his mother's income had reverted to him, he would like to know more of the source from which it came, that he had learned from her diary of her bitterness toward her father, that there was much to be explained, that he hoped he and I could blot out the feud and become friends."

"Apparently you have. Does he intend to stay in this town?"

"He has kept his residence here, wants to live in his house.

12

When he arrived a month ago he told me he would like a job at the lab. He was here two weeks. At the end of that time Prexy asked him to head the Science Center to take the place of the man who has been requisitioned by the War Department. Tim requested time to think it over, went back to Washington, and M.I.T., and returned about an hour ago. I don't know what or if he decided. Of course the appointment will have to be okayed by the trustees."

"Head of the Science Center. That's going some for a man his age. What did Henry Lander, your guide, philosopher and friend, say to his coming to this house? Apparently he had it in for his mother."

"He said a lot. 'Don't see him. He is after this property.' The Judge can't dictate to me. He was so emphatic that I wrote Tim Grant to come. He has a sensational service record as a leader and organizer. I'm not so cocky—I wasn't calling you," she declared as a black cocker spaniel dashed in from the balcony. "Go speak to Debby."

The dog sniffed at the blue house coat, jumped into the chair on the arm of which the girl was perched, and with nose on his fluffy paws regarded her with eyes shining like jet buttons. She stroked his silky head.

"He's a beaut. Where did he come from?"

"I needed a dog for a model. He was Best of Show."

"Is it to be assumed that he discovers the dead body in the latest story?"

"How did you guess?" Molly B.'s mouth tipped up at the corners, her eyes shone with laughter. "As I was saying, I'm not so cocky about the desirability of Tim Grant's presence in this house as I was. I am sure Henry Lander will try to block his appointment to head the Science Center. I have a premonition of trouble."

"It is only your plot-nerve tuning up. Prexy must think the late Major's arrival the answer to prayer, he probably made plenty of inquiries about him before he offered the job. That college president isn't taking on a pig in a poke. Why worry about Judge Lander? He is too keen about you and your business to risk an insult to your guest, and Tim Grant looks as if he had been around enough to keep his hands off the legal throat if he did."

"I hope you are right, Deb, but, in the words of Sarah Allen, 'I have a feelin'' there will be fireworks, perhaps bombs, before, or if, Tim is appointed. Enough about me and my problems. You can't know how happy I am to have you here. Now that the drastic need of your help in Washington is over I hope you will make your home with me and give the college and the town that grew up around it the benefit of what you have learned in the bigger world outside. With the influx of GI wives, you can help immeasurably. You have proved an ace secretary, time to polish other facets of your mind. Perhaps already you have begun. Perhaps that is a manuscript clutched under your arm or do those black covers contain your last will and testament?"

"Wrong guess. They contain an intimate record of my life for the last three years. While I am here I intend to edit the diary. You have given me an idea. Why not polish the creative facets of my mind? I can help with the GI wives also. Why should you be the only writer in the family?"

"I shouldn't, not with your flair for description and perceptive observation. You showed by your courage in returning to college after the breakup with Clive Warner that you can take disappointment, and believe me, taking disappointment on the chin and keeping on, everlastingly keeping on, is one of the toughest tests on the rocky road of authorship. I'll turn over my log cabin workshop on the island to you. Ask Sarah for the key."

"Thanks. May I put the diary in your safe where it will be secure from fire or inspection?"

"Of course." At the desk Madam Stewart wrote on a slip of white paper. "Here is the combination. Press the top of the panel at the right of the fireplace."

The panel responded to pressure. On her knees Deborah turned a small steel knob, consulted directions, turned, reversed, turned again. The safe door swung open revealing three laden shelves.

"Don't cover the folding money, Deb. It is my monthly payroll and cash for incidentals. Stella Dane put it there this morning after Ingrid brought it from the bank. I opened the safe for her. Ingrid has lived with me for years, has seen me through sad days and happy days and refuses to know the combination though important papers of hers are there."

"Has she explained why?"

"No. She doesn't confide in me as she used to. I'm worried about her. She hasn't heard from the aviator brother we visited in Norway before the war. She suspects he was active in the underground and thinks he may have been shot as a hostage. I have a suspicion she has hired a shyster lawyer to trace him, that she is using her money for something or someone besides herself, but, when you come to that, who isn't?"

"It's your job to get the papers."

The fierce whisper drifted through Deborah's memory like a sinister ghost as she glanced into the safe with its neat files of papers and velvet and satin jewel cases. Had it been the threat of a shyster lawyer she had overheard? That was

14

a dumb thought. He wouldn't be staying in the house and the soft closing of a door in the left wing had followed the second whisper.

"Would Ingrid employ a lawyer with Judge Lander practically in the family?" she inquired, as she made room for the bulky notebook on top of files of papers in the lower compartment. It filled the space between them and the shelf above.

"She doesn't like him. In all the years she has been with me I have never discovered the reason. Most women do."

She had something there, Debby told herself. The man was a wolf, not that he had ever whistled to her but she knew his type. They ran in packs in Washington. She never had trusted him. She hated the little intimate squeeze when he shook hands. She could understand Ingrid's reaction. She closed the safe door, slid the panel into place and rose from her knees.

"I now feel safe about my diary. I wish you wouldn't keep so many jewels in the house, Molly B. A thief trying to steal them might hurt you."

"I want them where I can enjoy them, what fun would they be locked in my deposit box at the bank? I might as well not have them. Roger gave me many jewels but some of those cases represent a novel. I make myself a present on a book's birthday to square never celebrating my own. Hold on to the combination, Deb, you may want to refer to the loose-leaf book when I am not here. Don't begin work yet. Keep out of doors till you get back your lovely color. You are too pale."

As Deborah tucked the slip of white paper into the deep V of her house coat, Ingrid entered.

"Still here and not dressed, Debby? It is time for sherry in the hall. Better scram."

As in her room Deborah slipped the lime and turquoise sheer over her dark hair, she remembered the safe combination. It should be locked in the desk. Where was it? Had it fallen when she removed the house coat? It wasn't on the floor. It wasn't in the room. Had she dropped it on the stairs? Suppose the person who had fiercely demanded "papers" found it? Would it be recognized for what it was and be used to further theft? That was a breath-snatching thought.

III

DEBORAH went down the spiral staircase with its beautiful harp balustrade step by slow step, looking at each tread. No slip of white paper to be seen. Had it been picked up? Halfway down the second flight she stopped and looked into the hall below with its black and white tiled floor, rich-toned Persian rugs, huge fireplace where a low fire burned, and its carved high-back chairs. The bleached cypress paneling made a perfect background for the assembled guests, for the human comedy being staged to the soft, radioed music of strings playing "To Each His Own," a setting which belonged in a past era of outsize, magnificent houses.

The chair in which Molly B. sat was of the throne variety —trust her for a touch of drama. Her tangerine frock was a foil to the pale blue of Sophy Brandt's, a small woman with knitting needles and the diamonds on her fingers flashing, who occupied a companion chair beside her hostess. Her blonde transformation was a mass of tortuous waves and curls, a bang reached almost to her heavily blackened eyebrows. A peaches and cream make-up, plus artistically applied eye shadow, gave her round face a touch of girlishness. Her reddened mouth drooped at the corners.

The girl in white must be Stella Dane. She was thin, almost to attenuation; pretty, though. Her hair, which reached her shoulders in a page-boy bob, shone like silver gilt. Her mouth would be lovely if she didn't appear so darn sorry for herself. Was it because she had had to go to work? Was the tall thin-faced man Burke Romney, the new science professor, who was adoring her with his eyes? To Sarah's "sad and sorry" she would add sinister. As he talked he raked his dark hair with long, bony fingers, with the result that he looked like the picture of an aboriginal head hunter. A girl he loved had better watch her step.

There was a dark red carnation in the lapel of Judge Lander's black dinner jacket. No wonder most women went all out for him. A six-footer, just heavy enough for his height, with a bold, old-man-of-the-mountain profile, clear skin with a touch of red at the cheekbones, and wavy white hair, he must be in the late fifties. His keen dark eyes could appraise, caress, invite a woman, could turn the blood of a lying witness to ice. At the moment his charm was turned on at high. He was toasting Tilly Farr, whose mimosa yellow satin frock made her lovely dark eyes and hair seem even darker.

The gold charms of her bracelet jingled as she raised her glass of sherry in response. Her tall, blond husband, Sam, in white—had it been his bag that had been brought to her room?—slouched against the mantel, his blue eyes half covered by heavy lids. His expression sent a disturbing quiver along Deborah's nerves. He had known Tilly practically all their lives. He must realize that flirtations, which were her meat, desperate as they were, never lasted. Perhaps he was fed up with them. One would never know from him. He was the quiet, pipe-smoking type. Was a storm of anger gathering beneath the surface? Was the ivory-handled revolver his? Why was she getting the shivers over Sam, whom she loved as she would a brother?

Ingrid Johnson turned from twisting the radio dial. Her blue eyes flamed as she looked at Tilly with her upraised glass. Why? Did she resent her response to the Judge? Could it be because of Sam? Perhaps she was in love with him. They were about of an age. That was a thought.

"At long last. Enter the late Miss Randall."

Clive Warner's greeting focused attention on her. Time was when his caressing voice and eyes would have set her pulses racing, but those had been the pulses of a nineteen-year-old girl. He was wearing white dinner clothes. Perhaps it had been his bag Sarah had opened in her room. The Judge and Romney were in black. The man with whom she had collided on the stairs was lighting a cigarette and listening to Stella Dane, his dark head bent. He was in white. That made three potential owners of the ivory-handled revolver. If it were his, perhaps Judge Lander wouldn't be so safe as she had thought. That was a grisly idea.

"Shall I tell you I love you?"

A tenor voice singing Cole Porter's song came over the air. Seemingly asking the same question, Tim Grant's laughing eyes met hers. What fun. She hadn't felt this sense of excitement when meeting a new man for years. Not since she had met Clive Warner. That meeting hadn't accelerated her pulses to their present quickstep. In the top-of-the-mountain mood she had recaptured since her arrival at Beechcroft, she nodded assent and ran down the stairs.

Scragg, the lean, saturnine butler, in dark blue livery with silver buttons, handed Madam Stewart a slip of white paper. Deborah drew a deep breath of relief. The safe combination had been found. With a mysterious voice at loose in the house demanding "papers" the memory of the lost directions would have been a major nightmare to her.

The delicious dinner was served on a satin-smooth mahogany Chippendale table, which was enriched with choice lace doilies and gleaming silver. Mammoth pink dahlias in the center matched the tall, thin tapers in superb gold-embossed crystal candlesticks which in turn matched the glasses at each place. The deepest green of the exquisitely colored, hand-blocked French scenic wallpaper was repeated in silken hangings at the open long windows and wide door to an enclosed porch. Dazzling crystal prisms of the huge chandelier chimed with each movement in the room. The chairs were Hepplewhite. The sideboard held two large silver wine coolers full of glistening dark green huckleberry branches.

Nothing in the room appeared to have changed since she was here a year ago, Deborah thought—how about the lives of the persons at the table? Had Molly B.'s been changed by Tim Grant, seated at her right? She appeared completely sold on him. At the moment he was listening to Stella Dane, who had switched on the fascination-current with particular emphasis on eyework.

Sophy Brandt at the foot of the table was giving a vitriolic imitation of the gardener, who was a character, for the amusement of Henry Lander at her right. The butler's eyes were murderous as they rested on her for a second. Ingrid Johnson at her left was at her sparkling best. There was a hint of appraisal in the Judge's eyes as he watched her. Was he thinking he had missed something in years past in not appreciating her charm?

Conversation was always interesting in Molly B.'s house. Tonight it ranged over the problems inherent in the occupation of foreign countries; the great contributions scientists had made to the Army, the Navy and the Air Force in the overwhelming success of amphibious warfare; the devastating possibilities of the atomic bomb; the lack of housing accommodations for returning servicemen; nationwide strikes, portal-to-portal pay, subjects which were being discussed in homes like this all over the land.

Later when card tables were set out in the book-walled library the shivers that had crept over Deborah at intervals combined in one frigid wave of spiritual tumult, as if her heart and soul were being broken and tossed as she had seen ice spin and crash in a spring breakup, as if her emotions which she kept buried deep had surged to the top. Was this the "go-to-pieces" state Sarah Allen had prophesied? Was it a return of the flu? Surely she wasn't such a goon that seeing Clive Warner would drag her self-control from its mooring and that was what was happening. She must make her getaway and fast.

She crossed to the long window open on the balcony in front of which her grandmother was standing beside Judge Lander. She heard him say impatiently:

"I see that Grant is back. You let yourself in for trouble when you invited him here, Molly B. I warn you now, I shall fight his appointment as head of the Science Center and I have influence. He is after Beechcroft, intends to own it if he has to marry your granddaughter to get it."

"Is that so? That would interfere with your game, something tells me, Judge." Tim Grant's voice was hoarse with fury. Evidently he had been smoking on the balcony behind them. Remembering Molly B.'s "I have a feelin' there will be fireworks, perhaps bombs," Deborah flung herself into the breach.

"Will you excuse me from cards, Molly B.?" Her throat tightened over what threatened to be a sob.

"Of course, honey. Ingrid will take your place." Madam Stewart glanced from Grant, taut and threatening, to Lander. "Tim, Judge, understand, both of you, that I will not permit quarreling in my house."

Deborah didn't wait for their response. She ran into the hall. Clive Warner, coming down the stairs, called:

"Wait, Deb, I have a lot to say—"

She shook her head and raced on. Across the broad terrace. Down the steps. Along the garden path, her frock shaking fragrance from the roses as it swished by. Waving leaves wove patterns on a moonlit lawn terraced to the lake.

"He intends to own it if he has to marry your granddaughter," the words singsonged an accompaniment to her flight. Under a great pine she flung herself to the ground and face on her crossed arms let the storm break. Why? Why was she crying, she demanded of herself as long, shuddering sobs shook her body.

"You will ruin that perfect frock on this dew-drenched grass, darling," a man's voice warned.

A turn. A spring. She was on her feet. The moon was broadcasting light like nobody's business. It silvered Tim Grant's white clothes as he faced her with a cigarette between his fingers, his lips widened in a smile, his grave eyes intent. The silence was broken only by the chirp of a lonely cricket and her spasmodic breathing.

"W-what do you m-mean, stealing up on me, c-calling me d-darling?"

"Don't talk."

She brushed impatient fingers across long drenched lashes.

19

He drew a handkerchief from his breast pocket and gently wiped the tears from her cheeks.

"Administering first aid is getting to be a habit with me, isn't it?" As her breath still came in little convulsive gasps he suggested, "Let's sit on the bench under the pine while you tell me what has made you unhappy so suddenly. I can't believe you are the lighthearted girl I met head-on coming up the stairs."

The tempest of emotion was passing but it still shook her like the thunder of a storm diminishing in the distance, still caught at her breath. She obeyed the hand on her arm like an automaton under remote control. He dried the bench with his handkerchief.

"Sit here."

"Still l-leatherneck technique?" she inquired with an unsteady attempt at flippancy.

"Not this time. It isn't a command, it's a request." She shook her head in response to the cigarettes he offered. "Mind if I smoke?" Another shake.

Silence, a curious throbbing silence. The light of his cigarette glowed and faded. Her breath came unevenly as she watched the thin spiral of smoke rise and drift away like a fairy spreading gauzy violet skirts in flight. She tried to speak but her voice wouldn't come. As if he sensed her attempt he commented:

"The white, vine-draped colonnade, the game house at the end, look as if they belonged in a world of magic in this light. It wouldn't surprise me to see a mermaid rise from the swimming pool in front of it."

"I c-can see a figure pacing the lawn between g-game house and pool." She cleared her voice. "I sound as if I stuttered. I don't really. It's—it's a hang-over f-from my weep-fest. He, perhaps it's a she, is smoking."

"If you don't, you know the consequences to you."

The threat echoed through her memory, started the quiescent shivers. Was the person who had whispered in the bay meeting a conspirator at the game house? Should she do anything about it?

"You are shivering. You would be cold after that emotional crack-up. Let's go in."

"No. I hear voices on the terrace. I'm a sight. My nose and ch-cheeks feel spotlight red, my eyes burn. I'll stay here till they cool to normal. P-please go and join the card players, Mr. Grant."

"Doesn't our relationship—if only by marriage—warrant our dropping Mr. and Miss formality? You didn't think I suggested a return to the house in self-interest, I hope. Not a chance when I am sitting pretty with a lovely girl in the moonlight. Ready now to tell all? Why the weep-fest?" He clasped his hands about one knee, strong, steady hands with long, sensitive fingers. They had been amazingly gentle when they touched her bruised lip, she remembered.

"That was my miserable cold departing in a typhoon of temperament, the way a thunderstorm ends in a terrific cr-crash. I don't know why it rolled up when I was so happy to be with Molly B.—she is such a grand person—or whence. Lucky I was the only wreck in its path."

"Don't be too sure of that. Sometime I'll tell you what it did to me. What started it? Must have been something. You were the life of the party at dinner."

"I don't know, honestly, I don't know. After I left Washington I had a week of New York whirl with friends and a handsome check from Molly B. to spend on clothes—and did I spend it! After dinner all at once I seemed to go to pieces inside. I still don't understand why."

"I do. Reaction. From having every waking moment packed with responsibility—I'll bet you even dreamed of your work—you see I've heard of your job, you now find yourself a lady of leisure with a flu hang-over."

"Let's hope that your diagnosis is correct. I would hate to think of myself as a chronic burster-into-tears. Let's tune in on another station. What a gorgeous night. So light I can see the roofs and chimneys of the large summer places across the lake, the outline of the hills and the twinkle of star reflections in the water."

"Look at this house. The lighted windows put the stars out of business with their shine. I hadn't realized what a huge place Beechcroft is. What do you think of Judge Lander?"

"As a man or as the money-raising trustee of the college? On the last count he is a wizard."

"You're telling me as if I didn't catch the how-much-is-he-good-for gleam in his eyes the first time we met before he knew who I was. You don't believe with him that I am here to cadge in on this real estate, do you?"

"It wouldn't be unnatural for you to want the house your grandfather built, it was your mother's home until she married. Now that we are on the subject this is as good a time as any to observe that should you as a last, desperate expedient think of marrying me to secure the estate, forget it, I have other plans."

"I hadn't thought of the marriage solution till the Judge mentioned it, but, now that you have definitely turned me down, I know what the score is. Okay, if that is the way you feel about it."

His voice was rough with anger. She watched him stride

21

away. Why had she said she wouldn't marry him? He hadn't asked her, had he? Was it a vibration of the brain storm she had just passed through? She forced back a sob. Darn. Was she about to go to pieces again?

He had stopped to speak to a man in white. Clive Warner. Now he was hurrying toward her. She couldn't talk with him. Where could she go to avoid him? She would have to pass him to reach the house. Better remain where she was and take it. She would have to sometime. Apparently he was set for a showdown. Unfortunate it should flash its coming-up number while little creepy chills from her emotional binge still slithered along her veins.

"What's the idea running out on the party?" Warner inquired as he dropped to the bench beside her. "Why did you beat it when I spoke to you in the hall? There is a lot that needs saying between us. You've been crying. Because of me? You don't hate me, do you, Deb?"

She remembered the tone with its suggestion of male invincibility. Crying because of him? How dared he think that? He was still sensationally good-looking with his fair hair and small mustache, and large brown eyes which could have the appealing softness of a setter's, when appealing softness was called for.

"Why don't you answer? I came back to the old job because of you. Going to forgive me, aren't you, Debby? Let me start where we left off?" His wheedling question followed her mental summing up almost as if he had waited for her verdict.

"Forgive you for what, Clive? For saving me from a life of unhappiness? Gratitude is the word that fits."

"Is that so?" He chewed at a corner of his mustache, a habit when he was angry that she remembered. "Because Odile let me down? It wouldn't have happened with you. It wasn't my fault that she wanted a divorce and got it."

Did he really think that was the reason she distrusted him? Had he forgotten that he had walked out on her seven days before they were to be married? He was putting on an act and who knew better than she that he was an expert at cajolery?

"It will be a shock to you, but I am not interested in you and your one-time wife, Clive."

"Is Grant responsible for that? I saw him beat it through the hall and out the door after you."

"*Grant?* Do you mean *Tim* Grant? Where did you get that absurd idea? I had forgotten he was in the world till a few hours ago when Molly B. told me he was here to talk business with her."

22

"That's a phony. How could you help knowing? Recently he came in for half the big Stewart estate, didn't he?"

"I wouldn't know. Better ask him."

"I won't have to ask him. Wasn't I hep to the family history when you and I were engaged? Didn't I know that Cobina Grant was furious that her father had willed Beechcroft to his wife? That business gag is a joke. Hold on, though, is it? Getting a stranglehold on the other half of the Stewart property would be big business, a master enterprise. Ever think what a body blow it would be to you if he put the scheme over, if he hypnotized your grandmother? You are her only legal heir."

"You did post yourself on the family history, didn't you? There have been plenty of cases where legal heirs didn't inherit. Molly B. may become furiously angry with me, Tim Grant will be Johnny-on-the-spot, and whoosh, there goes my inheritance. Believe me, I'm not losing sleep over it— and speaking of sleep," she tapped her hand over her lips as if to suppress a yawn, "sorry, but the conversation—if it can be called conversation—begins to be boring. I'm going in." He caught her bare arm and held it.

"Just a minute. Get this. When I saw you coming down the stairs before dinner I fell for you as hard as I fell the first time I saw you. I must have had a brain storm when—"

"Afraid to say it? I'm not. When you left me waiting at the church."

"You've grown bitter, Debby. I don't like it."

For an hysterical instant she thought she would shriek with laughter. The upsurge of emotion frightened her, fright steadied her. The fight for self-control hoarsened her already husky voice.

"Bitter? Who, me? I'm not bitter, I told you before that gratitude is the word. I'm not the only one, think of the war brides who wore my wedding dress we sent to the Red Cross. No use trying to fan embers where there isn't so much as a spark, Clive. There is nothing deader than dead love and believe it or not, any feeling I may have had for you is as cold as that stone bench. Now, having made my position crystal clear, good night."

She eluded his outstretched hand and ran toward the house. Voices on the terrace. Better dodge Molly B., who thought she was in her room. She slipped in through a side door and almost bumped into the butler. He was talking to Stella Dane.

"How soon?" she whispered. She saw Deborah and added in a normal voice, "I'll take the message on the phone at once, Scragg. Thanks for calling me."

An hour later in pale blue pajamas, Deborah rested her arms on the white rail of the balcony outside the open window in her room. Crickets in full chorus were spelled at intervals by the shrill call of katydids. The heavy fragrance of phlox rose from below. The moon beamed from the zenith, 240,000 miles from the earth, astronomers calculated. Garden, lake and even distant hills were washed in its silver light. The pool gleamed like a huge platinum platter, the colonnade and game house shone with the same mother-of-pearl luster she had seen the Taj Mahal take on in India.

A white figure paced the lawn in front of the game house. A spark gleamed. Another. That added up to two persons smoking. When Tim Grant left her in anger had he sent word to Stella Dane to join him there? Apparently he had gone all out for her at dinner. Were they the two who had conspired in the bay of the gallery? That thought started the shivers. Better tune in on another wave length.

"Okay, if that's the way you feel about it." Tim Grant's angry reply followed the switch. Would he have been so furious had there been no truth in Judge Lander's accusation that he would take any means to acquire Beechcroft? Clive, also, had declared that Roger Stewart's grandson was after the estate. Suppose he were? Who cared?

"Stop playing twenty questions and go to bed, Deb Randall," she advised herself aloud. She snapped off the bedside light before she added, "Unless I miss my guess they will be answered—and how. I don't need Molly B.'s mystery scout to warn me there is trouble round the corner." As she snuggled her head into the pillow a voice within her mused softly:

"Three men in white. One of them parks a revolver in his suitcase." The voice allowed time out for a yawn before it added, "Which one?"

IV

ARM on the carved oak mantel, pipe in mouth, Timothy Grant looked about the long room which took up the entire front of the third floor in the left wing. It seemed like getting home to come back to it after two weeks' absence. Was it because it had been his grandfather's study? "And I mean study," Madam Stewart had said when she had assigned it to him. "There Roger Stewart worked out many of the problems which later became successful experiments in the lab."

To his amazement he had been asked to head the Science Center that same grandfather had founded, which had contributed a team to a great scientific wartime research. When he had consulted his onetime instructors at M.I.T., to a man they had given an enthusiastic "Go ahead. You are fully qualified for the job."

Acceptance of the appointment meant tremendous responsibility, not only to the Center but to the world, unceasing effort to acquire the best men for the teaching staff, men who would develop social responsibility and moral sense in the students as well as a knowledge of science. Also, it would be up to him to deepen and broaden his own knowledge. So what? He intended to do that wherever he was, he had embarked on a profession of unlimited potentialities. Lander's threat tonight that he would fight the appointment had crystallized his indecision into determination. He would accept. His mother's house on the campus, now his, would be a fitting residence for the Head of the Science Center.

Grandfather Stewart had been part of a hazy dream of a dark-haired man's wink, of his hearty laugh as he tucked a five-dollar bill under his grandson's supper plate in the nursery.

"A little chicken feed for a growing boy, Timmy," he would say.

He had admired him enormously, had wondered if he, himself, would ever be so grand and impressive, had even as a youngster determined to follow his profession. That had been before Roger Stewart had married Molly Burton Randall. After that, if he were to believe his mother's diary, hell had broken loose between father and daughter and Henry Lander had assiduously fanned the flames of anger.

Lander! He repeated the name aloud and rapped his pipe against the mantel with a force that snapped the stem. The Judge couldn't know how near he came to having his block knocked off when he had intimated that Roger Stewart's grandson had come to Beechcroft with the intention of acquiring it. Who in these complicated days wanted a white elephant like this estate?

He had clenched his teeth to hold back the furious words that flocked to the top of his mind like shock troops rushing to attack, words from his mother's diary which before this he had set down as possibly the imaginings of a furiously angry woman for which allowance should be made. Now, he wasn't so sure. Lander's nasty outburst in the library had venom—might have been fear—behind it. He would wait and watch.

He crossed to the long window opened wide on a balcony, leaned against the frame and looked out at a moonlit world. There was frost in the crisp air. The lake was indigo, glinting with gold sparks. A faint, rasping chorus of katydids rose from below. Zowie, what a lonesome sound. How thick the stars. They were on the move tonight. That was the third meteor he had seen whiz through the field of gold. What a peaceful world this seemed after the tumult and horror of war, even with the undercurrents of envy and selfishness he had sensed beneath the surface these last few weeks. Tumult was too tame a word for the years he had spent in the midst of blood, horror and sudden death.

A little breeze whispered through the branches of a nearby giant beech and set in motion leaves showing a hint of autumn purple. It traveled on like a gossip trading her tidbits of news from house to house till every silver-tipped treetop in sight was titillating in sympathy, all except the majestic dark pine, which barely moved a needle, the tree under which Debby had flung herself.

She was too young to be shaken by such tearing sobs. When she had asked to be excused from cards her voice had betrayed emotional tension. Fearing that his own self-control would snap if Lander spoke to him, he had left the library, had seen her shake off Warner and dash through the hall. Hoping he might help, he had followed.

Was the ex-Captain responsible for her crack-up? During dinner Stella Dane had managed to get across the story of the broken-off marriage. If she but knew it he probably had more data about it than she. Apparently his mother had been obsessed to keep abreast of the happenings in the life of the granddaughter of her father's wife. The diary had been full of references and notes about Deborah Randall, clippings from newspapers and pictures of her cut from magazines. In the moment of encounter on the stairs he had realized that none of them had shown her aliveness, given a commensurate description of her brunette beauty, the perfection of her slender figure, the laughing brilliance of her gray eyes, the charm of her expression.

She had furiously resented his "darling." Why not? She couldn't know that in the months since he had received his mother's diary he had gone all out for her. Lucky he had controlled the impulse to catch her in his arms and hold her close till the storm of sobs passed. Believing as she did that his presence here was inspired by self-interest, she would have thought his effort to comfort her was because she was her grandmother's heir. It had been darn unfair to snap at her and leave her in a huff tonight, largely because he had been furious with Lander. What more natural than for her in her emotional upset to resent the slimy Judge's suggestion?

"Come in," he answered a knock at the door.

"How come you are on duty tonight, Miss Allen?" he inquired as the tall angular woman in rustling black silk began to fold off the green satin bedspread. "Where's the maid who is usually on the job?"

"She struck because she had to help with the dishes." Sniff. Sniff. "Strike if you don't like what you're asked to do. Strike if you want more pay. Strike if school conditions don't suit. The world's gone strike crazy." Impatiently she jerked her spectacles into place.

"I'm sorry you bothered to come. It is late and you must have had a busy day. I could open the bed myself if it has to be done, but believe it or not, there have been weeks on end during the last four years when I haven't seen a bed with sheets to say nothing of having one opened for me. I'll help." He folded back blankets to match her side.

"You have a voice and laugh like your grandfather, Mr. Timothy."

"Have I? I'll say we've done an A-1 job; this looks tight, neat and as hard to get into as a scientifically made-up hospital bed. Hey, what goes with my pajamas? You are not planning to tuck me in, are you, Miss Allen? I'm a grown boy."

A smile crinkled her face till it resembled the surface of crackled pottery.

"You get more and more like Roger Stewart, Mr. Tim. He was a great joker—at times." She folded the navy blue pajamas and laid them on the turned-back sheet. "Thanks for helping. I'd like fine to have you call me Sal, the way Debby does. Good night."

"Hold everything, don't go, Sal. Stay and tell me about my grandfather." He pushed forward a wing chair covered with green brocade, perched on the corner of the broad oak desk opposite and drew a package of cigarettes from the pocket of his brown velvet lounge jacket. "Smoke?"

Seated on the very edge of the chair Sarah stiffened her shoulders and sniffed.

"Do I look as if I did?"

"Sorry, my mistake. I take it you don't, but you never can tell about a woman these days. What sort of a person was my grandfather?"

"Roger Stewart was a fine man, a great man I've heard him called, if he was obstinate as a pack of mules. He was crazy about you when you were a youngster—made all sorts of plans for your education—you were to take his place as head of the lab, which was to become the greatest one of its size and kind in New England, if not the country. 'It's my dream,' he would say, 'I'll make it come true.' "

"It is one of the finest in the country, it gave invaluable help in the war."

"The townsfolk are awful proud of it, an' they're so stuck-up about the Science Center you'd think 'twas their idea. Your grandfather used to talk to me about his plans, he was mighty lonesome after his first wife died, his family and the lab being about all he cared for. Then he met the widow Randall who came here to visit her younger sister who had married into the faculty, she was Sam Farr's mother. My sakes, he fell head over heels in love with her at first sight an' she married him. She's a fine woman I can honestly say after livin' with her for years."

"It hasn't taken me but a few weeks to find out that. She is a grand person."

"It beat me why your mother up and fought the marriage. She wouldn't let you come to this house. That most broke your grandfather's heart. After that he wouldn't see her, or you for whom he had been building up the lab and started the Science Center. His wife tried her hardest to change his mind; all she got for her trouble was, 'Don't *talk* about it.' I don't know how she put up with his obstinacy, if't' been me I bet I'd up and swatted him. Much as I respected him I almost did once when I run against that streak."

"I'm here now to carry on, Sal. I am to head the Science Center, that is, if the trustees confirm the appointment."

"Now ain't that perfect." She clasped her heavy-veined bony hands to express enthusiasm. "I hope Roger Stewart knows his dream has come true, an' I have a feelin' he does. 'Hold fast your dream, Sarah,' he would say to me, as if I had any time, first raising a lot of kid brothers an' sisters, then hiring out for a job, to cook up dreams. I'll bet Judge Lander will be fit to tie when he hears the news."

"I take it you don't admire Lander?"

"Admire him? I don't trust him. More'n that, he's vindictive an' he thinks he runs this college. He's tryin' to oust the President, an' step into his shoes. I never could understand how a man keen and inventive as your grandfather kept him on as his lawyer after your mother sent him packin' when he wanted to marry her. That was before she fell in love with Dean Grant."

"Good Lord, Sal, how come you know so much about my family?"

"I've lived in this town all my life. What the Stewarts in the big house did, said and wore, and the Wild Danes' goin's on, provided half the conversation in the houses I visited, an' what went on at the college the other half. I came to Beechcroft soon after your own grandmother died, when Coby, as we called her, was in her teens. An' I've been here ever since."

"Then you were here when Ingrid Johnson came to be secretary to Molly Burton Randall, the novelist, who recently had become Molly Burton Stewart?"

"Certainly, I was here. How come you know so much about her?"

"No occasion to ruffle like a turkey cock, Sarah Allen. I think she is charming."

"It ain't only that, she's a fine person. She'd about lay down her life for Madam Stewart. She's changed a lot these last years, worryin' about her brother, I guess, but, land's sake, who ain't changed? Debby looked as if she'd cried her eyes out when I met her tearin' up to her room this evenin'. I expected it. She was all keyed up before dinner. Hope 'twasn't because of that Warner fella, who let her down once."

"Is she still in love with him?"

"More than likely she isn't. She always had a lot of beaux. Perhaps she was cryin' 'bout one of them, though it ain't like her to cry. When she was a youngster her face would get terrible red when she was hurt, but she wouldn't cry. I'd better get goin'. It's late to be settin' here gossiping, if it is with one of the family."

"Thanks a lot, Sal, for bringing me up to date about my grandfather." He opened the door. "Good night."

He unlocked a drawer in the desk and drew out a volume of his mother's diary. There were three of them bulging with clippings about politics, poems, many newspaper and magazine illustrations. This one covered the period of his grandfather's illness and death and extracts copied from his will plus her angry comments. He read on and on till the ultramodern clock on the mantel struck the hour sharply, quickly, as if eager to shake off the spell of the silent night and get on with the day in the hope that adventure lay ahead.

He counted. Four. Good Lord, he had been reading for hours. Thanks to Sarah Allen's description and the diary, his grandfather had materialized from the shadow world to become a three-dimensional personality. And now to bed.

He had one arm out of his brown velvet jacket when a scream came through the open window and set the air vibrating. What in thunder—another yell. Sounded as if it had come from the right wing, Madam Stewart's apartment. Halfway down the stairs he remembered the diamonds she had worn at dinner and took the last three steps in a leap. As he snapped on more light he thought he heard the soft closing of a door below.

He was not the only person who had heard the terrifying shriek. Doors opened overhead. Men with robes over their pajamas, women in house coats and mules catapulted down the stairs in a vivid stream of color. Debby Randall in a pale blue satin coat caught his arm as he tried the door of Madam Stewart's living room.

"Tim! Tim! Was it Molly B.? Someone after her jewels?" she demanded breathlessly. "I knew it would happen."

"The scream seemed to come from here. Good Lord, why doesn't she answer?"

"Perhaps she can't."

"That's a cheering thought, Deb." He shook the door. "Any other way to get in?"

"Oh, dear! Oh, dear. Perhaps Molly B. has been mur—" Tilly Farr in yellow velvet lounge pajamas shuddered and hid her face against the black satin shoulder of her husband's robe.

"Can't one of you tell me of another way to get into this room?" Tim Grant's voice was hoarse with anxiety.

"There are outside stairs from the terrace to her balcony, but—" The sound of a key turning interrupted Deborah's whisper. The door opened. Madam Stewart, belting a white Chinese Mandarin coat embroidered in rose-color iris and green gold dragons, stepped across the threshold.

"What goes?" She laughed. "Don't tell me that Ingrid's nightmare brought this convocation or is it a sunrise surprise party? I miss Sophy. She must be sleeping on her good ear."

Tim Grant could have shaken her as she stood there smiling while his nerves twanged like harp strings being brushed by a heavy hand. He was not the only one. Lander, in a dark green brocaded robe, which betrayed the bulge in his waistline, was scowling with impatience. Warner was nervously swinging the tasseled cord of his khaki-color house robe. Stella Dane in a flimsy violet negligee which revealed white pajamas beneath ran down the stairs and caught her employer's arm.

"Are you sure that awful sound was a nightmare, Madam Stewart?" she whimpered.

"Pull yourself together, Stella. Of course I am sure. Haven't I lived with Ingrid's nightmares for years? Accustomed as I am to them, I'll admit that when the first yell woke me from a sound sleep, it frightened the life out of me, my knees are still shaking like a mold of Jell-o. She has been warned to leave sweets alone. I noticed that she had a second helping of lemon chiffon pie at dinner."

"What's all the shootin' about?" Burke Romney sent his voice ahead as he ran down the stairs. The crimson corduroy of his lounge robe, which didn't quite cover the legs of his red and white striped pajamas, lent a tinge of color to his olive skin. "Who had a nightmare and let out those blood-curdling screams?"

"Smart fella, Burke. You recognized it for what it was, and took it leisurely," Clive Warner commented sarcastically. "The rest of us break our necks beating it to help a woman we fear is being mur—"

"Don't say it, Captain," Molly Burton Stewart interrupted sharply. "I use the word plenty in my stories, but I don't like it on the loose in my house." Her shiver was genuine. "Go back to your rooms, please. Ingrid will hear you. I don't want her to know she roused the household. She is sensitive about her nightmares."

"Gad, she should be," Judge Lander, looking slightly pontifical in his long green robe, agreed testily.

"Good night, everybody, and thanks for your concern about me. Pleasant dreams—there is time still for a few." Molly Burton Stewart blew them a kiss and closed the door. A key clicked.

"That seems to be that. Break ranks," Tim suggested and laughed. "Go ahead, all of you. I'll put out the lights I switched on when I arrived at this door."

Deborah lingered. Her eyes followed the figures hastily mounting the stairs. Still watching she moved close to him and whispered:

"Did you notice that Burke Romney was wearing black evening shoes with those red and white pajamas?"

"I did, Debby. I noticed also that the tips of the toes were wet as if he had just come in from outside. Leave it at that for the present, will you? Your eyes are enormous. Remember that emotional crack-up. *Please* go to bed."

"I'm going. Good night, good morning, rather."

He watched till she was out of sight in the upper gallery. What would she think if he told her that not only had he noticed the black evening shoes but, also, that Stella Dane's gold sandals were moist at the tips as if wet from dewy grass? Had it been a sentimental rendezvous?

"Nightmare," he said under his breath as he snapped off all but one light. "Nightmare, phooey. Boy, oh boy, what goes? What goes?"

V

WONDERFUL what a night's sleep can do—even if broken by screams at 4 A.M.—how it can change one's point of view, Deborah thought the next morning as, flat on her back on a bed of dried pine needles, she looked up through green branches at a luminous blue sky. She listened drowsily to the lap, lap, of water against the side of her canoe moored at the float on the white-sand shore of the island, the rasp of a distant saw, and the rhythmic breathing of the black cocker spaniel sprawled beside her in what appeared to be utter exhaustion.

Heavenly spot. No wonder the lake was surrounded by large summer estates, their boathouses the only part of them visible from this viewpoint. Already she felt made over physically, her cold but a wraith of memory. Now she was back to normal, why not check on her impressions of yesterday? Had her weep-fest been gathering in the offing, and so inflamed her imagination that a voice from the gallery bay had appeared to threaten, or was trouble really lurking round the corner?

She brushed away a bee buzzing too near her nose for comfort. The movement brought Cocky to his haunches with a grunt of disapproval. Laughing, she rolled over to elude his rough tongue on her throat left bare by the V of her white shirt, dug elbows into the soft needles, braced chin in hands and looked across the lake at the college boathouse where two scantily clad men were lowering racing shells into the water. She shook her head at the dog who had ingratiatingly laid an oversize pine cone on a fold of her navy slacks.

"No can play now, Cocky. Go hunt squirrels while Debby thinks."

He barked at the scolding chipmunk on a branch overhead before he trotted toward the woods. She picked up the train of thought. The campus appeared peaceful enough at present, it suggested no sinister mystery. The pinkish brick buildings which surrounded it and the white chapel with its heaven-pointing, gold-tipped spire were ivy-covered in the best New England college tradition. Grand old trees shaded benches beneath them. Scattered about were stiff, motionless figures, bronze tributes to departed prexies, a hundred or more years

33

gone, some of them. Iron lampposts which for decades had lighted students on their way now held electric bulbs instead of oil. The paths which crossed and crisscrossed the short grass were dotted with strolling or hurrying figures.

Toward the west stretched the long, two-story brick building with huge windows enclosed in an iron fence with ornate memorial gates, which was the Science Center. East of it a plane was landing on the college airfield. Not far away a dark depression marked the Bowl for athletics which Molly B. had given in memory of her son. She had named it the Bass Bowl because fishing for bass in the lake had been his favorite sport. Faintly across the water came the strain of the chapel organ:

> In heavenly love abiding
> No change my heart shall fear.

White curtains at the open windows of dormitories were blowing in the light breeze, even at this distance she could feel the stir of preparation for the expected students. The GI Bill of Rights had set an army of veterans on the march for an education. How would the close corporation of this small college, which was the faculty—and, in capitals, the Faculty Wives—take its share of the influx?

What effect would it have on the town itself? Molly B. had suggested that she stay at Beechcroft and help the GI wives get adjusted. It would mean resigning from the Washington job. Her boss would fume at first but there were girls in the office who could fill her place. Why not polish other facets of her mind? Why not take a postgraduate course in English, French, start Spanish and make a try at creative writing? For three years she had concentrated on one type of work. Time for a change of outlook and, boy, would living in this narrow world be a change from Washington!

Narrow? Was a world narrow from which a stream of students enriched by its teaching had taken their places in the country, especially in these last years when men of science had played such an important part in winning victory? There was a long honor roll in front of the chapel with many gold stars. Narrow is not the word to be applied to this college.

Her eyes traveled to the H-shaped Sewart house with its ells and porches sprawled on a rise of ground half a mile beyond the campus. Its walls were cream concrete, its balconies in matching tint were lacy ironwork, its gardens a mass of brilliant color, its greenhouses—empty now—a blinding dazzle of glass where sunlight struck them, its terraces verdant and velvety in their slope to the lake shore. The vines on the white colonnade showed a tinge of crimson, the rare purple beeches for which the place was named had taken on the pastel shades of autumn.

Her eyes rested contemplatively on the right wing. The entire second floor was Molly B.'s apartment. Her workroom faced the lake, then came the dressing room, bedroom, living room, all with outlook on lake and distant hills, and at the other end, the front of the house, Ingrid's suite. Tim Grant was right, it was a huge place. Was Judge Lander right also? Had Roger Stewart's grandson come here in the hope of acquiring it?

The question brought his curt, "Okay, if that is the way you feel about it," to the forefront of her mind after she had fought all the morning to keep it in the background. Why had she referred to Judge Lander's hateful suggestion that he would even marry her to get it? Must have been a backfire of her cry-fest. He had been friendly again when they met in the hall at 4 A.M. Had he believed Molly B.'s explanation of those screams? If he had would he have been alerted to noticing that Burke Romney's black shoes were wet at the toes? What did it all mean?

That question brought her up spang against the whispered words that had drifted from the gallery bay. What papers were wanted so desperately? Papers in Molly B.'s safe? Ought she to report what she had heard to her? Mysteries were her meat, mysteries which she created—would she be so keen in unraveling the real thing? Now that Tim Grant had appeared friendly she would confide in him. Perhaps he would laugh at her, tease her about her vivid imagination. She could take it. She might take a fling at hunting down a solution of the mystery herself. Where to begin? How did Molly B. commence a story? Did she locate the dead body first and work back from that or work up to it?

She couldn't start with a body yet—What popped that "yet" into her mind? The mere word "body" gave her the merry-pranks. Her best bet was to begin at the whispered command, "It's your job to get those papers." Working on the premise that the voice belonged to a person staying in the house, who was the most likely suspect?

"Why, Judge Lander!"

Surprise brought Deborah to her feet. Had she heard the exclamation or had suspicion, faint as shadowy wings, brushed across her mind? Thank heaven, she wasn't just hearing a voice, it was real. The tall, white-haired man in cream-color shirt designed with blue herons and slacks the shade of French mustard was frowning at Sophy Brandt, who simpered in response. A rowboat was tied to the float, had he come in that? The cocker spaniel leaped up on the woman's green plaid skirt in noisy welcome. Was she pale or did her Parma violet blouse and the matching scarf wound round her head above her yellow bang make her seem so?

"Stop staring at me, Debby, as if I had dropped from the skies," Sophy protested impatiently. "The houseboy brought me to the island an hour ago. Molly B. said she had turned her workshop here over to you. I had a lot of my duds stored in that log cabin. I have been packing them for the boy to take to the house. Can you do as well with an explanation as to why you are here, Henry?"

"Sure. I came with a message for Debby. Her boss will call her on long distance at one o'clock."

"My word, does he want me back so soon? Thanks a million for delivering the message, Judge." She glanced at her wrist. "It is twelve now. I'd better get a move on. Coming with me, Mrs. Sophy?"

"N-no. I'll wait to check on the houseboy to make sure he gets everything."

"No use inviting you to be personally conducted, Judge. You have a boat."

"I'll stay to take Sophy home in case the boy doesn't show up, Debby. From what I saw of him when he brought my bag—he had first left it in another room—I can't hand him much of an I.Q."

"How good of you to wait for me, Hen-er-y. I almost hope the boy won't come." The hint of sarcasm in Sophy Brandt's simper brought a wave of dark color to the edge of his white hair.

"They have turned us down, Cocky-me-lad. Come on. Something tells me we won't be missed from this twosome. If I see the boy on the lake coming for Mrs. Sophy shall I tell him to turn back, Judge?"

"No." At his explosive pronouncement she departed.

Sounded as if he were afraid to be left alone with the intriguing gal, Deborah thought as she sent the canoe through the glassy water with rhythmic sweeps of the paddle. She waved to the two men as the racing shells shot past neck and neck.

"Stop wriggling, Cocky, unless you have an urge to swim ashore. I haven't."

Curious how the certainty persisted that the meeting of the two she had left behind on the island had been prearranged, her thoughts trooped on. Why the rendezvous with Sophy? Sentiment was out as an explanation. Yesterday the Judge had given every indication that he had lost his head over Tilly Farr. It was incredible, he had such a cool, calculating head. He had been part of this college too long not to realize that the campus gossips never slept.

He must be aware that the faculty wives resented Tilly. She outspent, outdressed, outentertained them all and flirted with their husbands. In addition she had a biting tongue. They wouldn't turn a glass eye on the Judge's infatuation. It was difficult to imagine him in the role "of one that loved not wisely but too well," self-interest would always be paramount. He was discounting her husband's reaction, if he thought of him at all. Sam had blinked at flirtations, he would take drastic measures to stop scandal. His expression last evening as he had watched the two had given her the shivers.

So-o, the Judge's bag had been delivered first to the wrong room. Her room? Had it contained the ivory-handled revolver? No, he had worn black dinner clothes. Suppose he had? It didn't necessarily follow that he hadn't brought a white suit, did it? He was a snappy dresser. That explanation went for Burke Romney, too, which conclusion jacked the number of the possible pistol-packers to five.

Molly B. in a crisp green and white striped cotton morning frock was standing on the threshold of her living room when Deborah reached it on her way to change for luncheon.

"I've been watching for you, honey. Come in." She closed the door. "Have you been here to get your diary since you locked it in the safe?"

"No. Why?"

"Look."

Deborah's eyes followed her outstretched hand. On the floor at the side of the safe panel lay a bulky, black-cover loose-leaf notebook.

"My word, how did it get there?"

"Someone must have opened the safe, taken it out to get at papers under it, and in his or her hurry and excitement forgotten to put it back. What did you do with the combination I gave you, Deb?"

"Dropped it somewhere. I intended to tell you when I came downstairs, then I saw Scragg hand you a slip of white paper in the hall before dinner last evening, and thought he had found it and returned it to you."

"That wasn't the combination, it was a note from the cook —she has a passion for note-writing—to tell me that the butter had been stolen from the icebox so I wouldn't send out to inquire how come there was no Hollandaise for the broccoli."

"Did someone find the combination and unlock the safe? Wait a minute. Do you suppose the yell before dawn this morning had anything to do with it?"

"No. I told you it was one of Ingrid's nightmares. That loose-leaf book was not on the floor when I had breakfast in this room beside the fire."

"Have you looked in the safe? Golly, I remember that fat roll of bills. Anything missing?"

"I haven't opened it. I sent a messenger for Tim Grant. I'll ask him what I'd better do first. The moment I saw him I went all out for him. It's heaven to have a man upon whom to lean, Deb, and you'll have to admit that up to date I haven't been a leaner."

"How about the Lander person? I thought he was your port in every storm?"

"Henry is a crackajack lawyer, he has saved me a lot of money and care, but as a personal adviser he's not so hot. My regard for him is definitely on the down beat. I disapprove of his present point of view so much that whether to retain him as my attorney has approached the proportions of a problem. He is the 'if-you-had-listened-to-me' type. I don't want him to know about the safe complication. He would be sure it was the result of my carelessness."

"Looks as if it had been mine. Does anyone know the combination but you? Does Stella Dane?"

"No. When she brought in the payroll yesterday I unlocked the safe and closed it. Here's Tim, I hope." She opened the door in response to an authoritative knock.

VI

"WHAT'S cooking, Molly B.?" Tim Grant inquired as he entered. "Your SOS caught up with me at the house where I was unpacking books. It was so urgent I didn't stop to change. I'm pretty dirty." A wine-color shirt was open at the throat. He brushed a streak of dust from matching slacks. "The top of the morning to you, Miss Randall."

"Never mind your clothes. Come in, Tim, and close the door. I need your help."

"Boy, you sound mysterious. Is it a new brain child stirring?"

"If it were I would know what to do. Now that I am up against the real thing, I'm ashamed to acknowledge I'm stumped." She told of her reason for thinking the safe had been opened since Deborah had put in her loose-leaf book and closed it.

"Just a minute, Molly B." He stepped to the balcony of each open window. "No one there. What is beyond that door at the other end of the room?"

"That is Ingrid's suite."

"Ingrid, fair Ingrid, with the nightmare yell. Is she there now?"

"No. This morning she took our exhibit to the Flower Show in aid of the USO."

"Okay if I take a look-see?" He opened the door and disappeared. "No one there," he announced as he returned and closed it. "Now, let's get on with the mystery. Where were you at the time the safe was opened, Molly B.?"

"At the cottages I am having made over to house some of the married GIs. My conscience won't allow me to let them remain vacant when there is such a drastic need of housing."

"Bully for you. Have you opened the safe to see if anything is missing?"

"No. I didn't even touch Debby's notebook on the floor."

"I remember it, she had it under her arm when we crashed on the stairs. Leaving it out makes this look like an amateur job. Let's open the safe. First, we'll pick up the book." She handed him a large handkerchief. "You know all the ropes, don't you, Molly B.?" He laughed and dropped the white square of linen over the notebook before he laid it on the desk. "Now open the safe. Cover the knob first." On one knee behind her he watched as she turned and reversed till the door swung open.

"Whoever opened it didn't want money or he or she wouldn't have left that fat roll of bills. Does it look as if anything had been disturbed?"

"Some of the papers have been taken," Debby informed them breathlessly. "When I put in my diary there was barely enough room for it between the files of papers and the shelf above. Now, look at the space."

"What papers were there, Molly B.?"

"Mostly contracts with publishers, magazine editors, and movie magnates. Some of your grandfather's letters in which he suggested what disposal to make of certain holdings and this place eventually, though he left me a free hand as he had in the will, and Ingrid's personal papers."

"Ingrid's!"

"Why that shocked exclamation? Any reason why they shouldn't be there?"

"Certainly not and every reason why they should be. When you said 'Ingrid' I wondered if she would open the safe without first telling you."

"She doesn't know how, besides that she has been away all the morning. Someone must have picked up the lost combination for opening it."

"What lost combination? Come clean, gals, you're not telling all you know about this. Give. Give."

Deborah told of her discovery that she had lost the white slip of paper and why she had believed that Scragg had returned it.

"Why didn't you tell that at first? Where were the other members of your present family this morning, Molly B.?"

"Clive Warner and Burke Romney left early to attend an all-day faculty meeting. The Farrs departed soon after breakfast to look after the painters at their house. Stella Dane drove to the Town Hall with the silver bowl I am presenting for the most artistic shadow-box at the Show. I don't know how Sophy and the Judge put in their time, but not together, I'll wager."

"They—" Debby tried to cover the impulsive exclamation with a cough. Why tell that they were on the island—yet?

"You ought to do something for that cold." Tim Grant's amused eyes met hers. He was friendly again. Did it mean that he had forgiven her senseless refusal to marry him when he hadn't asked her?

40

"Let's get busy. Close the safe door and restore the panel," he advised. "We must get a fingerprint man here before we touch the papers or the jewel cases, and an expert to change the combination so that the safe can't be opened again except by you, Molly B. I happen to know that our county bank has both on call. I'll telephone—no, there are other extensions in the house, we won't take a chance at a listener-in. I will go for the men."

"Better tell the print man that our prints are on file in the Town Hall. During the war a fingerprint expert lectured at the college. I entertained him at dinner. He was so emphatic as to the importance of having the fingerprints of every person in the country on record that the next morning Ingrid, Deb, Sarah Allen and I trooped to police headquarters. You were here for a week end, remember, Debby?"

"Yes, I was terribly impressed."

"It's a break to have them on record. Hide the notebook. Be careful not to touch it with your fingers, Debby, though your prints must be all over it. The person who moved it from the safe may remember it was left out and try to put it back. One of you stay here till I return. If the men I bring are seen and questions are asked, say they are builders I have engaged to reproduce the windows and balconies of this room at my house. And, for the love of Mike, don't let a hint of what has happened get on the air." He stepped into the hall and closed the door.

"Quick, Deb, put the notebook in my bedroom, later we will lock it in my manuscript file," Molly B. advised before she sank into a deep chair.

"What do we do now, according to your formula?" Deborah inquired as she returned and perched on the arm of the sofa.

"I can't work it out because I can't believe that any person in this house is a thief."

"It might have been an outsider who knew of your jewels, we may find some of those cases empty. Then again, we don't *know* that anything was taken though I am sure that the space between the shelf and the papers below is a lot wider than when I squeezed in my notebook."

Was this the time to tell of the whispered threat she had overheard yesterday? No. She had better consult Tim first, Molly B. was upset enough as it was. For a creator of mysteries she was having a bad case of the jitters. This was the chance to introduce the questions she had formulated as she paddled across the lake.

"Why haven't you given me a hint that Cupid was busy around here, Molly B.?"

"Cupid? You don't think love has anything to do with that

silly flirtation Henry Lander is trying to start with Tilly Farr, do you? I don't like it. This college has been free of scandal. Occasionally a faculty wife or husband has cast a glance over another's wall, but it never developed beyond the yearning glance stage. I'm worried. Sam is a dear, but unpredictable."

"I was referring to the Judge and Sophy Brandt."

"Judge Lander and *who?*"

"You heard right the first time. Your pal, Sophy."

"Where did you get that crazy idea?"

"Unless my radar detector is off the beam they met at the island this morning by prearranged plan. Have you seen Henry in sports regalia? He's gone 'California casual.' His shirt looked as if he had crashed into a flock of migrating blue herons and some of them had stuck, his slacks were the color of mustard used to smear hot dogs. I flung sand in the gears by being there before them."

"Your radar detector is off the beam, way off. Henry Lander can't endure Sophy. She hates him. I have suspected that after her husband's death—the Judge was the legal adviser of his creditors—there was a battle royal between them. He knows that her take-off of him rates high on her program of imitations. He hates coming while she is here and she is everlastingly warning me against him. She declares he wants to marry me, but, as I am in full possession of my senses I know it isn't true. He wants the presidency of the college but even to gain that or Beechcroft I doubt if he would marry."

"Isn't the present Prexy still a popular and capable administrator?"

"He is, and a great gentleman with all that word means. The war increased his problems one hundred per cent; commonplace details as to menus for the dining hall, his O.K. on admissions, repairing of buildings, and dozens of questions that have been the business of others pile up on his desk. He has done a beautiful job, a mountain of additional work and *no* additional gravy."

"Does he want to give up?"

"No, not until retiring age, but someone, I hope it wasn't Lander himself, started a whispering campaign to oust him. Did the Judge and Sophy arrive at the island together?"

"She said she went over early with the houseboy to remove her belongings stored in the log cabin you have turned over to me. Ever heard of them?"

"No."

"I thought perhaps you hadn't. Her explanation was too glib. Has Mrs. Sophy a secret in her young life?"

"Probably several. I wouldn't know."

"You wouldn't. You never repeat unkind gossip or scandal, Molly B., do you?"

"I break the chain when it reaches me. As to Sophy and her secret, most of us have one."

"You've got something there. I mean a secret that she would make any sacrifice to keep from coming to the surface."

"What is it all about, Debby? Are you working up the plot to a mystery yarn and taking poor, harmless Sophy as the nucleus from which to spin your thread?"

"So, that's the *modus operandi?* I didn't know. Thanks for the tip. You are right, I have picked up the whodunit bug. There is plenty of material in my diary from which to spin."

"Then for goodness'. sake, stick to that, but watch out for libel suits. I speak as one who knows. Don't drag poor Sophy into the toils. Hear the luncheon chimes? You'd better go down while I stand guard here. It is always buffet, serve yourself. It won't seem unusual if we straggle in."

"Go first, Molly B. My Washington boss phoned that he would buzz me at one. That will provide an excellent reason for me to wait here until you come."

"When that boss calls tell him you are not going back, Deb. I want you, I want someone of my very own. I need you here terribly," Madam Stewart admitted, with tears in her eyes, before she stepped into the hall.

"Were you coming to report to me, Stella? We will go down to lunch together. Before you return to the Flower Show I want you to do an errand in town at—" The closing door shut off her voice.

That was Molly B.'s first move to get the members of the family away from the house as Tim had suggested, Deborah decided. Why had Stella come to the door? Had she removed the loose-leaf book from the safe and suddenly remembered that she hadn't put it back? Whoever it had been must have found the slip with the combination. Was the secretary carrying out the command, "It's your job to get those papers"? The Wild Danes had plenty of enemies. Was one of them twisting the thumbscrews? Apparently the person who had opened the safe had taken papers. It didn't look as if the jewels had been disturbed. Who knew? Every case might be empty.

Suppose the mysterious safe opener suddenly remembered he had moved a loose-leaf notebook, that he had not replaced it? He might seize the moment when he thought the household would be at luncheon to put it back. Better hide it and quick, as Molly B. had suggested.

She slipped behind the mirror screen, through the bedroom and dressing room into the workroom. The place had a fascination for her. Paintings which had been designed for the jackets of Molly Burton's books lent color—and an occasional touch of gruesomeness—to the cool, gray walls. There were full-page ads, photographs of the author along the years, framed letters from three world-famous persons who had taken time from their crowded lives to tell her they had read all night to find the solution of a mystery only to discover that they had guessed wrong as to the murderer, letters that would be as well worth stealing for the signatures as some of her jewels.

The drawer of the filing cabinet squeaked as she drew it out. What was that other sound? She dropped the loose-leaf book into the file, motionless, listened. Someone was moving in the living room, stealthily. She tiptoed to the screen and stuck her head cautiously around an end panel. The living room door was being closed quietly, very quietly from the outside. Chills pricked along her veins. Her mouth went dry. Her heart beat like an Indian war drum. Who could it be? Dumbbell, why was she standing here wondering?

The question released her taut muscles. She dashed across the long room to the hall door and opened it carefully. No one in the corridor. She almost fell over the balustrade in her excitement to see the hall below. No one in sight.

Back in the living room she leaned against the closed door. Someone had stolen out of this room, someone who was afraid of being seen. Had the person been concealed here since the safe was opened? If so, where? It would be a person who knew the arrangement of the rooms. Had Tim been overheard when he had said he was going for the experts? Nothing to do now but stand guard till Molly B. returned to take over. Meanwhile better close the drawer into which she had dumped her diary.

As she approached the filing cabinet in the workroom she glanced casually at the large flat desk upon which lay long pages of printer's galleys in imminent danger of being scattered by a breeze from the open window. She picked up an old-fashioned paperweight with a colored flower within its glass ball from the top of the bookcase, brushed her hand across her incredulous eyes and looked again. Under it was a slip of white paper. She could read the directions for opening the safe. Had someone after using it put it there for Molly B. to find?

VII

ON HIS way home from the village Tim Grant glanced at
the clock on the instrument board of his open maroon convertible. Three-thirty. There would be time for a look-see at
his own house. He had driven the fingerprint and safe experts to Beechcroft and back to the bank. Not a person had
they met coming or going. Molly B. had been waiting for
them in her living room. She had said that just as she returned from lunch the Washington call had come for Deb
and they had not had a chance to exchange a word.

The fingerprint man had reported that the safe had been
wiped clean, there were no prints. Ingrid Johnson's natural-
ization papers and letters had been taken and the file which
held Roger Stewart's suggestions to his wife as to the disposal
of Beechcroft and some of his holdings were gone. The
jewels were intact. Apparently the cases had not been
touched. Molly B. had shaken her head in disbelief.

"Who in this house, I still think it was an inside job,
would want your grandfather's letters to me or Ingrid's papers, Tim? Those last for blackmail? That's a stupid suggestion. There has been nothing in her life to warrant it, even
if she had money enough for a blackmailer to risk a prison
sentence, which she hasn't. Shall I tell her?"

"Not until after the Flower Show. She is carrying the brunt
of that, isn't she? Why give her more to worry about? Let
me tell her tonight after dinner."

"That is an inspired suggestion, I have dreaded it."

Had Roger Stewart's letters been taken for a blind or because someone had a vital interest in knowing the ultimate
disposal of certain parts of his estate, he wondered as the
convertible shot ahead. Taken for a blind, he'd bet that Ingrid's papers were the loot wanted. His mother had intimated in her diary that the Norwegian had been something
of a mystery girl when she came to Beechcroft, but the
suspicion might have been a part of her hysterical opposition to her father's new wife.

How did the opening of the safe tie up with the screams
at 4 A.M.? He still couldn't swallow that nightmare explanation. There was the matter of the sound of the closing door

in the entrance hall he had heard—could it have been a prowler frightened off by Ingrid's yell? The safe had been looted between Molly B.'s breakfast hour and noon. The more he thought of it the more baffling the mystery. Better drop it into his unconscious for a while. Could be, it would pop up solved.

Perfect day for the Flower Show. The air was tangy with the scent of spruce and balsam. The sky was cobalt blue, a few fluffy clouds drifted aimlessly as if they didn't care whether or not they arrived anywhere. Birds sounded off in the shrubs, squirrels chattered. No whining fighter planes overhead to tear this sky apart, thank God.

Four years had passed since he had seen the yellow of birch, the flame of swamp maple, the crimson pointed spearheads of sumac with its green leaves just beginning to color like the clump behind the straggling stone wall which glistened with mica. From the woods beyond the roadside bordered with pink-plumed joe-pye weed, purple towers of asters and a mint of goldenrod, came the rhythmic gurgle of a brook.

Grand country, New England. He had been sent west to school when he was ten but he never had forgotten it. His decision to return to the family home and the great enterprise his grandfather had conceived and raised to eminence hadn't been sudden, he realized as he drove slowly through cathedral quiet, along a road shaded by giant pines and spreading oaks. He had thought it had stemmed from statements in his mother's diary which were in urgent need of straightening out; now he knew that those had been but the occasion, that the motivating urge had been his determination, even as a small boy, someday to take Roger Stewart's place and forward his work.

He hadn't dreamed of starting as Head of the Science Center, he had planned on being an instructor for a beginning, or perhaps superintendent of a department at the lab. Judge Lander was working for the presidency of the college; if he made it there would be no place for Cobina Grant's son on the faculty. If the statements in his mother's diary were facts—it was up to him to prove if they were or not—the smooth Henry was not a fit person for the job. How had he retained Molly B.'s friendship through the years? He couldn't have pulled wool over the eyes of a woman keen as she—or could he? Even though younger, was he scheming to marry her? Being master of Beechcroft would add prestige to the president of the college.

Boy, but his honor had been a funny sight at 4 A.M. The mirror above the windshield gave back his grin. A gentleman so rotund at the waistline shouldn't appear at the door

46

of a lady he might be courting in a green brocade lounge robe that pitilessly revealed his curves, which thought brought him up spang against the memory of the frightened group. What was behind the yell that had assembled it? Nightmare? No, though he would stake this car that Molly B. really believed that had been the cause of the screams.

As he approached Beechcroft a girl stepped between the gates into the road ahead and held up a thumb. Her sports frock was white with a glisten of gold belt. No hat. Curious, this hatless fashion. Must save heaps of money. It was Debby Randall. Her hair shone like wavy, blue-black satin in the sun. Were her lovely legs stockingless? He couldn't tell at this distance. She wasn't waiting there by chance. What had happened? He stopped the car.

"Taxi?" She settled into the seat beside him. "What goes?" he asked, as he drove on. "Must be something world-shaking for you to hold me up."

"Right. This is a holdup. I have something to tell you. With each person at Beechcroft a potential suspect it had to be away from the house. We don't know who is watching or listening."

"Have you told Molly B.?"

"No. You and the experts were on her heels when she relieved the guard, after luncheon, the guard being yours truly, in case you've forgotten. Then the call came from Washington. By the time my boss had rung off her living room door was closed. I figured that meant no admittance, that you were all busy within. After I changed my clothes, had lunch and returned to her living room, she had gone. I had to tell someone what I had discovered, so here I am."

"I'm all ears. Brief it for me."

As they passed fields dotted with clumps of juniper, patched with granite boulders, dotted with black and white cattle who stopped chewing their cuds to watch the car, she told of the softly closing living room door, of the discovery of the slip of white paper.

"Period. What do you make of it, Tim?"

"Nothing so far. The return of the safe combination knocks my theories into a cocked hat. You say you haven't told Molly B.?"

"No. It was quivering on the tip of my tongue when she came into the living room but I didn't have a chance. Then, the more I thought of it the more I felt that you should hear it first."

"Bright gal. If you haven't seen her since the visit of the experts you haven't heard that the jewels weren't touched." He told what was missing.

"*Papers!* Ingrid's and Molly B.'s? I wonder—"

"Don't stop to wonder. Talk. I've suspected you were holding out on me. Come clean."

She repeated the whispered words that had drifted from the bay in the gallery, told of the sound of a door closing in the left wing, of the voice singing, "From the desert I come to thee."

"On the third floor? Lander, Romney and Warner have rooms there and I'm bunking in my grandfather's onetime study which takes up the entire front of the left wing."

"Perhaps it was you I heard? Perhaps you have a dark secret in your life. Molly B. says most persons have."

"Could be, except that as I haven't qualified as the daring young man on a flying trapeze I couldn't have coasted down two flights of stairs and flown up one and a half before colliding with you and if that isn't enough, there isn't a radio in my room."

"Don't be touchy, Tim. Of course it wasn't you. And while we are on the subject of your touchiness, I would like to make it clear that I haven't the slightest belief that you are here to get Molly B.'s share of your grandfather's property by marrying me—is my face red and not entirely from sunburn—or charming her. Now, can't we be friends?"

"We can. What say we work together on the solution of the Beechcroft Mystery? How's that for a title?"

"I'm all for it. I have an urge to try my hand at fiction. Getting at the truth about the safe opening will give me something to start on."

"Does that mean you are through in Washington?"

"Yes. When my boss phoned today I told him I wouldn't be back. He didn't expect my return until January but from his heated protest you would have thought I was walking out without notice. Perhaps I have made a mistake, perhaps I am qualified only for that kind of work—intelligence flash —perhaps if you are appointed Head of the Science Center you'll give me a chance as your secretary."

"No dice. I don't want you as a secretary."

"Don't bite. My suggestion was merely my idea of the light touch. I couldn't qualify. I haven't a scientific cell in my brain—if that is where scientific cells are located. The other day I read that a recent experiment conducted by scientists indicated that a person of average intelligence must concentrate for six hours on the fundamentals of the atomic problems in order to understand them sufficiently to pass them along to someone else. Six hours. Ye gods, those scientists are optimists."

"Boy. Can you read a thing once and quote like that?"

"Marine, I cannot tell a lie. Knowing that I was coming into a hotbed of scientists, that I would meet the brother-

48

hood at dinners, I boned up on it in case I was stuck for a subject for conversation. Am I good?"

"You are spectacular. Go on, spread the doctrine, that of understanding the effect of atomic war. The next war will lay this world of ours waste, the only remedy is in the hearts of men, in their determination that there shall be no more wars, that there shall be good will between the nations of this earth."

"I have heard something like that before. 'And suddenly there was with the angel a multitude of the heavenly host praising God and saying: Glory to God in the highest and on earth peace to all men of good will.' That is what you mean, isn't it?"

"Exactly. One reason I am so keen to head the Science Center is because I will have hundreds of GIs to whom to teach the doctrine, to turn into Johnny Appleseeds covering the country, perhaps the world from east to west, from north to south, sowing the seeds of the Brotherhood of Man till lasting peace is a reality, not a hope.

"How the dickens did we get switched to my major soap-box oration"—his laughing eyes met hers in the windshield mirror—"the education of the peoples of the world as to the menace of atomic energy?"

"I started it. Of course you will be appointed Head of the Science Center. Didn't your grandfather first create, then endow it?"

"I don't want it for that reason. Either I am qualified to serve regardless of my background, or I am not. I realize that I'll have to go in fighting every step of the way, if I make it—to carry out my ideas. Lander will block me if he can. 'I have a feelin' ' he plays rough. He is a powerful factor in the college, an expert politician and money getter, he will go to town on those two qualities if he achieves the presidency."

"It will be horribly unfair if he does. Molly B. declares that Prexy has done and is doing a super job, but, the Judge has a way with the faculty wives."

"Do the faculty wives run this college?"

"They have a tremendous influence on the thinking of their husbands. Most wives have, haven't they?"

"I wouldn't know, having seen few women since I enlisted in the service. But if they can blur and blot out a man's sense of justice, I won't acquire one at present. I can't afford to have the issues of the next few years obscured."

"Cheerio, there are doubtless exceptions. You may be one of the men impervious to woman's wiles. I understand there are some. Isn't that your adorable house ahead? The four tall white columns give it a southern antebellum look. Why did we come this way?"

"I promised Molly B. I would report at the Flower Show. Had to come here first to check on the painters and paperhangers who are doing over the upstairs rooms."

"Are you planning to live here—alone?"

"Why the stunned surprise?"

"That's right, why? Perhaps you don't intend to live alone. My word, in spite of your views on matrimony recently expressed perhaps you are married."

"I am not. I can't live with Molly B. forever, can I? There are such things as housekeepers, at least there were before I joined up with the Marines. I'll get Sarah Allen to hunt up one for me. You are going to the Show. Wait for me while I check on the workmen and we'll drive to the Town Hall. We two sleuths should hang together."

"I'm not crazy about the word 'hang.' Perhaps we will. I'll go on with you. I had intended to return to Beechcroft and pick up the roadster. Molly B. and Sophy Brandt were driven to the Show in the antiquated but still impressive Rolls-Royce."

"You said a while ago you suspected that Lander and Mrs. Sophy had met by appointment on the island. Object, romance?"

"No, Molly B. says they detest each other. It might be money. Sophy had a beautiful home, diamonds galore, was a superb hostess, her establishment ran as if on oiled wheels, she was a social power. Her husband died suddenly leaving a load of debts, and a small annuity for her. One son, a bachelor, is a career diplomat, in Argentina at present. The other two are married and swamped with the expenses of a family. She ekes out her income by visiting friends and playing cards —for money—not at Beechcroft, though, Molly B. has views about that."

"No wonder the woman is bitter and unhappy. What a tragedy. A fine homemaker going to waste. Hey, that's a thought. Here we are. Come in and wait for me, will you?"

"It looks like that or walking to the Town Hall. I'll wait in the garden. I remember the view from there. It is something out of this world."

"The last four laborless years have reduced it to a jungle, but you may find a flower or two. Help yourself. Here we are. Hop out."

When he appeared an half hour later she was in the car with a perfect red rose in her hair and a small bunch of blue flowers in her hand.

"Sorry I kept you waiting so long but they caught me on long distance."

"No apology needed. I loved the garden. I found these bachelor-buttons for the lapel of your gray coat. Come here while I draw the stems through the buttonhole. Not so good. They hide your ribbon."

"Don't take them out. They are all right as they are. I shan't wear the ribbon when the GIs get here." He slipped behind the wheel. "All set? We're off on the first lap of our mystery hunt. From now on, so far as you and I are concerned, there is a suspect behind every bush, a clue at the end of every beckoning trail."

"My word, that has a professional sound. You wouldn't be a dick in disguise, would you?"

"I would not. 'Dick.' You've given me an idea, though. Scared? There was a quiver in your laugh."

"Not scared, excited. Your suggestion that a suspect was hidden behind every bush set my imagination galloping, and can it gallop."

As they entered the Town Hall with its flower-lined walls a captain of aviation, slim, rangy, blond, seized Deb in his arms and kissed her with a resounding smack that drew the astonished attention of every person within a radius of thirty feet, and flushed her face a brilliant pink.

"Light-of-my-eyes, where have you been? Didn't Pop put you wise that I was coming? I've only ten minutes in which to tell you I love you before I shove off again."

"My word, Gordy, haven't you grown up even in the service?" Deb laughed and tucked her hand under his arm. "Why go on the air about the tender passion? Let's find a quiet spot where we can talk. When your father phoned I wondered why he was so anxious to know where I would be this afternoon."

"Sure, he was anxious, he wants to keep his ace secretary in the family. So do I." They walked away together.

"That seems to be that," Tim observed under his breath. He bought a catalogue from a girl in USO regalia and was waylaid by another with a flat basket of boutonnieres. He shook his head and touched the bachelor-buttons in his coat lapel.

"Presented by a lovely lady. No can change."

He laughed and dropped a bill into her basket. On he went from exhibit to exhibit, from incredibly tall stalks of late delphiniums which ran the gamut of blues and purples, past tables laden with glass vases displaying gladioli in exquisite tints and shades and dahlias by the colorful score.

Canaries in golden cages were bursting their yellow throats in song, as if in competition with the wired-in music. He caught up with Molly B. in silver gray and a large red hat. She was standing before a shadow-box in which were arranged all white flowers, single dahlias, snapdragon, glads, one perfect lily, a faint mist of feathery gypsophilia in a pale green Lalique vase.

"Like it, Tim?" she inquired. "It won the silver bowl."

"It's all right. I would have put my money on that squatty gold affair with the yellow roses, but I'm no judge I'm such a push-over for color."

"So am I. It is food and drink to me. Have you seen Deb?"

"We came together. When she stepped into the hall she was seized by an aviation captain and soundly kissed. Those flyers get away with murder."

"A captain? He must be the son of her Washington boss, who was her father's best friend. What is he doing here?"

"Making violent love to your granddaughter was indicated."

"I wish the violent love-making would dent her heart. She is sweet and lovely with us all, but I have the feeling there are frozen depths that nothing has stirred."

He thought of the girl's tempest of tears under the pine tree. Unless he was mistaken the "frozen depths" not only had stirred, they had smashed. Apparently Molly B. didn't know of what Deb had called a "weep-fest."

"Don't worry about her. Being with you will swing her back to normal. Do we eat? I was so busy transporting the experts and changing my clothes while they were at work that I forgot lunch. I'm hollow to my toes."

"Did those men report anything more to you?"

"No. Nothing definite till tomorrow. We'd better sign off on that subject, Molly B. Even your whisper carries."

"You are right. Judge Lander will join us at tea. Don't start anything with him, *please*, Tim."

"Me, start anything? Here? Lady, do you think I am that crude? Watch me be a perfect gentleman. Here comes your granddaughter. She's the snappiest dish in the hall and the prettiest."

"I agree. That makes it unanimous. Take her to the tea-room. I have a table engaged. Ingrid is rounding up the others. I'll join you in a few minutes." She turned to speak to two girls who were holding out books for her to autograph.

"What became of the Great Lover?" Tim inquired as Deborah joined him.

"Already on his way to California and points west."

"Is he the plan to which you referred?"

"Plan? What plan?"

"Forgotten that you refused to marry me because you had other plans?"

"Be noble and cross off your memory book the fact that I refused to marry a man who hadn't asked me. As to the plan, I was referring to a career, and believe it or not, from what I have observed of the casualties it won't be matrimony.

Having answered that world-shaking question, we'd better follow Molly B. She is looking over her shoulder at us."

As if to separate Lander, seated at her right, and him as much as possible, Madam Stewart had directed Tim to the seat across the table from her. Sam Farr, in white, was at his left, and Tilly in yellow linen on his other side. Her right arm was covered from wrist to elbow with gold bangles which clashed with every movement of her hand. The sound drew the Judge's eyes to her like a magnet—was that her intention?

Deb, Sophy Brandt, Stella Dane, Romney and Warner, who had arrived late, filled out the table. Laughter and repartee, conversation, with the Judge grabbing the spotlight with his account of recent contributions to the college and his plans for its advancement, were accompanied by the tinkle of silver on china, the ecstatic trill of canaries which rose above the soft, radioed strains of "It Might As Well Be Spring," the scent of many flowers and the aroma of coffee and tea. Sam Farr touched Tim's sleeve and indicated Lander with a wave of his spoon.

" 'Upon what meat doth this our Caesar feed, That he is grown so great?' " he quoted softly. He raised a glass of water and hummed behind its shelter:

"Some day I'm going to murder the bugler . . ."

VIII

INGRID JOHNSON stepped from the long window to the terrace, the light from the room behind set the silver sequins on her midnight blue dinner frock shimmering. Tim Grant slid off the wall on which he had been perched thinking and smoking.

"Molly B. said you had something to tell me, Tim," she explained. "She sounded terribly serious. What have I done?" The exaggerated fear in her voice and the nervous laugh which followed he recognized as an act.

"You have done nothing, Ingrid, it is what has been done to you I have to report."

"To me?" The concern in her question was genuine.

"Let's go to the bench on the edge of the lake. We can't be overheard there. Swell night," he observed as they walked along the garden paths. "Not even a hint of September crispness. How did the Flower Show turn out?"

"A social success, but with the usual amount of heartburning and bursts of temper over the awards. I am exhausted from my efforts to keep things smooth, and to make myself heard above the crescendo trills of those indefatigable canaries. However, we made money for USO and that was what we were after. Next year there will be more than two hundred thousand veterans in hospitals, and a million and a half servicemen on duty, part of them the 'kid-brother army.' The United Service Organizations must continue to function. We can't let them die out."

"I should say not. Here we are. The bench is dry." He sat beside her. "In this light the island looks like a fragment of fairyland dropped into the five-mile-long lake. By the time I was ten I could swim from the campus boathouse to the island. I was sure then that making good as a swimming champ was my destiny."

"Funny how youthful ideas change. As a boy my brother's ambition was to be a jockey. He was a chemist assigned to work on explosives when the war started. Let's not stall any longer, *please*. Tell me what this conference is about, Tim.

It isn't that Molly B. wants me to leave and has asked you to break the news, is it?"

"Good Lord, no. What put that fantastic idea into your head?"

"Not so fantastic when you realize that Judge Lander detests me and is doing his best to influence her against me. She has a great respect for his opinion."

"He doesn't like me and is doing his darnedest to oust me from the neighborhood; so far he hasn't succeeded. Molly B. wouldn't cut you out of her life any more than she would carve out a piece of her heart. I brought you here to tell you that your papers had been snitched from her safe." For an instant she sat motionless, as if his statement had stunned her.

"My papers? Do you mean my citizenship papers and letters I keep there? How, when were they taken? Who could want them? Is anything else missing? Were the jewels or the money stolen?"

"No. Whoever opened the safe—"

"Was it cracked?"

"No. Someone got wise to the combination. The thief apparently wanted only your papers and Roger Stewart's letters to his wife."

"Those gone? Then they were what the safe-opener wanted, mine were red herring drawn across the trail. Molly B. has told me that in them her husband indicated what he wished done with this property, eventually. Who would be the most interested person to know? That's easy. Henry Lander. He's scheming to marry her to get this place. He's not so much younger than she, as you—"

"Not so loud, Ingrid. Voices carry in this clear air and it's hush-hush that the safe was opened."

"Sorry. When did Molly B. discover that the papers were gone?"

He told of the lost safe combination, of Debby's notebook on the floor.

"What do you make of it?"

"It must have been someone in the house and a first offender or he—or she—wouldn't have forgotten to put back the notebook. Come to think of it, I'm not so sure it was someone in the house. Now, I'll tell you something. I heard steps on the balcony outside Molly B.'s living room early this morning and yelled."

"You're telling me. Don't you know that you brought every guest in the house, except Sophy Brandt, to that door at 4 A.M.?"

"Molly B. didn't tell me that. She honestly believed I had a

55

nightmare and I let her think so. Between the first and second scream I would have sworn I heard footsteps going down the balcony steps. I've been afraid someone would come for her jewels, have begged her to keep the dog in her living room at night."

"Where does he sleep?"

"Scragg takes him to the service cottage. Cocky is a dear, but he runs away and then appears at an unearthly hour in the morning and barks on the terrace to be let in. I don't wonder Molly B. doesn't want him in her apartment. When the butler has him he barks under his window."

"Why didn't you tell Molly B. about the sound you heard?"

"With daylight came the suspicion that I had had a nightmare, they can be terribly real. No one else apparently had heard anything unusual. Why worry her? Then I was caught up in the Flower Show—caught is right, I felt as if I had been churned round and round in a squirrel cage before the day ended—and I haven't thought of those mysterious footsteps again until now. I believe—"

"Miss Johnson." Scragg's sleek voice brought them to their feet. How long had he been behind them? How much had he overheard?

"What is it, Scragg?" Ingrid inquired and clutched at Tim's sleeve. Was she *afraid* of the butler?

"Mrs. Carroll would like to speak to you on the phone, something important about the Flower Show, she said. She's holding the line."

"More heartburning because of the prizes, probably, Tim. The next time I have anything to do with awards I'll be older —a whole lot older. I'll answer at once, Scragg."

"Very good, Miss." The butler hesitated as if waiting for her to precede him, then turned and stalked toward the house.

"You don't have to run, Ingrid," Tim suggested as he kept pace with her through the fragrant garden. "You could call the Carroll person if she hangs up, you know."

"Scragg was so solemn, his voice scared me, suddenly coming on top of your news." At the long, open window on the terrace she stopped. "How did he know where we were? Something queer about that," she added in a whisper before she stepped into the room.

"Mrs. Sophy, what has happened?" Her concerned voice drifted out. "You are crying."

There was a muffled reply before Sophy Brandt came slowly through the open window and sank into a deep chair. Tim heard one sob and then another.

"Anything I can do to help?" he asked before he seated himself beside her. She drew a long ragged breath.

56

"I'm afraid you can't, Tim. Why, why does life have to get in such a mess when one is old?"

"Cheerio, lady, you're not old. You and Molly B. were classmates. Do you know of anyone, except teen-age bobby-soxers, who would call her old?"

"But she has her work. I have nothing. I can't write or paint, I can knit, play the piano, but who wants that with plenty of youngsters to do it?"

"You could run a house, couldn't you?"

"Certainly I could run a house, but who would engage a woman my age?"

"For Pete's sake, forget that age obsession. Some psychiatrist should start a movement to isolate the age bug. It does more harm than the boll weevil by the loss to the world of experienced workers. I would engage you. I had planned to ask you to live in my house and be my hostess."

"Tim." Excitement brought her out of her slump. Even in the dusk of the terrace he could see her cheeks redden slowly, light flame in her blue eyes. The diamonds on her fingers shot iridescent sparks as she clasped her plump hands.

"Do you mean it? In your mother's lovely house with its choice equipment? You—you are not just kidding me, are you?" The breathless, unsteady question tightened his throat.

"Now I ask you, Mrs. Sophy, why should I kid you? Here's the situation."

He told of his intention to have his own home, that because of the help the Center had been during the war there would be many scientists coming to the college whom he would want to entertain whether he were the Head or not, that together they would work out a budget, that during the year since his mother's death considerable income had accumulated which meant they wouldn't have to pinch pennies; suggested the amount of her salary and asked if she thought it would be fair.

"Fair? It is too much, Tim. I can manage a house that size with one hand tied behind me."

"We'll let it stand at that sum. Remember, you haven't taken a crack at housekeeping since the war, conditions are very different, I understand. There will be more to it than managing a house. I'm likely to jump a bunch of guests on you at short notice and with service and food conditions as they are you may have to hustle to provide both, then appear as an unstampedable and gracious hostess. How about it? Want the job?"

"Want it? It sounds like heaven. As to service I believe I can solve that problem. My mind has been running double track as you talked. When will I begin?"

"The workmen will be out tomorrow. How about looking over the house in the morning and making a list of what we'll need to carry on? You'll find it a mess. A lot of barrels of china, trunks of linen and some mirrored stuff were sent on from the New York apartment, most of the furniture was sold there. I'll have the silver sent from the bank. Is your answer still yes?"

"Double yes. I'll see that you have the most perfectly run house on the campus—always excepting this—Sarah Allen is an expert. Shall I tell Molly B.?"

"Sure. This isn't a secret compact. We'll drive to the—"

"Run to earth at last, Mrs. Sophy." Deborah stepped through the open window to the terrace. Little rivulets of silver glistened on her short-sleeve pink dinner frock. "Sam Farr is looking for you. Oklahoma coming up."

Sophy Brandt seemed inches taller as, with chin lifted, shoulders back, she crossed to the window.

"He'll get me, what's more my opponents won't see me for my smoke." Her laugh was unsteady. "Life begins at sixty-five, Tim."

Deborah's eyes followed her till she was lost in the distance of the lighted room, came back to the man leaning against a vine-covered upright of the terrace.

"What did she mean, 'life begins at sixty-five'? Where has she been? Imbibing at the Fountain of Youth? Mrs. Sophy entered the house as if she were the Queen of England and Empress of India, that is, as I think the personage would appear, my personal contact with royalty having been limited. What worked the miracle, Tim?"

He told her.

"Where did you get the crazy idea that Mrs. Sophy with her eternal knitting will qualify?"

"From you, this afternoon. Forgotten that you told me her house had run on oiled wheels, that she was a superb hostess?"

"Yes, but that was before she had become an unhappy old—"

"Did she look like an unhappy old—whatever you were about to call her—as she crossed the terrace? You said she had the mien of royalty."

"That's right, but—"

"Sophy Brandt has had no interest, has not been needed; that spells tragedy for man or woman—no wonder she has picked up the old-age bug. I believe she will make good in the position I have offered her."

"Suppose you marry? She will be out of a job and then the tragedy will be all to do over."

"That doesn't follow. My marriage at present, though I've

58

had the girl on my mind for some time, is a mere speck on the horizon, in fact when I look closely I can't see the speck. If I head the Center, the job will take all my thought and time."

"Don't put it off too long. She may not wait for you."

"It's tough but I have to take that chance. To return to Mrs. Sophy, if she makes good with me she'll have plenty of chances at a job. Can you see Molly B. deciding that she is through writing for years and years? I'll bet you can't. I am so sure she will make good that I'll invite you now to be our first dinner guest."

"And right off quick I accept. I have a ravishing frock I will save for the occasion, but I just somehow can't see Sophy Brandt presiding at the head of your table."

"You will. Debby, you couldn't suggest to her that she get rid of that—er—that er—hideous yellow bang, could you?"

"I could not. From now on, Pygmalion, Sophy is your Galatea—and yours alone—to shape to your fancy."

"Okay, you wouldn't be making a joke of my plan because you'd like the job yourself, would you?"

"In words of one syllable, I would not. I wouldn't marry you—"

"Boy, did that sound like a proposal? I hope I can do better than that when my big chance comes. Haven't I just told you that my heart-throb is already selected? I was talking about a housekeeper, not a wife."

"No goes for both. How did we get into this wacky discussion? I came to ask if you'd snagged any more clues to the mystery of the stolen papers? I heard Molly B. tell Ingrid that you wanted to talk to her."

"Let's get away from the house and I'll tell you. I'm beginning to believe every stone on this place has ears."

He waited till they were seated side by side on the white rim of the pool which reflected the lights from the game house windows before he answered her question.

"Molly B. asked me to tell Ingrid that her papers had been taken."

"Did she seem much disturbed?"

"No, she appeared more concerned about the Roger Stewart letters which were missing, she was sure hers had been taken as a cover-up. At once she suspected the fine Italian hand of Judge Lander. She told of hearing footsteps on the balcony of Molly B.'s living room, that she screamed, and heard them going down the steps. She had started to say, 'I believe' —when Scragg spoke behind us."

"I've had my suspicions that those yells weren't nightmare. Come on, let's go back to the terrace. I'm all creepy chills. The mystery is getting under my skin. Remember what I heard in the gallery bay, 'It's your job to get those papers—if you don't, you know the consequences to you.' "

"Take it easy." He slipped his hand under her bare arm as they started for the house. "Walk, not run, to the nearest exit. You are shaking with excitement."

"Sure, I'm excited. Whispered threats. Screams. Footsteps. Stolen papers. They convey a sense of doom. I have been thinking also that it was queer that Scragg should have interrupted Ingrid as she was about to say who she thought had been on the balcony."

"I had reached the same conclusion. Something tells me that the butler at Beechcroft will bear watching."

IX

THE haze over the hills meant a hot day tomorrow, even if it were the twentieth of September, Tim thought, as he stood at the window of the room which had been his father's home office, the room in which Dean Grant had talked over the most serious matters with student malefactors. It was spoken of still by the older alumni as the Dean's Den, he had been told. Pity some of them couldn't see it now with shadows cast by the low fire making grotesque patterns on the crimson leather chairs and books on the shelves, tinting with pink the white chrysanthemums in the copper bowl on the large, flat desk, the last being one of Sophy Brandt's touches that had turned this long vacant house into a home.

"Come in," he responded to a knock on the porch door.

"Who was the old duffer in the *Iliad* who was supposed to be the bearer of good news, Tim, or wasn't there one?" Sam Farr asked as he entered. "Anyway, I'm him, something grammatically wrong there, but we'll let it go in the interest of speed. You're Head of the Science Center, fella. Official notice will come later."

"Let's sit down, Sam. The news takes the stiffening from these old knees. I began to think Lander would block the appointment." He motioned to a chair across the desk from the one he pulled out.

Sam Farr produced a bag of tobacco from the pocket of his brown coat, filled a dark and smelly pipe, lighted it and settled into the crimson leather chair.

"Any questions?" he asked between puffs.

"Are you sure?"

"Sure I'm sure. Can you see me barging in here if I were not?"

"Was it a unanimous election?"

"No. Judge Lander had his knife out for you, did his darnedest to block it, but both the Board of Trustees and Faculty were at the meeting and snowed him under."

"Any others turn thumbs down? Let's have the whole awful truth, then I will know what I am up against."

"Warner voted with Lander. Romney refused, said he was too new here to register a vote."

"I don't get it. Why should that newcomer, Warner, have it in for me?"

"Warner isn't a newcomer. He was drafted from a teaching job here."

"I remember, he's back in the applied physics department. I still don't get a reason for his opposition to me unless he counted upon filling the position himself. He must know he isn't qualified."

"Probably does, but he's always been Lander's yes-man. Romney is in the cyclotron lab with its new atom-smasher."

"Quite sure I'm elected?"

"For good behavior and life, I guess, if you want it that long. M.I.T. and the brass in the Pacific didn't soft-pedal their praise of you as a scientist and organizer; if one believes them you are Science's gift to the world. Also, they bore down hard on your courage as a fighter—that's what you'll need in your new job, fella, make no mistake about that. You're all set unless—"

"Here it comes. Go on. Unless?"

Sam Farr tapped his pipe tree of ashes in a copper tray and slipped it into his pocket.

"Unless Henry Lander is made president of the college. There is a minority that will go all out for him, can't tell how much they can swing the others. If he gets it you and I will be expeditiously canned. The constitution of this college gives the president practically a free hand to hire and fire. The present Prexy consults the Board and Faculty."

"So what? You didn't come here to tell me this without having a remedy up your sleeve, did you?"

"Wise guy. I came to suggest that you use the weapon your mother provided and oust his honor from the Board of Trustees now, before he has a chance to get in his dirty work. She had the goods on him, hadn't she?"

"How did you know?"

Sam Farr relaxed in the chair and laughed. His blue eyes were glints of triumph between their sleepy lids.

"I didn't, till you confirmed my suspicion by that question. My people have been connected with this college for generations. Always there has been a Farr on the Board or the Faculty. Things get around. I'm not asking what, if any, charges against Henry Lander Cobina Grant handed on to you, I would rather not know, but if you have disabling ammunition, for Pete's sake use it—and quick." He rose.

"Having fired my shot—which I hope will be heard around the campus—I will depart." He stopped at the door. "Nice place you have here."

"It was my father's conference room when he was Dean."

"I've heard of the Dean's Den. I wonder what the GIs will

62

call my torture chamber. Drop in and see it. It's quite nifty. By the way, Tilly is agog with curiosity to know how Sophy Brandt is working out as housekeeper hostess."

"She's a fairy story come true. She went to New York and came back with a couple who had worked as cook and butler for her. They had retired from service. She persuaded them that a year or two in the country at spectacular wages would lengthen their lives no end. Then she produced a onetime personal maid, Mildred, who does what the man and wife don't. If there are any creaks in the domestic machinery I never hear them. Tilly will be able to judge for herself how the house is running. I phoned her this morning to ask if you and she would dine here tomorrow. Black tie."

"Black tie, says you. There hasn't been a white one worn here since December 7, 1941. Tilly will swoon with envy when she sees that butler. We have a GI and his missus who have taken over the housework in exchange for rooms, board and compensation. It isn't that we can't pay for experienced help. We can't get it." He cleared his voice, swelled out his chest and said in Henry Lander's platform manner:

"And in closing, sir, think over my suggestion as to spiking the guns of a certain person before he gets a chance to shoot. Having said what I came to say, be it for better or worse, I will now, like the Captains and the Kings, depart."

At the window Tim watched him stride along the garden path. How he hated Lander. His voice humming, "Some day I'm going to murder the bugler," echoed through his mind and left a curious premonition of disaster. Was Tilly too much of a fool to realize the trouble she was fomenting? It could be trouble without a ceiling. Ostensibly Sam had come to tell him of his appointment as Head of the Science Center, really to warn him that Lander was out to defeat him somehow, some way. How could he have known what was in Cobina Grant's diary unless he had read it? Nuts to that suspicion. Sam Farr wasn't a snooper. Had someone not so honorable given it a once-over and reported its contents to him?

He glanced at his watch. Time to investigate before Mark Taylor was due at the airfield in his own plane. Grand person, he had been a colonel in the Pacific, had been hospitalized for months since his return. He needed a few weeks in the country, this college town was the ideal place for him, they had decided over long distance. It would be a pleasure to have him around and Mrs. Sophy had been enthusiastic about his coming.

He unlocked a side drawer in the desk. The three volumes of his mother's diary were as he had left them. He must have put the ivory-handled revolver and cartridges in here with the books in the hurry and confusion of moving. They should

be locked away upstairs. Emboldened by the fact that he—
or she—was still undiscovered, the safe opener at Molly
B.'s might develop a yen to investigate this room, with the
result, violence. As he laid the gun on the desk Henry Lander
spoke behind him.

"The porch door was ajar so I took it as an invitation to
enter."

Talk of the devil and his horns appear. The proverb flashed
through Tim's mind as he waited for the Judge to explain his
call. He was formally dressed in an expertly tailored dark
blue suit with a white pin stripe, he must have come directly
from the Board meeting.

"I met Dean Farr on my way in, Grant. Doubtless he
brought you the news."

"He did. Mighty nice of you to hurry here to second his
congratulations, Judge."

"Cut the sarcasm. You know better than that. To get down
to business, I want you to refuse the appointment to head
the Center. I have a candidate for the place."

"So what?" Tim produced cigarettes, tapped one loose,
lighted it and slowly returned the package to his coat pocket.
His eyes, slightly smiling, met Lander's piercing dark eyes
under their neatly trimmed white brows. "Is that a command
or a suggestion?"

"Take it either way so long as you act on it—and quick."

"Wouldn't it be a good idea to wait until the appointment
is officially confirmed before I decline the honor?" He sat on
the corner of the flat desk. "So far, I have only Dean Farr's
and your say-so."

"I came before the official notification so you would know
what to do."

"That was good of you. Suppose I don't see it your way?
Suppose I intend to accept the appointment as Head of the
Science Center? Just what can you do about it?"

"I have discovered a little complication at the Center that
won't reflect credit on the Head. I'll wait till you are nicely
installed and then I'll break the news and ruin you."

"Ruin me! What the hell do you mean, *ruin* me? Get out
and quick before I kick you out. Hello, Romney. How long
have you been standing in the doorway?"

"To be exact, the first word I heard of the controversy was
the word 'kick.' I don't know what occasioned the threat."
Burke Romney's dark eyes glanced from Lander, glaring at
him, to Tim. "I came to congratulate you on the appointment
to head the Center, Grant." There was a hint of defiance in
his voice.

"You heard Grant threaten violence, Romney. Just remember that. What are you doing here, Sophy?" He spoke to the

woman who, with a purple knitting bag on her arm, had entered from the hall.

"I didn't know there was anyone here. Have I interrupted an important conference?"

"As you appear to be here to stay I'll take off." The sneer in Henry Lander's voice sent a wave of red to the yellow bang. "Come with me, Romney, I have something to say to you." He stopped at the door. "I meant what I said, Grant."

"You don't guess *I'm* playing for fun, do you, Judge? Close the door when you go out—you are going, aren't you, or did I misunderstand that 'I'll take off'? Thanks for coming, Romney. I'll see you again." The porch door slammed behind the two men. Tim tossed the cigarette into the low fire and squared his shoulders.

"Now I know where I stand, with the Judge, at least."

"Henry Lander is a dangerous man to antagonize, Tim." Sophy Brandt's blue eyes were clouded with anxiety. "He is cruel when he gets a hold on a person. There is a rumor that he has foreclosed on the Dane property. Too bad. The sons, wild as they have been, have been working like slaves to pay him. Be careful, Tim."

"Didn't you hear him threaten me? Do you think I'll stand for that? Do I appear like a turn-the-other-cheek guy? Forget it. What can I do for you, Mrs. Sophy?"

"That means that the subject of Henry Lander is closed, I take it. Just one word more. I did hear you threaten him, I wish I hadn't. I'm frightened for fear of what you may do."

"Take it easy. I won't do anything—at present. What's on your mind?"

"Have you time before you go to meet Colonel Taylor to give me the list of guests for our dinner tomorrow?"

"Just about."

"I brought my note pad. I'll write while you dictate." She settled into his chair at the desk with a little swish of her amethyst and white print frock, patted her matching turban, laid her notebook on the desk, recoiled.

"My goodness, where did that vicious thing come from?" With the tip of her forefinger she pushed the ivory-handled revolver cautiously to the middle of the desk. "I'm scared to death of firearms."

"Sorry, Mrs. Sophy. It belonged to one of my service friends. His sister gave it to me when I took his last message to her in Washington." He picked up gun and box of cartridges, laid them on top of the diaries and closed the drawer. "It is harmless. It isn't loaded."

"If one is to believe newspaper stories it is the unloaded gun which shoots to kill. Now that the ugly thing is out of sight let's get on with the list."

"This being our first party, suppose we keep it in the family—in a way." Should he tell her they would make it a celebration of his appointment? No. He had not been officially notified. Lander still had a chance to get in his work. Sam might have been mistaken.

"What are you waiting for, Tim?"

"Mentally checking the guests. We'll ask Molly B., of course, Deb, the Farrs, Ingrid, Warner—"

"Why Clive Warner? It might be unpleasant for Deborah. You know they—"

"Sure, I know that their marriage didn't come off, darn lucky for her, if you ask me, but she's bound to meet him at every social function of the college. As we have started out to invite the Beechcroft family—pro tem—we can't omit him. List Stella Dane, let's include her brother, Mort, Burke Romney, and Judge Lander."

"Henry Lander." Sophy Brandt clutched her pencil in fingers that trembled. "After the way he spoke to you a few moments ago? He is fighting your appointment as Head of the Science Center, isn't he?"

"So is Warner, I have been told. We don't want the Judge to think I am afraid of him, do we? Jot down his name—unless he will spoil the party for you, Mrs. Sophy."

"For me? Where did you get that curious idea, Tim? I was thinking of your welfare."

"Don't worry about me. The dinner won't be too much care for you, will it, Mrs. Sophy?"

"Care? I love planning meals. Believe it or not, since I've been here I feel as if I had been born again." She blinked her lashes and swallowed hard. "Don't get uneasy, Tim. I won't burst into tears. This is where I came in. Any suggestions before I go?" She dropped pad and pencil into the purple knitting bag.

"U-m-m, yes, I have one, Mrs. Sophy." He thrust his hands into his gray coat pockets. "It isn't exactly about the dinner." He cleared his throat and settled his tie. "You may be hurt and I hate like the dickens to—"

"What is it, Tim?" She caught the lapels of his coat. The blue eyes that looked up were dark with terror. "Are you afraid to tell me I am not filling the bill? Not doing the job to suit you?" She bit her underlip to steady it before she added, "That you don't want me here?"

"Gosh, no, Mrs. Sophy. It's only that—"

"Please, Tim, please tell me. I can take it, really I can." He caught her shoulders hard.

"It isn't what you think, Mrs. Sophy. You're a bachelor's dream, you're grand. It's—it's—boy, I feel like a heel to

66

mention it, but it's—I *hate* that yellow bang. Could you—would you—"

Her laugh was a hysterical mixture of mirth and tears.

"Is that all?" She unwound the length of printed silk on her head, snatched at her forehead, and pulled off the fringe of yellow hair. It dangled from her unsteady fingers.

"It is so little to do for you who have done so much for me, Timothy. Sometime, sometime perhaps I can do more."

The next evening when Tim entered the living room before dinner, for a startled instant he wondered whence the white-haired woman in the orchid-color frock? She was readjusting the crimson glads that matched the brocade hangings to a shade, in a tall silver vase. A guest of Molly B.'s perhaps? She turned.

"Mrs. Sophy! For the love of Mike, what have you done to yourself?"

"Don't you like me this way, Tim?"

"Like you—you bet. Those short, silvery curls all over your head are a knockout. Who performed the miracle?"

"Mildred, my onetime maid. Not much of a miracle. My hair has been like this for years, covered by what is known to the trade as a 'piece.' You said you hated the fringe, I thought you might be allergic to yellow hair, so off it came. I strive to please."

Her unsteady gaiety tightened Tim's throat. A chance to be of use had changed her from a pepless, unhappy old woman to an efficient person with courage, belief in her power to achieve, and with sparkle, definitely with sparkle. He cleared his voice.

"Boy, and do you succeed in pleasing. You'll be the sensation of the evening."

She was. He wasn't so absorbed in his duties as host that he missed the exclamations of arriving guests.

"Sophy Brandt! What have you done to yourself?" from Tilly Farr. "Sophy, you're a dream. You look years younger," from Ingrid Johnson.

"Pygmalion, you've made a spectacular start on your Galatea," Deborah Randall admitted beside him. "I didn't think you could do it. Mrs. Sophy is lovely. She is wearing her famous necklace and bracelets of moonstones and diamonds. That means this is an occasion."

"Certainly it is an occasion." He dismissed the idea of telling her of his appointment. Let someone else do it. "Is that gold frock you are wearing the swankest in your wardrobe you promised to break out for my first dinner?"

"It is. If you wish more details my pearls are the string Molly B. gave me when I made my debut."

"I recognized them."

"How come?"

"Oh, I get around. Here comes Mark Taylor. Thought you needed a new interest in your life so imported him." He presented the dark-haired man with a short stubble of red mustache to Deborah.

"My friend, Colonel Taylor, late of Okinawa, Miss Randall."

"Even better than I dreamed," Mark Taylor murmured tenderly.

"I wouldn't swear to it, but I think I've heard that one in a movie and a whole lot more impressively done," Deb challenged. "You—"

"Enter our internationally famous author," Tim Grant's voice interrupted. "Mark, make our prettiest bow to Madam Roger Stewart, alias Molly Burton. I was afraid you were giving my housewarming the brush-off, Molly B."

The wall mirror above the fireplace reflected her mist-gray satin frock brocaded with silver feathers, the full, sweeping skirt, that swayed and swirled when she moved, the corsage of pink camellias, the emeralds and diamonds at her throat, her brilliant, smiling dark eyes.

"Not I, Tim. I sent Deb ahead to tell you I was held up by a long-distance call from my publisher. He suggests that while I am checking the galleys I add—heavenly day, what has Sophy done to herself?"

"Now you know why I hadn't explained our late appearance to Tim," Deb suggested, "I was knocked in a heap—" but Molly B. was already on her way to greet the hostess of the evening with Mark Taylor beside her.

"She didn't hear a word I said. Lucky Mrs. Sophy sprang her sensation before the real news of the evening broke."

"And what is the real news of the evening, Deb? Have you an announcement up your sleeve?"

"As if you didn't know that the campus is buzzing about your appointment as Head of the Center. Here comes Judge Lander. Look, Tim. He is staring at Sophy as if he couldn't believe his eyes."

"I see him. I didn't think he would come."

"Why, Tim?" ;

"We had a showdown yesterday."

"Oh, dear, does that mean war between you? Mrs. Sophy has gone white except for the touches of rouge on her cheeks." Her voice dropped to a whisper. "What *is* there between them? Fear? Hatred? Tragedy?"

"Find out and I bet we'll have a thread which will unravel the mystery of the opened safe, which gives you a rough idea of the trend of my suspicions. Meanwhile, Deb, don't look so frightened. This is a party. Strike up the band."

X

DEBORAH stopped her impetuous dash to the garage and caught at the flame-color sports coat thrown across the shoulders of her white crepe shirt, which her sudden stop had started slipping. Ingrid, with her arms full of pink and wine-color glads, stood in the middle of the cutting garden. Her frock made a patch of powder blue among the orange, tan, lavender and crimson flowers. She was talking to a man, a young man in tweedy brown, who stroked his right cheek as if something irritated it.

"Don't come here again." Ingrid had raised her voice in her insistence. Apparently the man said something. "I haven't decided," she answered tensely. "I don't know what to do. It's driving me crazy. I will let you know. Don't come here again. Go. Quick before—"

Deb slipped into the garage. She hadn't intended to eavesdrop. Surprise had held her motionless. They had been too engrossed in each other to notice her. She waited until Ingrid had crossed the terrace and entered the house before she drove the cream-color open roadster to the highway.

Who was the man? His back had been toward her. Ingrid's "I don't know what to do. Don't come here again—I will let you know" had been terrified. What was "driving her crazy"? Molly B. suspected she had hired a shyster lawyer to trace her brother, that she was using her money for something or someone besides herself. Was the young man the lawyer? Better sign off on Ingrid. She was strictly honorable. Whatever was going on was her business. When the trouble—or problem—got too big for her to handle alone she would turn to her best friend, Molly B.

She drew a deep breath. What a day for early October. It shimmered with iridescence where sunlight sifted through the scarlet, gold, red and rust of autumn leaves. The hint of frost in the fragrant air set her blood tingling. This morning she had awakened with the sense of expectancy, the world-is-mine buoyancy she hadn't felt since her second year at college when it had been her usual reaction to a new day.

This place certainly had what it took to lift the spirit. The sky was a clear blue, the hills flamed with brilliant color, the lake was an indigo mirror bordered with autumn tinted reflections along its shore. Ivy on the buildings around the campus seemed darker in contrast to the pinkish brick. She could make out figures seated at open windows, students studying. Paths were alive with men coming and going plus a woman-trundled baby carriage or two. Workers were busy in faculty gardens probably planting tulips and lilies for a spring border. Overhead a flock of geese flew in wedge formation on their way south for the winter. The Science Center stretched its white and glass front against a background of hills gay as if spread with mammoth Oriental rugs.

Eyes on the road, Deborah mentally reconstructed the ceremony of Timothy Grant's installation as its Head. It had been impressive. More emphasis had been laid on his invaluable help and courage, his achievements in the department of amphibious warfare as the Marines acted as shock troops seizing one defended beachhead after another, than on the fact that he was the grandson of the founder of a great and growing-greater institution to forward scientific research.

His acceptance had been brief. His voice had hinted at emotion under rigid control as he pledged his best effort toward the increase of usefulness of the Center, the rich possibilities of its future, of his realization of the honor conferred. It had had the solemnity of the dedication of a life to a purpose. He had raised his eyes to the balcony as if speaking directly to the GIs leaning forward in absorbed attention.

"On us, the new international Americans of this middle decade of the twentieth century, rests the responsibility of preventing more wars, of sowing the seeds of good will among men and nations from one end of the world to the other."

Applause had been thunderous. Judge Lander, on the platform, had kept his hands in his pockets. The day of the Flower Show Tim had said:

"I realize that I will have to go in fighting every step of the way, if I make it, to carry out my ideas."

He had made it. The fight had begun. Henry Lander's stand-off attitude had made that clear. Tim wouldn't quit. What quality was it in some persons which kept them fighting for what they wanted, often in what seemed a hopeless situation, until somehow, in some miraculous way, they succeeded? What was the thing which wouldn't let them give up, which nine times out of ten pulled them through? Molly

B. had it. So had Tim Grant. Would it come to her in a desperate need?

A shout attracted her attention to the side of the road. Clive Warner was waving. She drew up beside him.

"Did the hail mean that you want a ride? I'm on my way to town."

"Give me a lift as far as the crossroads, will you?" He slid into the seat beside her. "I started to walk, but when I saw you driving as if your thoughts were anywhere but on where you were going, I decided you needed someone with you whose feet are on the earth. I'd give a grand to know what you were thinking."

"Don't be a pinchpenny. What's a grand in this age of billions? However, I'll tell you for nothing. I was remembering that ceremony day before yesterday and thinking what a tremendous responsibility Tim Grant has taken on for so young a man."

"Why waste sympathy on him? He wanted the job. He didn't have to take it to make a living as the rest of us do."

"Wanting it makes the responsibility greater, I would say. Just to keep the record straight, I wasn't sympathizing. I think he is lucky to know the sort of a job he wants. Wish I were as certain as to which facets of my mind I would better polish next. I have registered at the college for first-year Spanish, postgraduate English and French, but that doesn't help me decide what I want to do. I seem to have lost my sense of direction."

"I can settle the question for you. Marry me. Make Clive Warner your career. Don't stare at me as if I were a curiosity. I mean it."

"Apparently my eyes reflected perfectly my state of mind. After what happened your assurance is incredible. In case you expect an answer, it is no, a double-barreled NO."

"Then the gossip going round the campus is true?"

"What gossip?" She could have bitten out her tongue for providing the lead he wanted.

"That Madam Stewart invited Grant here with the idea he would fall for you, marry you and you'd be on velvet for life."

"And just why would marrying him put me on velvet for life? After all, you know, Molly Burton Randall had a sizable fortune when she married Roger Stewart. Only a short time ago you were convinced that I was her heir, barring the tragic possibility that Tim hypnotized her into leaving her property to him."

"Time marches on, Debby, comes the light. The latest campus bulletin has it that income and real estate are not hers to will, that her husband left letters instructing her—"

His next words didn't register. She thought of the opening of Molly B.'s safe and remembered that Ingrid had told Tim she was sure the theft of her papers was a herring drawn across the trail, that Roger Stewart's letters had been the loot wanted. So far no clue had developed as to the thief. If their contents already were being buzzed about the college, she had been right. Tim should know of it at once.

"Hold up a minute!" Clive's exclamation brought her attention back to him. "Isn't that a trailer in the field? Looks as if the occupants had set up housekeeping. What d'you know about that."

"It must belong to the onetime aviator GI who came from Montana with a wife and baby to register at the Center. Tim Grant told me about him. I must ask her to join the GI Wives group that is to meet at Beechcroft Tuesday afternoons."

"Something doing every minute with you, isn't there, Deb? To return to Grant, quite a dinner party he threw the other night. And man, what a cook, what a cook! What were those birds?"

"Jumbo squabs stuffed with fresh mushrooms and wild rice. Nice, weren't they?"

"Nice! That's a masterpiece of understatement. They fairly melted in my mouth. And the dessert, apricot sherbet, someone said, but it seemed more like cream."

"There was cream in it. I haven't seen *petits fours* since 1941. I was terribly tempted to tuck one in my bag."

"Wasn't Mrs. Sophy a knockout as a hostess at the head of the table? Between her diamonds and her wisecracks she fairly twinkled. The opening of his house has thrown fresh brush on the fire of speculation as to Grant's future plans. The conferences of the UN have taken second place as table topics in campus households. A man doesn't take on the responsibility of a house unless he has matrimony in mind."

"You've missed your vocation, Clive. You should be editing a mouse-in-the-wall gossip column instead of wasting your talent teaching applied physics." She knew by the way he bit at the corner of his mustache and the faint red tinging his cheeks that this was not the first time he had been accused of spreading gossip. "In case you think well of the suggestion, here's a tidbit. Tim Grant is planning to be married."

"To you?"

"*No.*"

"Then how do you know?"

"He told me. From what he said I figured he lost his heart to a girl he met in the Pacific theater." Having begun a story she might as well make it good if she had to amplify it from

72

her imagination. Tim had admitted he was in love. Clive was as good as a coast-to-coast broadcast when it came to spreading news, this gem would stop the silly story about Molly B.'s matchmaking plans.

"In the Pacific theater? Must have been a nurse or a Red Cross worker."

"You may be right, he said he didn't expect to marry for some time. Probably waiting till she gets out of the service."

"Sounds reasonable. Know anything about this Mark Taylor who is visiting Grant?"

"Nothing, except that he is a onetime Colonel, has come here in the hope that country air will lick malaria—isn't his skin yellow?—and is most entertaining. Why is he on your mind?"

"He isn't. Burke Romney is pestered with the idea that he has seen him somewhere before in a position of authority. Has a hunch he is a sort of mystery man."

"A mystery man. How exciting. Why doesn't Professor Romney quiz him tonight at Molly B.'s buffet supper in celebration of Tim Grant's appointment? My word, but it will be a full house. The neighbors in the large places around the lake and all the Trustees, Faculty and wives have accepted, not a regret in a campus load. The demand for sitters will boost the price sky-high."

"Sounds like a big time. It will be the last celebration for Romney and me as part of the Beechcroft household. We have found rooms at one of the boarding houses."

"When do you move into your new quarters?"

"Tomorrow. Going to miss me?"

"Not a miss."

"Playing hard-to-get, aren't you, Deb. I like it. I don't mind working for what I want. I'll win."

"Been gazing into your crystal ball or have you contacted the 'Are You Worried? Consult Me' columnist? Here we are at the crossroads. Good-by."

"Here's your hat, what's your hurry." He laughed and stepped from the car. "I'll be seeing you."

Playing hard-to-get, was she. The roadster shot into the main street of the village, scented with wood smoke, bordered on each side with flaming maples. Two small boys were scuffing through fallen leaves in the gutter. Past beautiful old houses which dated back to the beginning of the college, some snuggled behind high box hedges, all with gardens a riot of autumn color; past the white high-steepled church, with its honor roll listing the local boys and men who had left this quiet town to fight, to die, many of them, in the deadly coral and the fearful jungle of Pacific islands.

Was there no way in which she could penetrate Clive Warner's colossal conceit with the fact that she detested him? Thank goodness he was leaving Beechcroft, she wouldn't see him every day.

Playing hard-to-get. She'd show him. She sent the car ahead with a speed that eased her anger. A shrill whistle penetrated her preoccupation. She stopped. It wasn't a cop who appeared beside her roadster.

"What's the big idea running through that red light?" Tim Grant inquired. "Girls who can't keep their minds on the road need a guardian, and here I am Johnny-on-the-spot."

"Perhaps I don't want you."

"Could be, but you're going to get me." He placed a florist's box in the car and swung into the seat beside her. "Whither in such a hurry?" he inquired as she drove on.

"To market to call for fresh mushrooms ordered for to-night's party. How does it happen you aren't at the Center?"

"This being Saturday I have stopped to draw a long breath. Mark Taylor picked up that box for me at the airport. I had planned to walk home but I'd a lot rather go with you even if you don't want me."

"I didn't say I didn't want you."

"We'll lay that on the table. Molly B. phoned me she would like to talk with me about the blowout this evening. She wants Mrs. Sophy, Mark and me to spend the night at Beechcroft so we can have a talk-over-the-party fest after the guests have gone."

"That talk-over snack party has become a tribal rite, it is the icing on the evening for her. This appears to be my pick-up-passenger day. I dropped Clive Warner at the crossroads." Why had she said that? Would she ever learn not to tell of everything that happened?

"Now we are getting somewhere. What did he say that made you so furious you ran through a red light?"

"That is my secret. He won't have many more chances to make me furious. He and Burke Romney are moving into new quarters tomorrow. He said something which may interest you, that Romney is pestered with the idea that he has seen your guest, Mark Taylor, before, that he has a hunch he is a mystery man."

It was several minutes before he replied, so long that she wondered if he had been thinking of something else and hadn't sensed what she told him.

"Suppose he were," he said finally, "I can't see why Romney should be pestered about him, no reason for him to have the jitters about a mystery man," he added after a moment of consideration, "or is there? I haven't announced it, but Mark is to be Dean of Students at the Center, I had that in mind when I invited him to come. Here's the market. I'll get the mushrooms for you."

"No, I have a message for the proprietor."

When she came out with the package he was standing by the roadster.

"Let me drive, will you?"

"Afraid I'll run through a red light and we'll land in the hoosegow?" She laughed. "It would put the skids under our party to have the guest of honor in jail."

"Could happen. All set?" He slipped behind the wheel. "Great town, isn't it? Driving along this street is like driving through a flaming forest. I like these old houses. They may be old but their music is modern. Listen."

From an open window drifted a man's voice:

Rumors are flying
And I'm not denying—

The song jolted her conscience.

"I didn't intend to tell you, Tim, but the 'Rumors are flying' warned me you ought to know before tonight."

"Know *what?* You haven't gone and got engaged to Warner again, have you?"

"Do I appear to have so little self-respect?"

"No, you gave me a scare, though. Love works in a mysterious way its wonders to perform."

"It isn't a joking matter."

"You're telling me. Forgive me, Debby, relief made me flippant. What's on your mind you think I ought to know? Has Lander started to get me so soon? 'Tain't regular."

How could a man with that indomitable mouth when angry have a smile that warmed the very cockles of one's heart?

"Will he stoop to come to my party?"

"Yes. He has arrived and settled bag and baggage in the game-house suite. I wasn't referring to him. Come hell or high water here's where I lay my cards on the table and ease my conscience. Clive brought up that silly gossip about —about—"

"A marriage having been arranged by Madam Stewart between Deborah Randall, spinster, and Timothy Grant?"

"You've heard it?"

"Sure, I get around. It's had a complete campus coverage. Go on. Then what?"

"I told Clive it wasn't true and to drive home my point informed him you were planning to be married."

"What was your authority for that statement?"

75

"Don't scowl. You told me you were in love, didn't you?"

"If I remember correctly, and I do, I told you also that marriage was a mere speck on the horizon."

"That is why my conscience is acting up. To make an impression that would stop the silly story about us, I was specific. I told him you met the girl while you were in the Pacific theater." He was silent as if considering, then nodded.

"That's right."

"Thanks for taking my breach of confidence calmly. Probably the story is at this moment starting a phone-to-phone round of the campus."

"Don't lose sleep over it. I would rather it hadn't broken yet, the marriage is such a long way off. It will die out in a day or two, some other news will drive it off the airways. Now that we are on the subject, have, you ever been in love?"

"I don't care to talk about myself."

"Don't stall, play fair. I've told all to you."

"I thought so once. Now I know that I wasn't, not as you think of love."

"Don't know what it feels like to see a face that sends the blood pounding through your veins, your heart racing its engine, meet eyes that plunge into your soul and glow there, do you?"

His husky voice tightened her throat. In an effort to relieve the tension she said lightly:

"No. Frankly, it sounds terribly uncomfortable."

"You're darn tootin' it is until the other person reciprocates—then it could be—heaven. Better try it."

"Nice of you to take an interest in my love life, but it is apparent, even to this girlish intelligence, that men do not care for me that way."

"Says you. Why? Mark Taylor has psychoanalyzed you perfectly. He has observed even in the short time he has been here that men are all set to fall for you—I hope he isn't speaking from experience, he has had it plenty tough already—but the way you appraise a guy with your outsize gray eyes the first time you meet him scares him off. That is what he says. I say, you are gay enough on the surface, but hard and bitter underneath, Deb. Don't give that heel Warner the satisfaction of knowing he had the power to spoil you for real love."

"I will ponder those words." She laughed. "I didn't appraise you with outsize gray eyes the first time we met, did I? I practically crashed into your arms. Which profound observation takes us to the side entrance of Beechcroft."

He followed her through the hall to the terrace.

76

"Perhaps that crash is why we have been friends from the start. We are friends, aren't we, Deb?"

"Friends and co-operatives. Our internationally famous author calls detectives 'operatives' in her whodunits, I've noticed. That reminds me, how could I have forgotten? You're just in time," she added as Madam Stewart came through the long open window. "Come here, Molly B. I have news which I think bears on the safe opening."

She repeated the rumor Clive Warner had told her was making the rounds of the campus as to the ultimate disposal of the Stewart estate.

"Did ex-Captain See-All, Know-All Warner say where it is to go eventually?" Madam Stewart shrugged distaste. "I don't like that word 'eventually,' it has a gruesome sound. Here's hoping it is a long way ahead. I have plots for ten more novels at least before I sign off."

"Clive said he heard that the property, income from the lab and real estate, wasn't yours to will, that your husband had left letters; that word 'letters' shot my memory back to the safe opening and I lost the rest."

"The most important, I would say. What do you make of it, Tim?"

"That the person who took the papers from the safe has talked out of turn. We must track down the beginning of the gossip."

"But, that's the catch, Tim. There was nothing in the stolen letters about the disposal of the property. I confess, I had given Ingrid the idea that there was, I told you that also, Deb, for reasons I needn't go into now. Those important letters, which by the way contain only suggestions and leave me a perfectly free hand, are in my deposit box at the bank."

"Then someone is spreading that lie for a purpose, which belief sends me back to the hunch I have had all along, that Ingrid's papers were the loot wanted—that she knows it—and why."

XI

DEBORAH stood on the top step before the front door of Beechcroft saying good-night to each guest, a custom of Molly B.'s she had taken over. The Trustees, Faculty and their wives, the lakeside neighbors had departed on a wave of "Such a brilliant celebration of the installation," "The best party ever," and so on ad infinitum.

She lingered after the last red taillight had glimmered out between the ornate iron gateposts. Perfect night. The boom of the chapel clock striking the hour reverberated through the autumn silence broken only by the faint sound of motor horns and the distant rumble of a freight train. Even the trees tipped with a silver mist were motionless. Eleven. College parties ended early. The crisp air was refreshing after the warm, flower-scented rooms.

The sky was cloth of gold. The planets polka-dotting it were no more brilliant than the lighted windows of the Center visible from this side of the house. Work went on there night and day. As professors and teachers had greeted Tim Grant through the evening she had caught scraps of their conversation and had been impressed again—or was it oppressed?—by the magnitude and importance of the job he had taken on.

Apparently it was not disturbing him. He had been laughing, cordial, had appeared carefree. Once she had seen his eyes narrow, his mouth set in a hard line when Judge Lander on his arrival had greeted the hostess resplendent in white lace glimmering with crystal beads, and had ignored the guest beside her. Someone had spoken to Molly B. The breach of courtesy had gone unnoticed by her, but not by Sophy Brandt standing near. If eyes could kill hers would have stabbed into the brain of the suave white-haired man. Hate like that would set off a mine of potential tragedy not too deeply buried and the explosion would injure everyone within reach.

A shivery thought for the end of a perfect party. She turned to enter the house. From the shadow of the shrubs a man with hat drawn low over his eyes took a quick step toward her. His hand rubbed the side of his face. Her heart

78

broke into quick-step. This was the person who had been talking to Ingrid in the cutting garden. Had he come to see—

"What's the big idea?" Tim Grant demanded behind her, and the advancing figure disappeared as completely as a rabbit in a magician's fingers. Cocky dashed from the doorway, down the steps and along the drive, conscious guilt in every pad of his black paws.

"Cocky, how did you get out? Cocky, come here!" Deb called. The dog stopped for an instant, looked back, and dashed on toward the entrance gates.

"Darn. That's the last we'll see of him until he appears sometime tomorrow yelping to be let in and fed."

"Let him stay out. He'll learn." He laid a white cardigan across her shoulders. "I picked this out of the coat closet. Want another crack at a cold?"

"It isn't even chilly. Perfect night. I hated to go in." Would she tell him about the man who had vanished when he appeared? No. He was Ingrid's business. She had said, "Don't come here again. I will let you know." Why had he come?

"It is a corking night, Deb." Tim Grant's voice cut in on her thoughts. He lighted a cigarette and dropped the package back into a pocket of his dinner jacket. "Molly B. told me you were speeding the parting guests, but I knew where you were. Your American beauty frock, like the white plume of Henry of Navarre, has been in the thick of things all evening. Mrs. Sophy and Mark have been at the piano in the game house playing for dancing every minute since supper. They were a smash hit. I heard that Mrs. Sam and the Judge put on a continuous performance as dancers and stargazers during the evening."

"Henry Lander is a wonderful dancer, light on his feet as a feather. It was a super party. Molly B. never does things by halves. That goes for you, if these sensational orchids are an example. Purple for Mrs. Sophy, white for Molly B. and me, and green for Ingrid. Thanks for my share. It has been a red-letter night for the college as well as for you, hasn't it?"

"It has for me in more ways than one. You'd be surprised to know how many times this evening it was hinted archly, just hinted, that I am in love with a girl in the Pacific theater. I have you to thank for starting that gossip."

"Don't minimize Clive Warner's share in spreading it."

"I'll give him due credit. It strikes me that for a girl who has been the top attraction of the blowout, has had the male members of the party—those three instructors, if you insist

79

on particulars—hanging on her words with Romney shadowing her, your eyes and voice are very solemn."

"We'll check the 'top attraction' comment first. I have taken to heart your criticism that I'm hard and bitter underneath, plus Mark Taylor's as to the appraisal in my outsize gray eyes." She laughed. "I've turned over a new leaf, from now on when I meet a man 'I'm all smiles and blushes,' Sarah Allen speaking. I live to learn. As to the solemnity in my voice, I was thinking as you spoke behind me that after four years of excitement and danger it will be difficult for you to be contented in this small community where life goes on day after day with nothing much happening."

"Forgotten the safe opening, haven't you? There will be compensations here. Life isn't smooth as a trotting park, Deb. From all I hear and read the home front—even this quiet portion of it—can use a few fighters to advantage. Thanks for thinking of me. It means—pause here for station identification—

"Molly B. sent me for you. The snack party is on. Scragg has set two tables laden with eats in the library. Listen. Mark is playing. He's a wizard at it. Can't read a note. Plays by ear.

" 'They say that falling in love is wonderful,' " he sang softly to the accompaniment of the piano. "I know, I've tried it. Better come in, Deb, the water's great," he advised as they entered the library.

"Your eloquence almost persuades me to try it."

"Try what, Debby?" Clive Warner inquired. "Have you ever been told that you have a carrying voice?"

"Such seems to be the consensus. Haven't you heard that I'm scheduled to speak at the Town Hall rally? With 1,172,000 more females than males in the country women will have to take a big hand in politics. Do I see chicken salad or—are my eyes playing tricks?" She settled with a tired little sigh into the chair Mark Taylor drew forward. "In my effort to see that everyone was served I forgot to eat. Sal, you treasure, are those hot crispy rolls, or is that silver plate you're holding a mirage?"

Sarah Allen offered the silver plate with one hand and with the other impatiently pushed up the steel-bowed spectacles.

"They are, Debby. I told the cook to leave a panful risin' for me to slip into the oven. I knew Madam Stewart wouldn't eat nothin' till now." She glanced over the two square card tables. "Anything more you want? There's plenty of coffee mousse with raspberry sherbet the caterer left."

"If we want it we'll get it ourselves, Sarah. Go to bed.

You've been on the move every minute of the day. Tell Scragg we won't need him, either. Now scram."

"Yes, Madam. You'd better send Debby up. She has taken two steps helping to my one. I'm glad you had such a fine party, Mr. Timothy. Your grandfather sure would have been proud. Good night, folks."

They sat in a semicircle around the low fire. On one side of Molly B. Sophy Brandt in violet crepe, with the orchid corsage, her moonstones and diamonds shimmering at her throat, Ingrid in an off-the-shoulder glittering black frock on the other. Tilly in white which glimmered with gold sequins with each movement of her lithe body sat on the floor, her head against her husband's knees. What was going on behind the eyes that looked down at her from under heavy lids? The eyes of Judge Lander seated opposite were on the same business. Deborah shivered. Something in the attitude of the two frightened her. She sensed tragic undertones.

Did Tim? He had taken Mark Taylor's place at the piano and was playing softly. Stella Dane, her silver-gilt hair reaching to the shoulders of her pale green frock, leaned an elbow on the shining mahogany as she talked to him.

"How about a monologue, Mrs. Sophy? Give us the low-down on the Trustees, the Faculty and wives, your This Is How I See Them act," Warner urged.

"Shall I, Molly B.?"

"Yes, but without malice, Sophy. I won't have my recent guests ridiculed. Wait a minute before you begin. Where's the bracelet that matches your necklace?" Madam Stewart inquired anxiously.

After a second of hesitation, Sophy Brandt patted the gold mesh bag with the moonstone and diamond clasp in her lap.

"Here. The clasp broke. Luckily I saw it in time."

"I'll say it was lucky, it might have been trampled out of shape had you dropped it. Now, on with the monologue, 'With malice toward none, with charity for all,' Mrs. Sophy."

Deb had not known that Tim Grant's arms were crossed on the high back of her chair till she heard his voice behind her.

"I don't feel malicious tonight, Tim. Life seems a wonderful thing." For an instant her eyes rested on Henry Lander bending forward watching Tilly Farr, whose gold bangles jingled when she stirred. "I've been thinking of what FDR said at the beginning of the war, 'The only thing we have to fear is fear itself.' I don't intend to allow fear of the future to get its vicious talons hooked into me again." She laughed. "Having proclaimed my new philosophy of life, I'll give you the highlights in the world of education."

As she told them off Deb could see the men and women as

81

clearly as if they were parading through the room, nothing unkind, just tricks of voice and manner that made them individuals; Prexy rubbing his hand across his chin, the English professor whirling the gold pencil on the end of his watch chain as he talked, little incidents of the evening, that brought a friendly laugh.

"You're a genius, Mrs. Sophy," Burke Romney's approval followed the applause. "I'll bet you could get a job as entertainer on Broadway. You left me out of the faculty imitations."

She repeated what he had said, voice and diction a perfect reproduction of his.

"Gee, I judge by the applause that you have me down cold. I didn't know I talked like that. You're better than a dictaphone. Try some of the others."

"No. Enough is enough. Better to leave my audience wanting more than have it thinking, 'Why does she talk so long?' Did Sarah Allen mention coffee mousse and raspberry sherbet, Deb, or did I dream it? Sounds like the end of a perfect day to me."

"I'll get it, Mrs. Sophy, in nothing flat."

"You'll need help, Miss Debby," Burke Romney suggested and followed her across the room.

"Thank goodness this day of unceasing activity has come to an end," Deborah thought as after helping carry the leftovers from the snack party to the pantry she mounted the spiral stairway slowly. Doesn't look so much like the end from this viewpoint, she decided, as she saw Stella Dane waiting outside her door.

"Haven't you called this a day yet, Stella?" she whispered.

"Not till I've said what is on my mind." Anger shook the low voice. "Just because I work for a living, don't think you can put anything across on me, Deborah Randall. Lay off Burke Romney. He's been hanging round you all evening. I saw him first. He's mine."

"My word, you haven't fallen for that male menace, have you? If you have you won't have to scratch out my eyes, dearie. Another girl's heart throb is definitely off my wave length. Good night and good hunting."

She entered her room, the quickly closed door shut off Stella's reply. She leaned against it to listen. No sound in the gallery, Stella had gone to her room at the front of the house. What a scene. It would look well in technicolor. That crack about working for a living was funny. As if Deborah Randall hadn't worked to a fare-thee-well for the last three years.

Healthy fatigue is a powerful soporific. She couldn't have told how long she had slept when the voice roused her. She

82

glanced at the illuminated dial of the clock on the table beside the bed. Four. Who was on the prowl at this hour? She listened. Was someone talking on the terrace?

Without turning on the night light she tiptoed to the balcony. Sounded like Henry Lander, a furiously angry Lander. She couldn't hear the other voice. Who was it? Had the man who had flashed in and out of the shrubs while she stood on the front steps been looking for the Judge instead of Ingrid? Silence below.

She went back to bed. If the guests would kindly cut out arguments under her window she would like to finish her quota of sleep.

She wakened suddenly. Now what? Listened. The great house which had been so full of laughter and voices a few hours ago had lapsed into tomblike quiet. In a near-by tree a bird roused with a sleepy twitter. Must have been the whir of the tall clock on the stair landing preparing to strike which had wakened her. Right. One. Two. Three. Four. Five, she counted. Nothing stirred on the balcony. The windows framed oblongs of sky spangled with fading stars and the faint spread of dawn behind the hilltops.

Her heart caught and tripped on. That sound wasn't the clock. She cautiously snapped on the bedside light, and glanced furtively at the door which opened on the gallery. The knob turned. Was it a trick of her imagination which had been geared to high since the opening of Molly B.'s safe? No. It turned again. Cautiously. Slowly. She swallowed her heart, which had shot to her throat. Thank heaven the key was in the lock.

"You know the consequences to you if you don't." Memory of the hoarse threat set gooseflesh rippling along her arms. Was it only yesterday she had said to Tim, "in this small community where life goes on day after day without much happening"?

"Who—who's there?" she whispered. Dumb question. The person who had turned the knob had counted on making a secret entrance. Why? Her pearls and the diamonds which had been her mother's were the only jewelry she had worth stealing. Jewels. Was this another attempt to get at Molly B.'s? Had the safe opening been an unsuccessful attempt to snitch them? Had the letters and papers been taken to obscure the real intention?

There were five men in the house—Tim, Sam, Mark Taylor, Clive and Romney. Judge Lander, in the game-house guest suite, wouldn't be of much use. It was almost day. It would be foolish to rouse any of them now. In a short time the servants would be stirring, a thief would vanish before an awakening household. She would watch and listen.

She sat up in bed hugging her knees, hardly breathing for fear she would miss a sound, and watched the light behind the hills change from violet to pink, from pink to a lovely crimson, and lights appear in the campus houses and dormitory windows. Sunday. Another day. What would it bring?

XII

DEBORAH'S attention wandered from the sermon though her eyes were on the face of the eloquent young preacher standing in the high pulpit of the college chapel. The soft rainbow light from a memorial window rested like a halo on his blond hair. Who had tried her door last night and why? Molly B. beside her stirred restlessly.

"Hear that pesky dog," she whispered, and Deb realized that the distant sound which had throbbed an accompaniment to her thoughts was Cocky at his vociferous worst. Evidently he had returned to Beechcroft after his runaway night out. She forced her attention to the preacher. He closed his sermon, as he had begun, with the text:

"Thou hast made him a little lower than the angels."

The Psalmist's belief in the heights man could achieve was a rock to which to cling in this day of suspicion and turmoil, she thought.

"I do not ask, O Lord, that life may be a pleasant road," the congregation sang fervently. Came the benediction:

"And may the Grace of God which passeth all understanding be and abide with you all, now and forever more."

"Amen. Amen," chanted the choir. The organ swelled into the postlude and the worshipers filed out slowly.

"There wasn't an empty seat in the chapel, which doesn't look as if this church has lost its prestige," Molly B. reflected aloud, as Deborah drove the cream-color roadster toward the campus gate. "That has been named as one of the major difficulties with which the home must contend. I couldn't stay to talk with people. That dog was an outrage. I would recognize Cocky's bark-whine, bark-whine, if I heard it in Hiroshima."

"Too bad you didn't stop, I'll bet a lot of your friends felt cheated. You're looking very special in that all-black costume with Tim's white orchid. Probably you were the only person who noticed the barking dog. Beechcroft is half a mile beyond the campus, but with the Sunday stillness and the air so clear it sounded next door. He has stopped now. Doubtless discouraged, he has curled up somewhere and gone to sleep. He dashed by me last evening when I was speeding the parting guests. I suspected he would make a night of it. It was a grand party. None of your house guests showed up for church, I noticed."

"Tim drove Sophy and Mark home. She said she was all in. Perhaps she danced too much last night. And can she dance. My news scout reported that when she wasn't at the piano the Faculty and Trustees gave her a rush. To Tim and his faith in her goes the credit of her renascence."

"Just shows that age is a state of mind. Her comeback is nothing short of a miracle. Wasn't it lucky she didn't lose that sensational bracelet? How fast the leaves are dropping."

"In another week or two the hills will fade to yellow brown and we'll be on the threshold of winter and my work will begin again. Think you can take it, Deb, after the stir of Washington?"

"I can. Looks as if life here would be anything but dull, with Judge Lander and Tim Grant feuding and the suave Henry muscling in on the presidency of the college and Sam's wife. How come that you like him, Molly B.?"

"I've intimated to you before that deep in my heart I don't, but he was a sort of legacy from my husband, who made him executor of the large fund he left to the Center with unrestricted power to administer it. Loyalty to Roger has kept me loyal to the Judge. Listen, that confounded dog has broken out again. The bark is coming from the game house. Is everyone on the place stone deaf? He must be locked in."

"If he were we wouldn't have heard him from the chapel. I'll bet it is pure deviltry." Deb stopped the roadster at the side door at Beechcroft. "I'll go for the pest. Shall I bring him to you for discipline or paddle him good and plenty at the scene of his crime?"

"I'll turn him over to you. Deal gently with the erring one, he's kind of young," Molly B. reminded and laughed. "As you see, my anger is petering out."

"Cocky. Cocky," Deb called as she ran along the colonnade. The barking stopped. A low whine came from inside the game house. Was the dog caught somewhere?

She pushed open the half-closed door. The lights were on. Queer that Judge Lander hadn't snapped them off when he came in last night. Perhaps he had been too hot under the collar after the angry argument on the terrace at 4 A.M. to think of them.

A peach of a room. There were crimson damask hangings at the tall windows in the eggshell white walls, banquettes and chairs were upholstered to match. Red roses on the grand piano scented the air. A long white glove and a coffee cup and saucer, reminders of last night's festivity, lay forgotten beside the crystal bowl that held the flowers.

86

Cool. Still. A sort of shivery stillness. The mirrored wall above the great fireplace gave back the motionless figure of a dark-haired girl in beige with a white orchid corsage and an emerald-green hat. The whining had stopped as if the dog were listening. She ran across the Persian rug to the door of the badminton court.

"Cocky, Cocky, you little dev—" Her voice broke. The silence of death caught her throat in an icy grip. She drew her hand across her eyes and looked again. The dog jumped on her with a frantic yelp. She caught him up in her arms and held his shivering body close, pressed her free hand over her lips to stifle a scream. She wasn't dreaming. In the middle of the marked-off court lay something covered with a hanging which had been pulled from its cornice. One clenched hand was visible, and the sole of a boot. Was it a man? Asleep? Dead?

"My God, Deb, who is it?" Molly B.'s voice roused her from the coma of horror. "Who—who—is—"

Deb dropped the dog and caught her as she swayed. She half carried, half dragged her to a bench, pulled off her small black turban and forced her head to her knees. She held it there till Molly B. resisted.

"I'm all—right now," she whispered. When Deb raised her head she rested it against the wall and closed her eyes. "Is—is someone under that—that covering or did I dream it?"

"You didn't dream it." Deb forced her voice through stiff lips.

"Who—who—is it? Does that shake mean you don't *know?* We must find out." She rose and steadied herself by a hand on the girl's shoulder. "I've been a weak sister long enough. We've got to pull off that—I'll do it, Deb, I'm all right now."

"We'll do it together." Side by side they tiptoed nearer as if afraid a sound might disturb the horribly quiet figure. Molly B. made two attempts before she gripped the crimson hanging and pulled it back. She stared incredulously.

"Henry Lander!" Her voice rose and cracked. She closed her eyes, shook her head as if to clear her sight. Looked again. "Henry Lan—der?"

"Hey, what the dickens are you two girls doing? What goes on here?" Tim Grant hailed from the outer room. "Playing badminton on the Sab—" His voice died in a choked rattle as he appeared in the doorway. With a whine the dog jumped on him.

"Lander. *Lander?*" he whispered incredulously. "When—what—?"

"We don't—know." Deb shook uncontrollably, her teeth chattered. "We heard Cocky barking—I came to find him—then, then Molly B. came—and—she—"

"Fainted. Imagine me—me—Molly Burton, mystery writer, fainting at sight of—" Tim caught her shoulders, shook her and cut off her high, hysterical giggle.

"Quit it. Stop it!" He shook her again, before he led her back to the bench. "Watch her, Deb, while I—" He knelt by the body on the floor.

Was it only yesterday he had said that some other news would drive the gossip about himself off the airways? Here it was, in the middle of the badminton court. Deb shivered.

"I'm sorry, Tim," Molly B. whispered. "I'm all right, Deb. We must phone for the doctor."

"Too late." Tim Grant drew the hanging over the white head and rose from his knees. "I'll send for the police."

"Is it mur—"

"Looks like it, but I don't know. I didn't touch him. Where's the phone here?"

"In the closet beside the back door. The number is—" He was out of the room with Cocky whining at his heels before she finished.

"What's all the shootin' about?" Sam Farr inquired gaily as with Tilly in a soft green frock beside him he entered from the front room. "Til and I saw you three people beating it here one after the other and Old Man Curiosity—Well, I'll be damned." His wife shrieked and hid her face against the shoulder of his brown Shetland jacket. His arms went round her. "Who—who *is* it?"

"What's going on?" Clive Warner demanded, as, followed by Burke Romney, he entered. "Lunch is served. Scragg's running round in a circle, said everyone was here. We nominated ourselves a committee of two—*hell*, what's happened?"

No one spoke. Clive's bulging eyes, the pallor that whitened Romney's face, proclaimed the question was answered. "Who —who—is it?"

"Henry Lander," Molly B. whispered.

"Lander?" Deb's eyes were on Sam Farr as he repeated the name. There was a glint in his eyes between their narrowed lids as they swept from face to face. Suspicion vibrated along her nerves. Nothing definite, just a queer hunch that someone on the place had done this awful thing. She fought back the memory of Tim Grant's bitter, "Perhaps that is your game, Judge?" of the hatred in his eyes last evening when Henry Lander had ignored him.

"Snap out of it, Deb." Clive Warner laid his arm across her shoulders. "You're standing here as motionless and white as a snow girl."

"You're not much rosier yourself, Clive." She shrugged herself free.

88

"So that's what is left of Henry Lander." Sam Farr's voice broke the eerie silence, his eyes were on the shapeless heap on the floor. "He was too slick, too smooth. Somebody's come to the pay-off. Who can it be?"

"He was my friend, Sam, remember."

"My apologies, Molly B., for speaking harshly of the dead —no matter what he deserves."

"Dead?" Ingrid Johnson inquired from the doorway. "What is going on? Scragg is on the verge of a nervous breakdown because the popovers are ready and no one has come to— Oh, my—"

Sam Farr shook off his clinging wife and clapped his hand over her mouth.

"Yelling won't help, Ingrid. It's Lander." As she moved her head impatiently he asked, "Promise me not to scream?" She nodded, whispered:

"I promise."

She sank down on the bench beside Molly B. and covered her chalky face with her hands. She was shaking. From shock, of course, who wasn't, Deb thought. It couldn't be because of regard for the Judge, she detested him; why had her eyes been terrified unless she knew or—

Memory chilled her heart to a standstill. Did Ingrid suspect that the man with whom she had talked in the cutting garden had done this horrible thing? Did she know that he had been on the place last evening?

"They caught the prowl car," Tim Grant announced as he entered. "The chief will follow. He was at dinner."

It seemed but a moment before the police swarmed in. Two at first. Then four. They arrived without benefit of shrieking sirens as they arrive in movies. Apparently this homicide squad had perfected a gumshoe technique.

The short, chunky chief followed. Deb drew the first long breath she had drawn since she had seen the motionless heap in the middle of the badminton court. It was Sandy McGregor, who had been a rosy-faced, smiling traffic cop who held up traffic for her to cross the street in her younger days. The village children had adored "Mac." The years had sharpened his eyes to bright blue steel, drawn reddish skin tight over prominent cheekbones, had stenciled his jutting nose with purple veins. He ran a chubby hand over the shiny pink oasis entirely surrounded by an iron-gray crew cut before he shook hands with Molly B.

"I'm glad it is you, Mac," she said.

A sergeant kneeling beside the body looked up.

"Shot, Chief. If we could get the room clear—"

Shot. Deb had a sudden breath-snatching memory of an

ivory-handled revolver in a suitcase. To whom had it belonged?

"Sure, sure. Folks, move into the other room while the medical examiner determines the time of death." McGregor drove them ahead of him like a flock of sheep. "Peters, come with me. Go to it, boys," he flung over his shoulder before he closed the door behind him. He seated himself in the chair that Tim Grant pushed forward. The blue-uniformed officer who had followed him drew a chair beside the checkers table, on which he dropped a stenographer's notebook.

"Better sit down, all of you. This isn't going to be short," McGregor warned.

Last evening the long, crimson banquette against the east wall had been taken over by laughing, happy women resting from a dance, some of them tapping sandaled feet to the rhythm of "For Sentimental Reasons," jived on the piano by Mark Taylor, Deb remembered. Now, white-faced Ingrid sat in the center, her hands clenched in the lap of her electric-blue frock, motionless as a stone woman. Sam Farr, with Tilly clutching at his sleeve as if she never would let him go, on one side of her, Clive Warner and Romney in golf clothes on the other sat stiff and tense, their eyes on the chunky man in the middle of the room.

"Better sit down, Deb," Tim Grant suggested.

"Come here, honey." Molly B. indicated the chair beside the one on the edge of which she perched as if ready for the Go gun in a race.

"All right to smoke, Chief?" Tim Grant inquired as he took over the piano bench.

"Sure, go ahead." Four cigarette lighters flashed simultaneously. McGregor cleared his throat. "It was my job through the war years to spot every newcomer to this town and to find out why he or she was here. I know all you college folks, but where does he fit in?" He pointed at Burke Romney, who shifted his feet uneasily.

"Professor Romney is in the cyclotron lab at the Center," Tim Grant explained.

"Hmm-m, that's the department with the new atom-smasher, isn't it? Who recommended you for the job, Professor?"

"Judge Lander."

"I guess that gives you the green light, the Judge didn't pick any phonies. There's one other stranger to me, the man who explained the how-come of Romney."

"He is Timothy Grant, my late husband's grandson, Mac— Chief," Molly B. corrected hastily.

"Well, well, well, is he now? The new Head of the Center. What d'you know about that?" McGregor beamed at Tim. "I read about you but I was so busy checking on the crowd your installation drew, I didn't see or hear you. I sure am glad to meet you. Your grandfather backed my first appointment on the force. Hmm-m. Old friendships don't count in my business, though," he growled as if suddenly remembering the gruesome job at hand. "I shall do my duty at no matter what cost to my personal feelings, Madam Stewart."

Did he mean that already a member of the household was under suspicion? The thought dried Deb's throat.

"Who found the body?" McGregor sprang the question with the suddenness of a steel trap.

She swallowed her heart, which had zoomed to her mouth, controlled a schoolgirlish impulse to rise, hold up her hand, and forced her voice through stiff lips.

"I—I did."

"Tell how you happened to find it."

She told of hearing the barking dog while in church, of driving Madam Stewart to Beechcroft, of locating the bark as coming from the game house, of running along the colonnade, finding the large room lighted, of hearing the dog whining in the court beyond.

"And then—and then—" Her voice gave out.

"That will do for you, Miss Deb. Who came next?"

Breathlessly Molly B. told her story, the others followed in order of their appearance in the badminton room.

"Hmm-m, what is it now?" McGregor demanded as the sergeant entered with something glittering and swinging from his fingers. Deb's world whirled and steadied. It was a moonstone and diamond bracelet. Molly B. leaned forward eagerly, then with a low exclamation settled back in the chair.

"Where did you get this, Sergeant?"

"Clutched tight in his fist, Chief."

"Might have been snatched from a wrist or a wrist might have been wrenched free and left the bracelet. Anybody recognize it?"

"It's Mrs. Sophy's, she told us last evening—" Romney stopped short in his eager explanation.

"Go on, what did she tell you last evening?"

"I missed it from Mrs. Brandt's arm," Molly B. carried on. "She said that the catch had broken and she had the bracelet in her bag."

"Hmm-m, Mrs. Sophy Brandt, the woman with the yellow wig. I know the lady, she has visited here for years. Drop the bracelet on the table, Sergeant, we'll come back to that later." He waited till the officer had left the room.

"Can any one of you recall the last time you saw or spoke to the Judge?" he asked. Peters at the checkers table picked up his pencil.

It turned out on questioning that after the snack party the women had carried the dishes in the library to the pantry and the men had adjourned to the smoking room. It was twelve-thirty when they said good-night in the hall. Supposedly the Judge had gone to the guest suite he occupied in the game house—his presence in the badminton court indicated that—and the others had gone to their rooms upstairs.

"Any reason to think he didn't come directly here?"

"I heard his voice later." Deb answered the question in the steel-blue eyes that probed hers.

"How much later, Miss Deb—Randall?" McGregor was having difficulty in observing the formalities, in keeping old memories in the background. "And where?"

"I had been sound asleep when I woke suddenly. I listened. Someone was talking on the terrace below my´window. Queer hour for conversation, I thought, and glanced at the illuminated bedside clock. It was just four. I tiptoed to the balcony and distinctly heard Judge Lander's voice."

"Did you hear what was said?"

"Not the words. His voice sounded choked, as if he were arguing angrily."

"Did you hear the other person?"

"No. Whoever was there must have been speaking very low."

"Anyone else present hear the Judge's voice?" Each head shook a negative answer.

"Queer you were the only one, Miss Deb. Hear anything more?"

"No. When the voice stopped I went back to bed. Surprisingly enough I dropped off to sleep. I was again roused by a sound. I snapped on the bedside light. The knob of my door was turning." From the corners of her eyes she saw Tim Grant's quick look at Clive Warner, who was lighting a cigarette. Did he think that Clive would dare come to her room?

"Sure of that? Sure that knob turned?"

"Yes. It turned. Stopped. Turned again."

"Then what?"

"I whispered, 'Who's there?' no one answered. Just then the clock on the landing struck five."

"You didn't call anyone?"

"No. I thought of it, when the sky began to grow pink. I decided that if it had been a burglar he would be afraid of the light. I watched and listened, barely breathing, till I heard the servants stirring in the house."

"And nothing more unusual happened?"

"Nothing." Deb felt as if all the life had been drained out of her. How long would she be kept on the witness stand? The sergeant entered and bent over his chief, said something in a low voice.

"He's sure of that?" McGregor asked.

"Yes, sir."

"Hmm-m, that's all." The sergeant closed the door to the badminton court softly behind him. McGregor drew himself out of a slump as if preparing to do battle.

"Let's go back a little, Miss Randall. You said it was about four o'clock when you heard Judge Lander's voice on the terrace beneath your window?"

Deb had a terrified sense that he was trying to trap her. Why be frightened? She had told the truth. The reminder steadied her.

"I didn't say 'about,' Chief McGregor. I said that it was just four, and I mean four, by the bedside clock when I tiptoed to the balcony."

He leaned forward.

"Sure, you said 'just four.' I don't know who you're trying to shield with that story, Miss Randall, or why. The medical examiner reports that Judge Lander has been dead since between 1 and 2 A.M."

XIII

McGREGOR'S accusation that she was shielding someone brought Deborah to her feet. Tim rose impulsively to go to her but a look from the chunky man in stage center stopped him. He might do more harm than good to the girl by interfering in her testimony. What had she heard?

"I'm not trying to shield anyone," she asserted indignantly. "I heard Judge Lander's voice on the terrace at 4 A.M. this morning."

"How come you know it so well that you could recognize it two stories below?"

"I told you it was raised in anger. I have visited in this house for years, you know how long, Sandy McGregor, you used to hold up traffic for me. During that time Judge Lander was legal adviser first to Roger Stewart, then to his wife. I'd be pretty dumb if I didn't recognize his voice when I heard it, wouldn't I?"

"Atta girl, don't let him get you down," Tim encouraged under his breath. For the first time since he had entered the badminton court and seen the motionless figure his mind settled to normal thinking. Was this crime tied up with the theft of the papers from Molly B.'s safe, and the threat Deb had overheard, "If you don't, you know the consequences to you"? What was on McGregor's mind now?

"If you are sure you heard the voice of the Judge, Miss Deb, the next step is to find out who he was talking with. Sit down, you've told your story. I want a report from each person present as to where he or she was from the time the snack party broke up in the hall till 5 A.M.," he announced blandly, and boy, could he be bland. "What's your business here, Miss Dane?" he growled as Stella appeared in the doorway. The long, sinister face of the butler loomed above her shining hair, his livery made a dark blue background for her white gabardine frock.

"We came to find out how come police cars were shooting all over the place. Scragg had about lost his mind because you'd all rushed to the game house and the popovers—" Her voice caught. "What is it? Who are you after now, Sandy McGregor?"

94

"Not the wild Danes this time, for a wonder."

"Sit down, Stella." Molly B. motioned to a chair. "Scragg, you'd better remain also. Never mind lunch. Judge Lander is —is gone."

"Gone?" Stella Dane echoed stridently. "Has he at last beaten it from this burg? You won't catch me crying about it. I loathed the old wolf. My two brothers will beat the drums—"

"Softly, softly, sister," Sam Farr interrupted her hysterical outburst. "Don't talk without advice of counsel. We are all before the bar of justice. The Judge is dead. Murdered."

"Dead. Mur—" Stella slumped into the chair and stared into space. Her face was colorless. Had she suddenly remembered that Lander had recently foreclosed the mortgages on the estate of her family, that her brothers had been muttering threats? Tim's eyes flew to the butler, who stood straight and tense against the wall. His eyes burned in his masklike face. Had he previous knowledge of what happened in the game house between 1 and 2 A.M.?

"To return to the point at which we were interrupted by new arrivals." McGregor attempted to cross one fat leg over the other and gave it up. Peters gripped his pencil. "Dean Farr, where were you at the time of the shooting?"

Through Tim's memory echoed Sam's voice humming, "Someday I'm going to murder the bugler." Could he have done this awful thing? He had made no secret of his detestation of the man.

"There seems to be a question as to the time," Sam Farr answered coolly. "Tell me when the crime was committed and I'll tell you to a minute where I was." His lazy voice tinged with amusement, his ironic eyes, deepened the color in McGregor's already sufficiently ruddy face.

"Mrs. Farr, perhaps you can be more explicit. Did you and your husband go upstairs together after you had helped clear away the dishes left from the snack party?"

"We did," Tilly asserted eagerly, "and we were together till we came down to breakfast."

"I can testify to that fact," Stella Dane corroborated. "My room is next theirs and I heard them fighting furiously. I figured that Dean Farr was objecting to the Judge's marked attention to his wife."

"Thanks, Stella. I guess that ties it." Sam's sarcastic comment brought a surge of color to her white face.

"What do you mean, Dean Farr? Don't you understand that I am trying to—"

"Pin the murder on Dean Farr?" McGregor interrupted smoothly. "You have provided a motive, Miss Dane, that's what we're after. Professor Romney"—Burke twitched as if

95

an electric current had been applied to his body—"Judge Lander recommended you for the job you hold at the Center. Did you know him before you came here?"

"We met several times in Washington. When he told me of the work the Center had done for the government during the war—he was very proud of it—I jumped at the chance of a professorship here. I knew I would learn a lot. We became friends."

He knew he would learn a lot. The words left an imprint black as a carbon copy on Tim's mind.

"Were you sufficiently friendly for him to speak of having recently been threatened by letters or a person?"

Had McGregor noticed the professor's surreptitious glance at him, Tim wondered.

"No, sir, he confided that his ambition—and determination to be president of this college—had stirred up a lot of opposition and bitterness. Apparently that didn't cut much ice with him, he laughed when he spoke of it, but he was a little upset about Madam Stewart's affairs."

"What are you driving at, Burke Romney?" Molly B. demanded. "There is nothing in my affairs to upset the Judge, the use of my stories on the radio without permission didn't worry him."

"It wasn't that. He felt that your husband's grandson would make trouble," Romney explained in a sorry-but-you-asked-for-it voice. "He was convinced that he was after Beechcroft, which had been his mother's home."

"Sit down again, Mr. Grant."

Tim hadn't realized that Romney's nasty crack had brought him to his feet. He obeyed McGregor's growl. Time enough to settle with Romney later. Was the guy out to frame him? Nuts. Hadn't he come to his house to congratulate him on his appointment? Why the dickens did he have it in for him now? Had he heard that since the new Head of the Center had taken office his dossier was being given the once-over? So was that of every other worker in the Center; each government employee was being given the Loyalty Test by order of the President. While he was in Washington the War Department had assigned to the Center—in the event he was installed as Head—the job of secret research on a certain new explosive. It was on the supposition that other countries might slip in observers—it was being done—that the check-up was in progress.

"That makes me out a dope," Molly B.'s angry comment cut in on Tim's reflections.

"Godamighty, stop fighting," McGregor commanded irascibly. "Let's get back to this investigation. It's getting nowhere fast. What time did you go to your room, Professor?"

96

"At the same time the others went up. I said good-night to Warner and closed my door. Remember, Clive?"

"That's right."

"Did you stay in your room, Mr. Warner?"

"To be honest, I didn't, Chief. I had left a flask of Scotch I bought in the village in the morning in my sports jacket pocket and I went down to the hall closet to get it.'"

"Who's selling liquor in the village? It's illegal. We'll come back to that later. What time was it when you left your room?"

"I wouldn't say exactly, shortly after I said good-night to Romney." The surge of color McGregor's reprimand had brought to Warner's face faded, he chewed at the end of his mustache.

"See anyone on your way up or down?"

"He met me in the hall, sir." Scragg picked up the story. "I hope I'm not butting in, sir, I could see the gentleman didn't want to drag me in, but I've nothing to worry about."

"What were you doing in the hall that time of night?"

"I went in to clear up, thinking the dishes would be left in the library and they shouldn't be found there Sunday morning, but they had been taken to the pantry."

"What did you do after you found there was nothing to do, Scragg?"

"I opened the front door and whistled to the dog, who I hadn't seen since afternoon. When he didn't come I went to the service cottage and went to bed."

"What time was that?"

"I really couldn't say, sir."

"That's helpful. Mr. Grant, perhaps you have some idea of time. Where were you between the final breakup of the party and, we'll say, 2 A.M.?"

Here it comes, Tim thought. For a moment the great room was so still that a burst of song from a bird in a vine outside the window set the air a-quiver.

"I changed to tweeds and walked to the Center, Chief." A hushed sound of consternation rippled like a wave around the room. It wasn't necessary to add that he had slipped the ivory-handled revolver into his pocket. That was for Mc-Gregor to find out.

"Why break out at that time of night—or morning?"

"I've been the Head of the Center since Thursday." With an effort Tim kept his voice smooth in reply to the skeptical query. "I still feel an overwhelming sense of responsibility, as if the weight of the world had been dropped on my shoulders. Important work is going on here, night and day, because of it this town has an unusually large and competent police force, but you don't need to be reminded of that,

Chief. I wasn't sleepy. Decided to walk across and take a look-see at what was going on."

"Meet anyone on the way?"

Would Mrs. Sophy, leaning over the balustrade of the gallery whispering, "Where are you going, Tim?" come under the head of meeting a person? He'd take a chance that it wouldn't. Why drag her into this mess?

"Why are you hesitating, Grant?" McGregor prodded.

"Thinking back to be sure I hadn't met anyone on the way or return."

"You had reason to dislike the deceased, I gather from the testimony of Professor Romney."

"Dislike is too tame a word, Chief. As the reason for my—call it contempt of Henry Lander—has to do with someone who has gone—"

"There will be no pussyfooting about this, Mr. Grant. We are dealing with murder. The Judge made trouble between your grandfather and his daughter, your mother, didn't he?"

"So I have been informed."

"I know he did. I heard the stories that flew around at the time."

"Don't repeat them here, Chief."

"I don't like the threat in your voice." McGregor's ruddy color deepened. "It ain't necessary. I'm not a fool. Hmm-m, hmm-m," he burbled. "We'll come back to that later." He pulled out his fat watch.

"You folks go to your lunch, except Professor Romney, Mr. Warner and the butler. Guess you can get along without him for one meal. Be in the library in just one hour, every mother's son and daughter of you. I've got more questions to ask and they ain't going to be easy.

"Just a minute," he added as with one impulse they surged toward the door. "Have Mrs. Sophy Brandt present. Perhaps she can tell how her bracelet came to be in Judge Lander's fist."

The group assembled later in the book-walled library reminded Tim of the directions on a theater program, "The curtain will be dropped to indicate the passing of an hour."

It was the same cast of characters which had been in the game house with the addition of Mrs. Sophy and Mark Taylor. She was knitting steadily on something that was a pink heap of wool in the lap of her lavender and white print as she sat beside Molly B. When he had told her why she was wanted at Beechcroft he hadn't explained that a shot had ended the life of the Judge. She had turned so white he had flung his arm about her shoulders.

"I'm all right, Tim," she had protested. "Henry Lander

isn't worth a faint. There will be many on the campus who will draw a breath of relief. His shadow darkened several homes. I wonder why Sandy McGregor wants me."

Perhaps he should have told her about the bracelet clutched in the dead man's fist, he thought now, as he watched the steel needles and the diamonds on her fingers flash, but it had seemed at the time better that her answers to McGregor's questions be unpremeditated.

The royal blue hangings at two long windows were the exact shade of the lake they framed. Early afternoon sunlight streamed in and set the gold lettering on bookbindings gleaming, it played up the pallor of the women, the apprehension in their eyes.

Chief McGregor entered like a squat tugboat under full steam and dropped heavily into a straight chair in the center of the room. He cleared his throat. Each person responded with a start before straightening tensely. Peters, at the flat desk, picked up his pencil.

"We'll take up the examination where we left off," McGregor announced mildly. "You folks understand, of course, I'm not putting this quiz over because I think anyone here is guilty of murder. I must get every scrap of information while it's fresh in your minds. People have a way of forgetting. 'Twouldn't be natural if you didn't."

He must have thought that up while we were at lunch, Tim decided. He must have realized that his previous questioning had had a third-degree tinge. Now he was looking from one face to the other as if deciding where to begin.

"Dean Farr."

Tilly gasped and clutched her husband's arm. He gently shook off her hold to light his pipe.

"Right here, Chief McGregor."

"You had words with Judge Lander in the smoking room after the snack party, didn't you?"

"I told you, Sandy McGregor, that my husband and I were in our room together." Tilly's reminder was shrill.

"Skip it, Til." Sam's usually lazy voice was sharp with warning. "I'll answer all questions. I guess you'd call it 'words,' Chief. I told the amorous Judge that if he didn't quit ogling my wife, I'd make it my special business to stop him. Grant heard me, so did Warner and Romney, you got the information from the last-named, didn't you?"

"What reply did the deceased make to your threat?"

"For Pete's sake, Chief, stop calling Lander the deceased, it gets my goat. The man I'm talking about was alive. He replied with that infernal smirk of his that he was human, that when an attractive woman invited—that's when I told him that if he weren't an old man I'd knock him down—I'll bet that 'old man' hurt more than what hit him later. Line up your next suspect, Chief, or have you settled on me?"

During all his life to come whenever he heard the scratch of pencil on paper would he relive the tense moments that followed Sam Farr's damning admission, Tim wondered? Was the setting of the book-lined library indelibly printed on the screen of his memory? McGregor carefully fitted the fingers of his two hands together.

"Warner, you hit it up with highballs after the snack party, didn't you?"

Arms folded across his chest, Clive stood straight and defiant against the mantel.

"Suppose I did. That doesn't mean I'd kill a man, does it?"

"It might mean that you didn't *know* you killed a man."

Tim hoped that never again would he see a flash of terror such as leaped to Warner's eyes.

"My God, you can't think I would forget a thing like that?"

"Has happened. You had a row with the deceased, I understand."

Warner glanced at Romney before he answered.

"Right, I did. I am in wrong with the government, it claims tax evasion. I rowed with Lander because he wouldn't smooth over the matter for me. He's done it for others."

"He's dead. He can't answer the accusation. You have provided a motive. We'll take that up later."

He questioned each one again as to their whereabouts between the time they said good-night in the hall and five o'clock, with practically the same answers. He passed over Mark Taylor lightly, left Sophy Brandt till the last. Tim had an uncomfortable hunch that he expected to get a valuable lead from her.

"Mrs. Brandt"—he cleared his throat. The flashing needles stopped, picked up and went on steadily. He pulled something from his pocket and swung it in a glittering circle. "This yours?"

"My bracelet! Where did you find it?" Sophy dropped the knitting into her lap and bent forward eagerly. If her surprise was an act, Romney was right, she did belong on Broadway.

"Then you knew you had lost it?'"

"Yes. The bracelet bothered me when I was playing for dancing in the game house, it kept unclasping. I took it off and laid it on the piano, and incredible as it may seem, came back to the house and forgot it."

"Hmm-m, when at the so-called snack party Madam Stewart noticed it was not on your arm you told her it was in the bag in your lap. How come?"

"I told her that first, because I was ashamed of having been so careless, second because I knew she would worry if she thought it was missing, it would be an unhappy end to the grand party. I planned to go to the game house and get it after the others had gone to their rooms."

Good Lord, why had she admitted that, Tim asked himself, it was the very lead McGregor wanted.

"Did you go?"

"No."

"Why not?"

"I lost my courage in this era of bag snatchers. There are a lot of strangers on this campus. You can't have forgotten the holdups that have occurred on this very highway, Chief McGregor. I belong to the generation of women who almost never went out after dark without a male escort. The colonnade looked poky when I started out. I went back to my room and took a chance that the bracelet would be safe."

"You are sure you left this on the piano?" The glittering thing swung from McGregor's stubby fingers. "Perhaps you can tell how it came to be in the fist of the deceased." Even that didn't crack her composure.

"I can't, Chief McGregor. Maybe Henry Lander picked it up from the piano just as he was—was shot."

How had she known the Judge had been shot? He hadn't told her. As he watched her face Tim remembered her frightened question when she had spoken to him as he went down the stairs—was it only this morning?—recalled her warning to him in the Dean's Den about Lander. "He's cruel, once he gets a hold on a person," she had said. He remembered her tearful promise. "It is so little to do for you who have done so much for me. Sometime, sometime, perhaps I can do more."

Good God, had she shot Lander thinking it might help him? Had she already planned it when she had reported, "The only thing we have to fear—is fear itself"? It was a crazy suspicion but it started drops of sweat on his forehead.

"Mrs. Brandt, think hard." There was a third-degree edge to McGregor's voice. "Are you sure you didn't go back to the game house for your bracelet?"

"I told you I lost my courage and went to my room."

"Hmm-m. That's queer." He drew a crushed purple orchid from his pocket. "I understand that you were the only woman at the party who wore a flower like this. The sergeant found it near the elbow of the deceased."

XIV

STANDING at the window of his office at the Center, hands thrust hard into the pockets of his gray coat, Timothy Grant looked across fields to Beechcroft, which gleamed like a white cutout against the blue of the lake and the yellowing hills where the roofs and chimneys of summer houses were visible now that the heavy foliage had thinned. His eyes followed the shadow of a plane as it skimmed the surface of the water which sparkled with gold coins of sunlight. It was Mark Taylor's returning to the airfield. He had flown two Canadians to Ottawa.

His attention shifted to the colonnade and game house at Beechcroft. Two weeks had passed since Henry Lander's body had been found in the badminton court. In spite of days crowded with conferences with the heads of many divisions at the Center to decide matters of operation, great and small, it had been the longest two weeks he ever had known. If McGregor had a clue to the mystery of the tragedy he was keeping it under his hat.

Unseeing eyes on the outside world, he reviewed the inquest. News of the murder had spread by the time Molly B., Deb and he had arrived, a crowd was streaming into the room in which the hearing was to be held. Reporters were scribbling in notebooks, photographers were focusing cameras. The result of the autopsy was read. Deb was asked the exact time at which she discovered the body, to describe the voice she had heard at 4 A.M. Molly B. and he had been put through practically the same examination McGregor had used.

There were questions about the party: had Judge Lander appeared disturbed at any time during the evening; was it known that he had enemies? After all the time spent and the questions asked the verdict had been, "Murder by person or persons unknown."

An impressive memorial service had been held in the chapel followed by burial in the cemetery where the great of the college lay. Now, after days of shock and speculation, life was returning to normal. That was right. Why should the lives of hundreds of students to whom Henry Lander was but a name—to many not even that—be shadowed by the tragedy?

It was shadowing him. He couldn't rid himself of the suspicion that Mrs. Sophy knew more, a whole lot more, about the shooting than she had told; when it came to that, she hadn't told anything. That Sunday afternoon in the library at Beechcroft he had been so impressed by his hunch that in some way she was involved that he had gone to his room in the west wing to make sure that the ivory-handled revolver was in his suitcase where he had tucked it under his dinner clothes when he had returned from the Center. It wasn't there. What had become of it? Did Mrs. Sophy know? He hadn't made inquiries. It seemed wiser not to let the fact be known that it was missing. It would put whoever had taken it on guard.

If Mrs. Sophy were aware that she was on his mind she gave no hint of the knowledge. She carried on smoothly, efficiently, so gaily sometimes that he accused himself of having gone nuts on the subject. Yesterday she had entertained for him the two visiting scientists from Canada who had come to look over certain arrangements at the Center with the idea of copying them. Only one fact kept his suspicion alive. Not once had she mentioned Lander's death, not once had she referred to the bracelet and orchid which had been found in the badminton court that Sunday morning. The omission had a sinister significance which brought him back to his conviction that she knew something about it.

For the hundredth time he asked himself if he ought to tell McGregor of his hunch and answered as he had answered each time before. "No." It was only a hunch. Why drag her into it? He hadn't a shred of fact with which to back it up. The missing gun might have been stolen by a servant. The chief had the reputation of being one of the keenest law enforcement officers in the state. Apparently he had rested the investigation with the dramatic display of the purple orchid. Of course he hadn't. He was paying out plenty of line. Someday he would give it a quick snap and land his suspect. Meanwhile someone was in possession of his revolver. He could inform the chief of that without involving Mrs. Sophy. He answered the buzz of the interoffice phone.

"Yes. I'll see him." He snapped off the connection.

McGregor calling. Uncanny that he should appear almost as if he had been materialized by his thoughts. The chunky official chugged into the room.

"Can you spare me a few moments, Mr. Grant? They told me in the outer office that your appointments for the day fitted together snug as bricks in a wall."

"This happens to be a chink between bricks. Sit down." He waited till McGregor had taken the chair opposite his at the desk. "What's on your mind?"

"Any dictaphones concealed under chairs or in the walls?"

"Nary a one. We leave that to men in your field. This visit has to do with Judge Lander's taking off, I assume."

"Sure, I haven't had anything else on my mind—hardly anything else—since it happened. Looked as if I dropped the case pretty sudden when I came up for air with that orchid, I suppose."

"It looked like a piece of unfinished business to me."

"Sure, I want them all to relax."

"Relax? You're crazy. Do you think any person in the college or town will relax with a killer on the loose? I'll bet a lot of them are asking themselves, 'Who next?'"

"That's a cheerful suggestion. They'll forget. I just called on Madam Stewart to ask if she would give some parties for the GIs and their wives to sort of pull the college back to normal. That poker-faced butler of hers gives me the creeps."

"You've got something there. If you're looking for a guy who isn't telling all he knows, watch him."

"Says you. I'm no rookie in this business, Mr. Grant. We won't find out anything from anyone till folks are off guard."

"What was Madam Stewart's reaction to the party suggestion?"

"She was shocked at first, the deceased being such a friend of the family, then she caught on and said, 'The GIs have had more than their share of horrors, why should their lives be shadowed? They are making good in their studies, they deserve all I can do for them.' Then she said that curiosity seekers were swarming over her place, couldn't I do something about it? I've put two men on the job to keep folks off. The game house has been sealed since the crime. She'll give four parties, too many students to have them all at once."

"She is a grand person."

"Sure is, smart as they come, too. I buy all her books, can't say I read 'em all, but we village folks have to stand back of home talent. She spends most of her life thinking up mysteries, seems as if she ought to solve this one. Do you think she knew Lander was married?"

"Married!" Surprise brought Tim half out of his chair. He sank back with a thud. McGregor's grin indicated supreme satisfaction at the effect of his bomb. "Where did you get that phony information, Chief?"

"From his will, probated yesterday. I've been watching for it, oftentimes you can get a lead from the way a man leaves his property. Except for a few legacies he left everything to the college to found a law school, apparently hadn't a relative, but, there was a codicil in which he said that if a woman sayin' she was his wife put in a claim for his property, nothing doing. She had left him a few months after they married years ago, and he divorced her for desertion. That isn't legal language, but that's what it boils down to."

"Why mention her in the will if she was no longer his wife? Sounds to me as if he weren't too sure of the legality of the divorce."

"Yeah, I figured it that way too. Also that the ex-wife might have had something to do with his snuffing out. You may be surprised to hear it but I hate the word 'murder,' I by-pass it whenever I can."

Tim remembered the hatred between the Judge and Mrs. Sophy. Could she be the divorced wife? Now he was crazy. She had had a husband and three sons, hadn't she?

"There's another angle to it, Madam Stewart told me." Tim forced his mind to attention. "She said to ask you about the safe opening. You could tell it better than she."

He told of Ingrid's scream, of her later admission to him that she had heard footsteps on the balcony, and had yelled; of finding the loose-leaf notebook on the floor by the safe; of the discovery that papers had been taken; of the return of the lost combination.

"Hmm-m, know what the Norwegian woman's papers were?"

"She said letters and her citizenship papers. I have an idea—"

"Don't stop. Go on. You can be a great help in this. Don't hold out on me."

"Then you don't suspect me of having shot the Judge?"

"I'm not committing myself," McGregor grinned.

"In that case perhaps I'd better tell you that a revolver of mine is missing."

"Godamighty. How come?"

Tim told when and why he had carried the ivory-handled revolver, of his discovery that it was not in his suitcase.

"Why didn't you tell me this before? Why? Because you've got an idea who took it, right?"

"I haven't the faintest idea, didn't know that anyone knew I had it with me. When I decided to spend the night at Beechcroft, I made up my mind I would walk to the Center after the party and that I'd better pocket the gun, there have been so many holdups lately."

"You're telling me. We'll go back to that later. Loosen up. What's the idea you swallowed a minute or two ago?"

"I had an impression that Ingrid Johnson, the Norwegian woman to you, knew why her papers were stolen. It is only a hunch. I haven't a bit of evidence to back it up."

"A hunch has solved a mystery before this. What do you make of the voice Miss Deb heard on the terrace at 4 A.M.?"

"That she had a vivid dream. What else could it be? According to the medical examiner the Judge had been dead two hours at the time she claims she heard him arguing. No one else heard the voice, at least no one has admitted hearing it."

"There are them that aren't telling all they know—you amongst 'em, Mr. Grant. Dream or not, it puts Miss Deb in a mean spot. I thought at first she had cooked up the story to shield someone, Dean Farr perhaps, he's her cousin and he sure had a motive, or Warner, who walked out on her— women have queer ideas of loyalty to a stinker—tax evasion's a pretty serious thing, and some men don't know what they're doing when they're high. He could have had it in for the Judge. I'm convinced now that Miss Debby is sure she heard the voice. Mrs. Brandt hasn't told all she knows about the shooting. I'm laying for her, but quiet, very quiet."

"Has the gun been found?"

"Not hide nor hair of it. 'Twas a .38 did the work. What was yours?"

"A .38. Mine couldn't have been used because I had it in my pocket at the time the Judge was shot, and I was at the Center."

"I know, I checked on you. I'm having Mrs. Brandt tailed to make sure she isn't meeting anyone on the q.t. It hasn't been hard to find out that she hated Lander like poison. She has sons who might have done the trick thinking he was blackmailing their mother."

"That's crazy, Chief."

"Maybe. Someone shot him, didn't they? I have a man following Miss Deb, too. Someone may suspect she knows more about that voice on the terrace than she's telling and get rough. She has so many irons in the fire my operator's threatened with a nervous breakdown trying to keep up with her. She rides, she rows to the island, hikes to the village, attends classes on the campus and drives to all kinds of society goings-on. There goes the buzzer. I guess that fills the chink allowed me." Halfway across the room he stopped.

"You couldn't lend a hand looking out for Miss Deb, could you? Maybe give her a job here at the Center where you could keep an eye on her? My man will take over after she leaves the office, and I have an efficient pipe line into Beechcroft." He chuckled. "You wouldn't guess in a million years who it is. Whatever you do, make it quick. She was the prettiest, cutest, politest kid I held up traffic for. I'd hate to have anything happen to her."

"What do you mean, *'happen'*? Is that a warning?"

"It ain't anything else but." McGregor closed the door between them.

XV

ALL day in the chinks between appointments, "I'd hate to have anything happen to her" bobbed up in Tim's mind like a jack-in-the-box.

What had McGregor meant, he would have time only to think before he had to turn his attention to the business at hand.

At five o'clock, with the last interview on his engagement pad disposed of, hands clasped behind his head he tilted back in the desk chair and concentrated on McGregor's question, "You couldn't lend a hand looking out for Miss Deb, could you? Maybe give her a job at the Center where you could keep an eye on her?"

Having her where he could keep an eye on her was just what he didn't want at present. The work he had shouldered needed his single-minded concentration, and how could he concentrate when the girl he loved, had loved since the day in the Pacific theater when he had found her picture among the pages of his mother's diary, was in his employ? His dream of her as his wife, living with her in the home he had inherited, had carried him through the tedium of idle days in a top-of-the-wave spirit. How could he tell her or show that he loved her with the infernal gossip going the rounds that he was after Beechcroft? As from a far country came a voice:

"Hold fast your dream."

He threw off the spell and forced his thoughts back to McGregor and his warning.

"I'd hate to have anything happen to her."

The words ghosted through his memory, leaving a shivery trail. That settled it. He must give his best to the Center. He must guard Deb. It was up to him to co-ordinate the two. He had succeeded in putting through difficult assignments in the service, assignments that at first had seemed impossible of achievement. This was just one more.

"Whatever you do, make it quick," McGregor had said. Had he been tipped off that trouble threatened or had the warning been merely from abundance of precaution? He grabbed the telephone and dialed the Beechcroft number.

"Miss Randall?" he inquired. "Mr. Grant calling."

"Miss Randall is not at home," Scragg answered.

"I'll speak to Madam Stewart." It seemed but an instant before Molly B. inquired eagerly:

"Any news, Tim, about—about anything?"

"No. I want to speak to Deb. Thought you might know where I can get in touch with her." A click as if a receiver in another part of the house had been laid softly in its cradle. Had the butler been listening?

"She went to the island—"

"For the love of Mike, to the island—after what's happened? Did she go alone?"

"She said she was going there to work. Here she is. You can ask her yourself." He heard her say, "Tim wants to talk with you, honey."

"Deborah Randall in person. What's on your mind, Timothy?"

"A binge. My head is bursting at the seams with problems. How about dinner and a little stepping at the Country Club across the lake? I hear it's super."

"You mean tonight?"

"Sure, I mean tonight. What help would a night next week be to my addled brain? How about it? Why don't you answer?"

"My word, but you are the impatient swain." She laughed. "I took a moment to visualize my engagement pad and one more to think what I would wear. I'll go. Thank you prettily, Marine. What time?"

There was a sharp touch of frost in the night air. The sky was so thick with stars that it had the effect of moonlight silvering the earth. The maroon roadster purred along as if skimming over black velvet. Deb drew a long breath and snuggled her chin a little deeper into the collar of her mink jacket.

"This ought to clear your addled brain, Tim. It's heavenly. All your days are crammed with problems, aren't they? Was this one especially hectic?"

"You've said it and the maddening part of it is, it needn't have been, but my secretary mixed appointments, messed things up good and plenty till there was the dickens to pay." She couldn't know that up to date he hadn't settled on a personal secretary.

"Aha, retribution has caught up with you. Remember how snootily you turned me down when I applied for the job? You didn't even ask for a rain check."

"You bet I remember. For the last week I've been bolstering my courage to ask you to take it."

"You're not kidding?"

"Sure, I'm not kidding. If you would take over for a couple of months—" McGregor should have solved the mystery of the tragedy by then—"it would help me over a stretch of rough going. The problems I have to solve are enormous—I like that—but the petty annoyance of a bungling secretary gets my goat."

"How do you know I wouldn't be a bungler?"

"Were you in Washington?"

"No. Here's where I droop my long eyelashes shyly and admit that I was the answer to an undersecretary's prayer."

"How about being the answer to a scientist's?"

"This is so sudden. I'll have to think it over. It would mean transferring the classes in which I've registered to evening sessions, those and my writing—you wouldn't know to look at me that I'm a coming novelist, would you? It's a temptation. I'd like to be really useful again, to have that what-a-big-girl-am-I feeling that goes with being an important man's right hand. Do you really want me?"

"Didn't I get across how much? Looks as if watching the traffic has cramped my selling style. I not only want you, I need you. Decide 'Yes' or 'No' by the time we get back home, will you? I'd like to feel settled one way or the other." Also, I'll have to get busy on another plan to keep my eye on you if you turn this one down, he told himself. "How are things going at Beechcroft? Getting back to normal after the shock?"

"Molly B. is, but I can't make Ingrid out. She's so tense, so brittle, that I'm afraid if I touch a finger it may snap off. I have been burning midnight brain cells wondering if I should tell you what I overheard."

"You should tell me everything. We are living in the midst of a mystery, remember, where the most innocent happening may prove a beckoning trail."

"You are doubtless right, but, I have an uneasy feeling of disloyalty to Ingrid."

She told of the conversation she had overheard in the cutting garden, that the same man had appeared in the drive after she had said good-night to the guests at the installation celebration.

"Why didn't you tell McGregor?"

"I thought it was Ingrid's business. She is one of the most forthright persons I know, if she felt the man had anything to do with the mur—mystery, she would tell of it. I can't bear the thought of getting her involved. Perhaps the chief knows already. Maybe he has noticed a man who rubs his right cheek as if something irritated it."

"What's that?"

"Don't jump at me."

"Sorry. I was reading the sign telling which turn to make. You were saying something about rubbing a cheek. I got that much. Here we are."

On a raised platform musicians in gaudy regalia, the South American motif, were playing, "For you. For Me. Forever More," when the maître d'hôtel drew out a chair for Deb at a small table against the wall with its brilliant mural of an Argentine village.

"The dinner has been ordered," Tim informed the dark-skinned, dapper man, who immediately gathered up the outsize menus he had presented. "Except something to drink. What will you have, Deb?"

"Iced coffee with plenty of cream."

"Make it two."

"Did you notice his horrified expression before he melted away? I suspect I've thrown sand in the gear of his department by my order, but I don't drink."

"I've noticed that, and that you don't smoke. I don't know much about you, really, Deb. So many things have crowded in since we—"

"Met in a head-on collision." He loved her low laugh. "Life has been just one queer happening after another, since then, hasn't it? Have you seen Sandy McGregor? I thought he would haunt Beechcroft; if he has been there I haven't seen him. Is he still on the trail?"

"Can you see him giving up? Not a chance. Let's forget him. This is a party. Is that ruff of black tulle on your head supposed to be a hat? I like that sparkly black frock you're wearing. The green clips are perfect with it."

"I strive to please. The frock is known in the fashion world as a 'go-everywhere.' The music is divine. What an array of instruments. Woodwinds, piccolo, three horns, xylophone, harp, piano and strings. The management has gone all out for effect. No wonder the place is crowded. The music is so firm, so spirited. It sets my sandals tapping." He laughed.

"Or, 'Why are we sitting here?' says you. What are they playing?"

"As Time Goes By."

"Why let any more escape? Come on."

They wound in and out among couples the majority of whom appeared content to swivel in one spot, cheek to cheek.

"How we doing, as time goes by, Deb?" Tim inquired.

"As dancing partners we'd steal the show at any night spot, Marine. Look at the doorway. We are not the only Beechcrofters with a get-away-from-it-all urge."

"Romney and Stella Dane. He's made a quick recovery.

He phoned yesterday that he was fighting a cold and wouldn't report for work. It beats me what he can see in her."

"It is what she sees in him that will count, my lad. She's a honey in that white frock. There's that man again."

"What man?"

"Don't look now, he knows I saw him. He's just sitting down at the table beyond Burke Komney's with the platinum blonde in silver lamé."

"You mean the redhead with the stubble mustache like Warner's? Where have you seen him before?"

"On the campus. In the village. In the front row when I spoke at the rally. Yesterday, I got so fed up with his constant appearance that when I saw his reflection in the window of the shop where I had stopped I wheeled on him and demanded, 'Are you following me?' It sounds corny, I know, but after what has happened, he gave me the jitters."

"We've danced round to our table. The fresh fruit cocktail is served." Tim drew out her chair, waited until he was seated opposite until he asked in what he flattered himself was a voice lightly amused:

"What answer did your mysterious admirer—you're a terribly attractive dish, Deb—make to that?"

"I'm glad you can see a joke in it. *I* can't. He said that he was in the town to prepare a poll on the progress GIs were making in their college work. I snapped, 'As I'm neither a GI nor a GI wife, you can learn nothing from me!' "

"What was his come-back to that?"

" 'Sorry to have annoyed you, Miss Randall.' He made me a bow from the waist and departed. My outburst did some good. I haven't seen him since until tonight, and he appears to have the platinum blonde on his mind. Listen!"

The great room settled into quiet as a soprano voice came over the air waves. It was Licia Albanese of the Metropolitan singing an aria from the first act of *La Traviata*.

"Beautiful, wasn't it?" Deb asked after the last lingering note had died away. "I love that—"

"Paging Mr. Timothy Grant." The voice began at the door. Tim stopped the boy when it reached him.

"I'm Grant," he said. "What is it?"

"You're wanted on the phone, sir."

"Excuse me, Deb." He rose and followed the boy.

"Alone, Tim?" a low voice inquired when he picked up the receiver in a booth. "Mark speaking."

"Go on."

"Just had a near crack-up taking off on the college airfield for a night flight. I'm not hurt. Had to get hold of you as soon as possible. Sorry to ask you to cut your evening short, but time counts."

"Where will I meet you?"

"Better come home. Fewer listeners there. My engine went bad. It had been tampered with."

"Sure?"

"Too darn sure. Listen close, when I discovered it I wondered—"

"Just a little louder. I can't hear."

"Wondered if the person who got Lander is after me."

XVI

MOLLY BURTON STEWART dropped the newspaper she was reading into the lap of her emerald-green satin dinner frock as Deborah entered her living room.

"How did the clinic for the GI wives go?" she inquired. Ingrid Johnson, standing at one of the long windows looking out at the darkening sky, turned eagerly to hear the answer.

"It went like a breeze after the first awful five minutes." Deb settled into a corner of the Empire sofa and crossed her feet encased in beige-strapped sandals which matched the color of her pleated wool skirt. Two large Chinese coins which hung from a chain about her neck repeated the gold threads in her beige sweater.

"What happened in the first five minutes?"

"Twenty GI wives reported in the library, Molly B. It looked like a frost and my spirit dropped to an all-time low, the girls were so correct, so stiffly polite. Then Scragg announced that tea was served on the terrace—it was warm enough to chance having it there—and we adjourned. They were crazy about the French paper in your dining room. Sarah Allen hovered to make sure that everything was in the best Beechcroft tradition, that the leaf-green wrought-iron table was set with your smartest outdoor china, glass and linen. With tea a thaw set in, those luscious little lobster salad rolls topped the trick." She drew a compact from the pocket of her skirt and regarded herself in the mirror. "No, I haven't."

"Haven't what, honey?"

"Acquired a bun of gray hair at the nape of my neck and deep wrinkles at the corners of my eyes. I rate them. I answered so many questions—I tried not to give advice—that I felt years older when the last attractive femme departed, and they were darned attractive and intelligent. I'm sold on the job of trying to help them with their problems."

"What did they want to know?" Ingrid Johnson asked. She rested an elbow on the mantel, the soft light of the fire turned her turquoise afternoon frock to pale violet.

"First, how, in cramped quarters, to keep a crying baby

from disturbing its daddy while he was studying."

"How did you answer that?"

"That husband would have to co-operate, Molly B., train himself to concentrate no matter what went on—it can be done, I know that from personal experience—or work in one of the lecture halls if he can't adjust himself at home. After all, I suppose having the baby wasn't entirely the wife's responsibility."

"That sounds reasonable, tell us another," Ingrid encouraged.

"The major problem was how to stretch ninety dollars a month to cover expenses. I couldn't do much with that one but be sympathetic, never having tried living on that amount to say nothing of providing for three persons on it. However, I mean to dig into budget figures and try to find an answer that will help, at least. I'll bone up before they come again. They were terribly disappointed not to meet our distinguished author, Molly B. They asked if you were a lavender-and-old-lace sort of person. I said on the contrary, you adored large hats and your clothes were hot-from-the-griddle models."

"That ought to sell a few books. You'd make a good public relations woman, Debby. Ingrid and I decided that the wives would feel freer to discuss their problems with you—you being kind of young—if we were not present."

"They discussed them all right. After tea and canapés, cakes and sherbets they let down their hair. One snappy brunette—I'm not mentioning names, you notice—lingered behind the others to confide that her husband went into violent rages and threatened her with a revolver. She was afraid of him. What could she do? She loved him, didn't want to leave him, was sure that his condition was the result of three years in a Jap prison. Tragic, isn't it? My word, you don't suppose the man went mad and shot Judge Lander thinking he was a Jap, do you?"

"I don't wonder the thought hoarsened your voice. Even though the woman told you in confidence, Sandy McGregor should be informed that a nervously overwrought man is on the loose with a gun, not only for the wife's sake, but for the safety of each person on the campus."

"You may be right but let's make sure the wife isn't a little overwrought herself before we put Sandy on his trail. She had a nice sense of drama. One of the girls said that the GI wife living in the trailer is terribly homesick. I promised I would call and invite her—"

"Living in the trailer? Don't," Ingrid protested sharply. "Excuse me, I hear my phone."

Deb's eyes returned from the quickly closed door at the end of the room and met Molly B.'s.

"What happened to her?"

"I don't know. Ingrid's emotions are stretched to the snapping point. I won't ask her, I won't force her confidence. When she is ready she will come to me, I am sure. She is working out something, trying to decide what to do about it, living with a problem. I shall wait for her solution without questioning. I trust her implicitly."

Deb thought of the man in the cutting garden and she recalled Ingrid's impassioned, "I don't know what to do. . . . It's driving me crazy." That had been before the tragedy in the game house, she couldn't then have been worrying about his implication in that. Ought she to tell Molly B. what she had overheard? No. She had said, "I shall wait for her solution without questioning."

"I wonder if I ever will be as wise, as sure, as poised as you are, Molly B."

"I'm not so very wise, as to poise—years ago I learned a little prayer, 'God grant me Serenity to accept things I cannot change, Courage to change things I can, and Wisdom to know the difference.' That has been a reliable beam to follow through dark days."

" 'Serenity to accept things I cannot change, Courage to change things I can,' that last is a thought to keep one fighting, Molly B."

"Sandy McGregor was here this morning." The statement derailed Deb's train of thought. "I promised to give four parties for the GIs and their wives. He thinks that a bit of social whirl will clear their minds of our mystery."

"Has he made progress in solving it?"

"I put the question. He shook his head. I asked him if each member of this household was still under suspicion. He said, 'Someone did it'—as if I had to be reminded of that—then added his stock phrase, 'We'll come back to that later.' "

"As a quiz master you wouldn't burn up the air waves, Molly B. Didn't he say anything more?"

"Just at that moment Scragg entered to tell me I was wanted on long distance."

"Were you?"

"Whoever it was had rung off."

"I'll bet there was no call. That butler is like a stock character in a movie, always entering at a climactic moment."

"Maybe, but he's a crackajack butler. He was trained at the Danes'. When they could no longer afford him he applied to me."

"Light breaks. That was why he was whispering to Stella the evening before Ingrid's nightmare."

"I can't imagine the saturnine Scragg whispering to any-one, but he has known Stella since she was a little girl. He may have a smoldering affection for her, feel a certain loyalty to the family. You'd better call on that homesick wife in the trailer and invite the couple to the first party next week."

"In spite of Ingrid's protest? It was a protest. That phone ring was an excuse for an exit, wasn't it?"

"We'll leave Ingrid and her reactions out of it. Call on the young woman tomorrow. How was the Country Club?"

"Super. The music was out of this world. Excellent food. A crowd, but a nice crowd. Your secretary was among those present looking like a dreamboat."

"I knew she was dining with her brother."

"Brother! Has she promised to be a sister to Burke Romney?"

"Was she with him? It is not my responsibility with whom she goes out, I would prefer she didn't lie to me, but I have discovered recently that she has done it quite often. She said she wanted to spend the night at home and asked for today off that she might help her brother with accounts. I assumed it had to do with the foreclosure of the mortgage. Did you dance?"

"Once, then Tim was paged for a phone call." Better not tell that his face was drained of color under its bronze when he returned to the table. "He explained that the call was on important business, brought me home, then shot off in his roadster, he didn't say whither. Hold tight to your chair. This item will make the room whirl. He has asked me to be his secretary."

"Heavenly day, why you? There must be at least half a dozen experts in his kind of work already at the Center."

"He claimed he had a tough day yesterday because the secretary pro tem. bungled his appointments. It isn't a permanent job he offers only until he gets the executive machinery under control. What do you think of it?"

"Because the progress of the Center and Tim's success as the Head is very near my heart, I say YES in capitals if you are willing to do it."

"That settles it. I'll sign on the dotted line. Did you know he has gone all out for a girl?"

"I suspected it. My study of motives behind actions has helped me understand the human heart—at least, my fans believe I understand it—I have seen that one-woman-in-the-world-for-me look in Tim's eyes."

"It's your imagination-plus getting in its work. How could you see it? She's still in the Pacific—not the ocean—the theater."

"What does that prove? Wouldn't he be likely to think of

the girl he loves? Wouldn't thinking of her bring that look to his eyes?"

"Hold everything, Molly B. I guess you're right. Who am I to question an authority on romance? As you approve I'll phone Tim I'll take over, he wanted an immediate decision. He didn't wait for me to answer last night he was in such a hurry to get away. Too late to reach him at the office, isn't it?"

"He and Sophy and Mark are dining here. Break the good news to him then."

They were having coffee after dinner in the library. The royal-blue hangings were drawn across the long windows. A brilliant dancing-dervish type of fire twisted and whirled, flamed and flared, made little whispering sounds and threw fantastic patterns on Molly B.'s emerald-green frock. Ingrid in bronze lamé presided at the low table with its silver appointments. Sophy in mauve was at the piano playing softly, Greig's "I Love Thee." Mark Taylor on the bench beside her was turning the music in response to her nod. Tim joined Deb on the sofa.

"What's the color of your frock?"

"Flame. Like it?"

"Suits me and what is more to the point, it's perfect for you. Having made which introductory, complimentary remarks, do I get a secretary?"

"How can I resist such a high pressure salesman? You do."

"Good girl. Start tomorrow?"

"Do you need me so soon?"

"That's the idea. Hours nine to five with time out for lunch, and Saturday afternoons off. No five-day week yet. Better have Molly B.'s chauffeur drive you to the Center and call for you."

"That's a wacky suggestion. You don't want a working girl, Marine, you're looking for what the columnists dub a socialite. When the weather is good I shall walk back and forth, and drive myself when it is bad."

"That appears to settle that—for the present." He rose and leaned his arm on the corner of the mantel.

"Heard the news, Molly B., about Lander's will?"

It seemed to Deb as if each person in the room stiffened.

"No, Tim. What has he done with his money? Wills fascinate me. Often they reveal the secrets of a person's life, his loves and his animosities, perhaps secrets which have been buried deep in his heart for years."

"Lander's does. He cuts out a wife who deserted him." He stopped to light a cigarette. "Anyone here have a suspicion he had one?"

118

He was looking through half closed eyes at Sophy Brandt, who appeared as startled as if the floor had opened and the Judge himself had appeared.

"Yes," Ingrid Johnson declared hoarsely. She rose. Two deep red spots burned on her high cheekbones. Her eyes were black with intensity.

"I was his wife when I came here to live with you as a secretary, Molly B. Remember that he recommended me?"

Molly Burton Stewart nodded and put her hand to her throat as if it were too constricted to let her voice through.

"I hated the deception. Thank God I can tell the truth now. He raged when I insisted upon telling you. He feared that the fact he was married would bog down his career. I was young enough, he was a lot older than I, and fascinated enough to agree to the secrecy until I came here. Then I refused to consider myself his wife while living in your house under false pretenses. Two months later he went to Reno for a divorce, grounds desertion. Since then, we have spoken to one another as seldom as possible."

"That was years ago, Ingrid. How could you keep the secret without telling me?"

"That was one of the conditions. Neither one of us was to let you know. As time went on the almost irresistible urge to confide in you died down, the marriage seemed like something that belonged in a dream world. For two years I have suspected that he was scheming to marry you, Molly B., to strengthen his hand here at the college. Had I seen an indication that he would succeed I would have told you the story. I hope—I hope it won't break our friendship." She bit her lips hard to steady them.

"Why should it, Ingrid? My love for you can't be uprooted by something that happened years ago. You have been a tower of strength to me. I think you were wise to keep the matter to yourself. What good would telling have done? Try as I might not to, I would have been aware all the time of the past relations between you and my legal adviser. That's why you stole your own papers, isn't it?"

"You knew that?"

"I didn't know it until this minute. I suspected it. Why and how did you do it?"

"Someone phoned me that the Judge had threatened a person with unpleasant publicity unless he produced my papers. Although the warning was in a strange voice, I heeded it. I suspected that the marriage certificate was what he wanted. The morning of the Flower Show, after you had gone to the cottage, I came back. I had found the combination Debby had lost the night before on the balcony where someone had dropped it. I opened the safe, removed my papers and a few of yours, as a blind—they are safe, Molly B., and in my haste forgot to replace the loose-leaf book."

"Was that nightmare yell part of your program?"

"Yes, Tim. I told you the other evening that I really heard footsteps on the balcony and screamed to frighten whoever it was. It confirmed what I had been told, that someone would try to find the papers, that is why I took them the next morning. Forgive me, Molly B.?"

"I have nothing to forgive, Ingrid. I—"

"Mr. Mortimer Dane," Scragg announced from the threshold. Had it been anyone but he Deb would have suspected a touch of pride in the butler's voice. The tall ruddy-faced man in coarse brown tweeds pushed by him into the room.

"Where is my sister, Madam Stewart?" His voice was aggressive, his eyes snapped nervously.

Molly B. placed the cup she still held on the low table beside her, Ingrid dropped back into her chair and stared at him wide-eyed. Sophy Brandt and Mark Taylor, still on the piano bench where they had remained as if frozen through Ingrid's story, regarded him with the surprise they would have bestowed on a Martian who had dropped through the stratosphere. Tim Grant stepped behind Molly B.'s chair.

"What's the idea, bursting in like this, Dane?" he inquired. "Take it easy. What's up?"

"Excuse me, Madam Stewart. So many terrible things are happening to girls that when Stella didn't appear today, I went haywire."

"Did she spend the night at home?"

"Yes. The maid reported that her white evening dress was in her room and that she carried breakfast to her about noon. She was to check some accounts with me, said you had given her the day off. I knew she would sleep late so didn't expect her much before one o'clock. Then I waited and waited. Phoned this house twice, thought you might have unexpected work that detained her. When after dinner Scragg said she wasn't here, hadn't been here today, I came to look her up." He drew his hand across his damp forehead. "Gosh, I'm scared. Sure she isn't here?"

"Yes, Mort." Molly Burton Stewart's voice was gentle. "I heard that she dined at the Country Club across the lake with Burke Romney last evening, perhaps he knows what plans she had for today."

"I'll get him on the phone—"

" 'Tain't necessary, Mr. Dane," McGregor assured smoothly as he stepped into the room. "Your sister's at headquarters. I've come to ask you to join her at once. Perhaps you can make her talk. There's a little matter of a .38 we found her hiding in the shrubs this noon, we'd like explained. She has refused to answer questions; we've held her, as 'twas a .38 that did for Judge Lander, you may remember. The gun she was hiding, she says she was picking it up—" he looked from face to face, his eyes rested on Tim Grant—"had an ivory handle."

Sophy Brandt's shoulder struck the keyboard of the piano with a crash of jangled notes.

XVII

THERE was a hint of smug satisfaction in McGregor's expression as his eyes flashed from the white-haired woman back to Tim Grant, before Tim and Mark carried Sophy Brandt to a chair.

"I—I'm all right," she protested. "I didn't faint, really I didn't. I have a heart twinge occasionally and one caught me as I was listening to Mr. McGregor. What did you say about an ivory-handled revolver, Chief?"

"Forget it till you're feeling steady again, Mrs. Brandt, don't fool with heart twinges, 'tain't safe. Miss Deb, I would like you and Mr. Grant to come with us. It would be nice for Miss Dane to have another woman present."

"I'll get a coat at once."

"Why not shoot along with Dane, Chief?" Tim suggested. "Miss Randall and I will follow in my car."

"That goes with me," McGregor agreed and waved Mortimer Dane ahead of him from the room.

The headlights of the roadster set the frost-whitened trees and shrubs that bordered the highway sparkling as if powdered with iridescent diamond dust as Tim drove under a slate-black sky dotted with a few blinking gold stars. Deb snuggled into her mink jacket. The crisp pine-scented breeze blew back her short hair. In her hurry she hadn't thought of a hat, she so seldom wore one. She lived over the moment when she had seen the ivory-handled revolver in the suitcase in her room. Was it the same gun Stella had been hiding or picking up from the shrubs?

"I suppose there are dozens of ivory-handled revolvers even in this college town, don't you, Tim?" she inquired.

"I wouldn't say 'dozens.' "

"What would you say? Have you a theory about the one Stella had? You haven't spoken since we started. Could you possibly be a little less wooden? I feel as if I were riding beside a robot."

"Whoa, take it easy, Debby."

"I'd like to talk, if you don't mind. Aren't we co-operatives in the Beechcroft Mystery? I'm fast getting the jitters, because, you see, I saw that kind of a gun at home."

"Where? When?" There was nothing wooden about the explosive questions.

She told of the suitcase which had been brought to her room and opened by Sarah Allen.

"Did you notice marks or an inscription on the gun?"

"No. There were three white dinner coats worn that evening. Whose bag Sarah opened has been the sixty-four-dollar question with me ever since."

"Did you take out the gun?"

"No. I covered it with the coat as soon as possible. When it comes to firearms I'm just a little Victorian-age girl. I don't like them."

"Neither does Mrs. Sophy, apparently, if the mere mention of an ivory-handled revolver brings on a heart attack. Ever hear of her having one before?"

"No, but that doesn't prove anything. I have been at Beechcroft for short vacations only during the last three years and she wasn't there at the time. See the trailer in the field. Isn't it brilliantly lighted for a trailer? The GI wife who lives in it is homesick. I intend to call on her and invite her to what Molly B. calls 'the clinic.'" She debated for an instant if she would tell him of Ingrid's objection, decided against it.

"What an explosive evening. First the news of Judge Lander's marriage crashed into the after-dinner calm, followed by Ingrid's confession that she had been his wife—and it's claimed that a woman can't keep a secret—that she was the safe opener. My brain still buzzes round and round and round from shock."

"What fool things women do."

"May I interrupt for a moment to observe that all men are not Solons at all times?"

"There's something in what you say, Deb. Now may I proceed with my reflections? Why didn't Ingrid tell Molly B. that someone was after her papers?"

"For the same reason, probably, that I didn't tell her of the whispers I heard coming from the gallery bay. Why stir her up till I knew what—if anything—they meant? The Judge must have had a stranglehold on someone and Ingrid knows who. Weren't you stunned by the announcement that she had been his wife?"

"By the fact that she had been married to him, yes, but my mother in her diary had declared that she suspected a love affair between the two when Ingrid Johnson came to Beechcroft to be Molly B.'s secretary, so I was prepared in a way. She had other suspicions of the Judge which I intended to follow up. He's gone. So that ends that."

"Will the facts we learned tonight tie in with the shooting

of Henry Lander? Do you think if I had told of the threat I overheard the murder wouldn't have been committed?"

"Good Lord, no. Don't get that on your conscience, Debby. I have a hunch that that leads into an entirely different trail— Here we are at the Town Hall. Dane's roadster is under the light. I hope he will be permitted to take his sister home."

"Just why have I come? What am I supposed to do?" she asked as they went up the steps.

"Be a moral support for Stella. By the way, better not mention the ivory-handled gun you saw in the suitcase."

"Don't worry, I shan't speak. I talked too much when I told of hearing the voice of Judge Lander on the terrace at 4 A.M. and didn't everyone, you included, think me the victim of a delusion?"

"Count me out, I'm sure you think you heard him." He opened a door which had the one word POLICE in big black letters on its frosted glass panel. They stepped into a large, brilliantly lighted room which smelled of stale tobacco smoke.

Stella regarded them in disdainful surprise, drew a compact from her pocket, and frowned at herself in the mirror as she reddened her lips. She didn't look as if she needed moral support, to say nothing of wanting it. The drab background emphasized her sultry beauty. She was wearing a skirt of brilliant green plaid with a black sweater and a broad silver belt. Her hair hung to her shoulders in shining waves. Her crossed knees displayed her lovely legs in beige nylon with eye-baiting success. Mort Dane's arm was across the back of her chair while he talked to her in a low voice. She kept shaking her head as if protesting. Each time she moved the mass of silver bracelets on her left arm clinked. McGregor entered through a doorway behind the large desk on a platform.

"Glad you got here at *last*, Mr. Grant," he greeted curtly as he dropped heavily into a high-back chair. Blue-uniformed Peters, notebook and pencil in hand, seated himself beside him.

Why McGregor's grouch? Had they been unusually long getting here? Deb questioned Tim with her eyes. He grinned and shook his head.

"Don't mind him," he whispered. "That's just an entrance line. He had to say something for a starter." In response to McGregor's glare, he straightened in his chair and thrust his hands into the pockets of his dinner jacket.

"Fire away, Chief," he encouraged. "Here we are as the doctor ordered. What's on your mind?" McGregor scowled at his levity before he looked at Stella.

"Miss Dane, I would like you to explain, so your brother

124

may hear, what you were doing with the gun you see on the desk."

Deb's eyes followed the indicative wave of his hand. She blinked and looked again. In the library at Beechcroft he had referred to an ivory-handled revolver. The gun he had told Stella to look at was a shiny blue snub-nosed automatic. Had he tried to trap someone with that first description? Was Sophy Brandt's collapse the answer? The night at dinner at his house Tim prophesied, in answer to her question, "What is there between the Judge and Sophy?"

"Find out and I bet we'll have a thread which will unravel the mystery of the opened safe." That mystery had been solved but not the secret of Sophy's relations with Judge Lander.

"I suppose your prolonged questioning is what is known as the third degree in circles in which you move, Sandy McGregor." Stella's acidulous voice broke the silence which had followed McGregor's reference to the automatic on the desk. "I can stand it as long as you can. Once more I repeat, I wasn't doing anything with the gun. Last evening I dined at the Country Club across the lake. After my escort said goodnight at the front door—"

"Just a minute," McGregor interrupted. "Didn't he wait to see you were safely in the house? There's lots going on these days that isn't nice, you know."

"He did not."

"Why?"

"That is my business and his."

"For gosh sake, cut out wise-cracking, Stella," her brother ordered roughly. "You're in a spot. Come across with what, if any, information you have. The chief wants to know why the guy who took you out didn't wait till you got into the house. Tell him that and where you found the gun."

"I've told him a dozen times that just before I went into the house last evening I thought I saw a glint under the shrubs beside the front door. So what, I said to myself, went in and snapped off the outside light. After my noon breakfast, I remembered the glint. Went out, looked under the shrubs and saw the automatic. Just as I lifted it to examine it more closely one of McGregor's hounds pounced and caught me with it in my hand. Apparently he has had our place watched, Mort. That's my story, I hope you are satisfied. As to why my escort didn't wait until I was in the house, I repeat that isn't anyone's business but my own."

"But I'm making it my business, Miss Dane." Deb wondered at McGregor's patience, it was so out of character. "We know now that the gun you had in your hand was the gun with which Judge Lander was shot. It was found on your property. Your brothers quarreled violently with the deceased, were heard to threaten him. Who knows that one of them didn't shoot him? How about answering my questions?"

The room was so still that the metallic clang of an elevator gate in the corridor sounded like an off-stage explosion. Someone passed the door whistling, "Jeannie with the Light Brown Hair," slowly, dreamily. Stella Dane's face was as colorless as on that Sunday in the game room when Sam Farr had told her the Judge was dead. Now did she suspect that one of the Wild Danes had shot him? Whatever she feared or thought, McGregor's suggestion had frightened her.

"You win. I'll talk." Her voice was flippant but her hands were unsteady. "Professor Burke Romney invited me to dine and dance at the Country Club. We quarreled on the way home. He was so angry that he didn't wait for me to get into the house. Do you require the details of that quarrel, Sandy McGregor?"

How dared she defy the man regarding her with half-closed eyes when perhaps the life of one of her brothers was at stake? Mortimer Dane was following the same line of thought apparently.

"Cut out the smart-aleck stuff, Stella. Can't you realize this isn't a cocktail party? Answer the chief civilly, get me?"

"Sure, I get you, Mort. Haven't I co-operated so far? If I have to go into the secrets of my young life—"

"That will do for that, Miss Dane," McGregor interpolated crisply. "Let's get back to where we were. You quarreled with Professor Romney. He said good-night and left you at the front door. You saw the glint of a gun among the shrubs and picked it up."

"I picked it up this noon, not last night."

"My mistake. You picked it up this noon. No reason to think the professor chucked it among the shrubs before he left, have you?"

"He couldn't have done it without my seeing him."

"And you didn't see him? Sure of that?"

"Certainly I am sure."

She was looking straight at McGregor as she answered. Was she telling the truth? She hadn't been truthful when she had told Molly B. that she was going to the Country Club with her brother. "I would prefer she didn't lie to me, but, I've discovered recently that she has done it quite often," Molly B. had said.

"How long have you been going out with the professor?" McGregor asked.

"He came to the college the last of August. I have been out with him since on an average of two evenings a week."

126

"He called at the house to take you to the Country Club, I presume? Rang the bell to get in, didn't he?"

"That is the usual program when a man takes a girl out, isn't it?"

"Honest, I wouldn't know it's so long since I've taken a dame stepping, but I guess you're right. Mr. Dane, did anyone call at your front door yesterday?"

The sudden and sharp switch of McGregor's spotlight brought Mortimer Dane out of his slouch with a jerk. He drew in his long legs and straightened.

"Gosh, I don't remember. The maid may, she would answer the bell. I was busy in my office with accounts all day, getting them in shape for Stella to help me with them this afternoon. No one called to see me—hold on, that isn't right. Scragg, our onetime butler, dropped in to ask about some back pay we owed him; he wasn't hounding me, he's been mighty decent about it. Before he left he said he'd noticed as he passed the house that the paint was peeling badly round the front door—he was with us so long he feels a sort of proprietary interest in us—said it should be attended to at once, so I went out front while he showed me what he meant."

"Hmm-m. That was yesterday morning and Miss Dane saw the glint last evening. That's interesting. Had the paint peeled?"

"Yes, it was pretty bad. I told Scragg I could see it was a mess but that we weren't spending money on repairs at present. He said, 'Don't let it go too long,' and walked off."

"I understand that Judge Lander had foreclosed the mortgages he held on your place, Mr. Dane."

"Then you understood wrong." The correction was tinged with satisfaction. "He had the papers ready, he was about to foreclose—for some reason held off—when he was shot. His property goes to the college. I'm hoping the Trustees will have a heart."

"That gives us a new angle on the shooting, doesn't it?"

"What do you mean?" Mortimer Dane's face looked as if the torrent of blood that had rushed to it must burst through.

"We'll go back to that later. You don't remember that anyone besides the butler came to the front door, Mr. Dane?"

"I—don't." He answered cautiously, like a man who suspects a trap.

McGregor spoke to Peters. He opened the door behind the desk, said something through the crack, closed it and returned to his seat. The chief fitted his fingers together, tilted back in his swivel chair and stared at the discoloration on the ceiling which resembled in shape nothing so much as the South American continent.

Was he waiting for someone? Deb glanced at Stella Dane. She was noticeably disturbed. Was she afraid of what was coming? The door at the side of the room opened. Burke Romney stood on the threshold.

"Is this my cue for an entrance, Chief?" he asked and raked his angular fingers through his hair.

"Sit down, Professor." McGregor indicated a chair facing the two Danes. "As you know, Professor"—he rolled the word off his tongue as if pleasantly savoring the taste—"there was a murder at Beechcroft, and—"

"Great guns, man, you didn't order me to report at headquarters to hear that crime rehashed, I hope."

"Mind your manners, Professor. Don't interrupt. Could be we have a new angle on it. It may interest you to know that we have found the gun with which the deceased was shot." He pointed to the automatic on the desk. "I say we, really Miss Dane was the lucky person."

"Lucky, where do you get that lucky, Sandy McGregor? I pick up a revolver I've never seen before and I'm kept in this stinking hole being third-degreed into confessing that I know where it came from. I say again I never had seen that vicious thing on the desk before." Stella's angry torrent of words might have been the harmless buzzing of a fly for all the notice McGregor took of it.

"Professor, you escorted Miss Dane to the Country Club last evening to dine and dance?"

"I did."

"She declares you left her at the front door before she entered the house."

"Right."

"She says also, that you and she had quarreled."

"One hundred per cent correct."

"She refused to tell the cause of the quarrel. Are you equally sensitive?"

Stella Dane started to her feet, sank back into the chair as her brother tapped warning fingers on her shoulder. She kept her burning eyes on Romney. Was there a touch of fright in their brilliance?

"I'm not sensitive about it. I'm ready to tell all." He stretched his mouth in what was intended for a grin but it didn't qualify. "The fireworks started when Miss Dane accused me of having fallen hard for Miss Randall. I—"

"Not here, Romney—"

"Sit down, Mr. Grant," McGregor interrupted Tim's furious protest. "You'll have your chance to talk later. I want to hear the professor's story without interruption, get it, *without* interruption, Mr. Grant."

Deb laid her hand on Tim's sleeve as he sat down. He

caught it and held it tight in his. The contact set her blood tingling, her heart beating like a trip hammer.

"Miss Dane had accused you of having fallen hard for Miss Randall." McGregor was on the trail again. "Take it from there, Professor."

"I admitted that I had. What could she do about it? To hear her tell it she could do a lot. But, that wasn't the entire reason I was off her, Chief." He paused and leaned forward as if to give what was coming dramatic impact. Stella Dane, white-faced, clenched her hands as if ready to tear him to pieces.

"I discovered that she was in the pay of Judge Lander at the time of his death."

XVIII

"WHY didn't Sandy McGregor keep on with his cross-examination, Tim?" Deborah asked as they drove away from the Town Hall. "He is the most maddening person. Why, after Burke Romney had declared that Stella had been in the pay of Judge Lander, did he say, 'That'll do for now. You may all go'? He has the darnedest way of scoring a point—like the time he flashed Sophy Brandt's orchid—then shutting off the current to leave one gasping with excitement."

"That's my reaction too. Then I remind myself that The McGregor is rated one of the keenest officials in the business and cooled down, but I admit I'm not hep to his system."

"Tonight he reminded me of a circus charioteer, clad in a Roman toga and helmet, holding innumerable white reins to guide his fiery steeds, Stella, Romney, and the rest of us representing said steeds. I could almost hear the calliope accompaniment as he raced round and round the sawdust ring. I bit my lips to keep from laughing each time I thought of it."

"It would be curious if someone driving an old-time horse and buggy with one set of reins beat him to the solution of the shooting, wouldn't it?"

"What do you mean, Tim? Are you on the trail of the person who did it?"

"Keep your seat, Debby, and don't grab my arm again or we'll land against a tree. Can't I have visions that make me grin as well as you?"

"You can. Why were we in that smoky police room? Just what did you and I contribute to the unraveling of the plot? Stella resented us. I felt like a butterfly fluttering on a pin when she glared at me."

"Romney's admission that he had fallen hard for you accounted for that. The green-eyed monster was gnawing at her vitals. It made me see red—"

"You're telling me. You were raring to have it out with him then and there. When you sprang to your feet was a moment to set the cameras rolling. That doesn't mean that I didn't appreciate your fury at having my name dragged into the mess. Whatever the provocation it was a low-down thing for Burke Romney to do."

130

"I wonder what was back of his statement. I thought he was a good egg, if a little on the poseur side with his hair-raking. He's keen at his job, the number one man in his department. Has he been making love to you?"

"Depends upon what you mean by that old-fashioned 'making love.'"

"Of course you don't have to answer the question, but I will remind you that we, who were staying at Beechcroft that tragic week end, are involved in a serious situation the solution of which so far is shrouded in a dense fog. Has he been carrying a torch for you?"

"Once, he appeared at the island when I was at work in the bungalow, his reception was so frigid he didn't come again. He has been dropping in for tea, has come several times for dinner, I charged up his presence to a passion for Stella, who was there usually, until—"

"Go on. Until what?"

"Until he began to invite me to dine and dance."

"Ever been out with him?"

"You wouldn't be qualifying for an 'Information Please' M.C., would you, Marine? I have not been out with him. I haven't time. I do a lot of studying evenings to make up for the hours I spend at the island writing—my mistake—trying to write. If you must know, his love-making, as you call it, hasn't been convincing. I felt that I was not being adored for myself alone, but because I happened to be Molly Burton Stewart's granddaughter."

"Why shouldn't you be adored for yourself alone?"

"I am fully in accord with your indignant question. Why shouldn't I? But the fact remains that I see the glint of Molly B.'s gold behind the love light in a man's eyes when they focus on me."

"Boy, what a hard-boiled viewpoint. It's too bad, and you such a lovely girl. Ooch, that pinch went right through my coat sleeve. I can see you headed straight for a life of single blessedness—if blessedness is the right word. I've got an idea. I'll invite poor lonely Deborah to be godmother to one of my children."

"It would be super. I'll present my silver porringer to the infant. I have been wondering what I would do with it."

"To kick through with that sure would be doing handsomely by the kid."

"Having settled the question of a godmother for young Grant to our mutual satisfaction let's tune in on another station. Isn't that the field where we saw the trailer? It's gone."

"Probably to the village on an errand. As the couple has a baby they couldn't go without the trailer, I suppose. The GI who lives in it has the deep scar of a burn on his right cheek."

Deb remembered Ingrid's passionate protest against calling on the wife. She hadn't appeared in the hall for sherry before dinner, had been a little breathless and late when she slipped into her seat at the table. She had offered no explanation. Molly B. had made no comment. The man with the scar on his cheek was doubtless the man with whom she had been talking in the cutting garden. Had she told him to leave town? Was a hurried trip to the trailer the answer to her lateness in the dining room?

"Mark Taylor reports that the same GI is a wizard in applied physics." Tim's voice brought her speculations to a full stop.

"Does he check on each student?"

"Not only on students but on every mother's son who has anything to do in the building from the highest paid professors and engineers down the line to the gatekeepers. He is of enormous help to me. He's an ace pilot, in case you're interested."

"Do the men like him?"

"Very much. Don't you?"

"Yes, but I'm not a scientist or a would-be. Trying to demonstrate a boy's chemistry set would tie my I.Q. in a hard knot. You'd better consider that before I sign on the dotted line as your secretary. When you spoke of Mark I remembered that Clive Warner told me Romney suspected he was a mystery man."

"Now that the war is technically over, though it does spurt up in spots like steam through the thin crust of the Yellowstone, he may have heard that Colonel Mark Taylor was one of the top secret workers in the amphibious division at the time when names were hush-hush. That is all the mystery there is about him."

"This may seem incompetent, irrelevant, immaterial, as they say in court, but in between paragraphs of our conversation I've been thinking back. Romney declared that Stella had been in the pay of the Judge. I believe that the voice I heard coming from the gallery bay was Henry Lander's. Her room is beyond mine and he was occupying one on the third floor in the wing for that week end, Sarah told me. Perhaps he was threatening her with immediate foreclosure of the mortgages on her home if she didn't get Ingrid's papers. Follow me?"

"To the ends of the earth," he declared with a fervor that set her pulses quickstepping. "I believe you have the solution to that angle, but who put Ingrid wise to the plot?"

"I haven't worked out the answer but I am sure that Scragg fits in somewhere. Perhaps he dropped that .38 under the

132

shrubs when examining the paint on the front of the Dane house yesterday. Perhaps he shot the Judge out of loyalty to the family."

"Perhaps you're right but you go too fast for me. Let's forget old man Trouble. Swell night, isn't it?"

Deb rested her head against the back of the seat, her face upturned to the sky.

"Perfect. A lot more stars than when we started out, they are so close now the heavens look like a fisherman's net of gold. Smell the balsams. What a beautiful world. Why can't everyone be decent? Why should there be sordid scenes like the one we have just left?"

"That question has been troubling the thinking portion of humanity for centuries, Debby."

"Wouldn't it be marvelous if only for this one night all the heartaches, crimes, quarrels, and sickness would stop and for twelve hours give to everyone in the world a sense of peace?"

"I said once that you were hard and bitter underneath, Deb. I take it back. You're the sweetest thing in the world." He bent his head and pressed his lips to hers.

"Tim." She sat up quickly. "I don't go in for that sort of thing."

"Sorry, Debby, neither do I. Charge my brain storm up to your vision of a world wholly at peace. It would be heavenly if only for a few hours. Here we are at Beechcroft. Am I forgiven? It won't happen again."

"Better not, if I am to sign up as your secretary."

"Where do you get that 'if'? You are my secretary, you promised. Come on. Watch out." He caught her as she missed the step. "Are your eyes too full of star dust to see where you are going?"

"Could be. You needn't hold onto my arm. My feet are on earth, if my head isn't. I wonder if there are still a few unexploded bombs in the house timed to go off immediately upon our arrival?"

There was no indication of excitement when they entered the library. The Farrs had walked down over from their home, it was an after-dinner habit. Molly B., who was listening to Sam as he stood back to the mantel, emphasizing the points in his discourse with a wave of his pipe, turned and smiled a welcome. Ingrid in a deep chair was gazing at the fire. Even its rosy light couldn't disguise her extreme pallor. Sophy Brandt was knitting something pale blue. Mark Taylor at the piano was drumming a soft accompaniment to Tilly Farr's voice as she talked to him. The shining mahogany reflected her yellow crepe frock and gold bangles.

"What happened at headquarters?" Molly B.'s question stiffened each person in the room to attention.

"You tell them, Tim," Deb suggested as he drew off her fur jacket. "After what I have heard and thought during the last hour I couldn't separate fact from fiction."

She snuggled among the pillows on the couch trying desperately to forget the feel of his lips on hers, his husky voice as he had said "to the ends of the earth," remembering, if he had forgotten for an instant, the girl in the Pacific theater.

"In case anyone here is interested the revolver that Stella picked up under the shrubs, which The McGregor declares is the murder weapon, was a snub-nosed revolver, not ivory-handled."

Sophy Brandt's steel needles stopped. She looked up at him, soft color flooded her face.

"Is that true, Tim?" Her voice was high, hysterical. "A snub-nosed—it's fun—ny." Ripple after ripple of laughter rose and broke in a choking sob. Tears ran down her cheeks. "Are you sure? It's the fun—" She laughed, shivered and shook. Sam Farr slapped her face hard.

"Stop it, Mrs. Sophy. You'll have hysterics."

"But, Sam—if you—knew—how fun—" she giggled.

"Okay, you can tell us the joke later." He shook her lightly. "Going to stop, Mrs. Sophy? Or will Tim and I carry you upstairs and call the doctor?"

"No, no, Sam. I'll s-stop. Really, I will." She picked up her knitting. A laugh gurgled in her throat. "I—I've stopped. Go on, Tim. Tell the rest of your story."

With his eyes on her he told what had happened at headquarters. She was knitting steadily, occasionally he heard the sound of a choked-back laugh. One big tear rolled slowly down her cheek. Sam Farr knocked the ashes from his pipe and dropped it into his coat pocket.

"The McGregor may be—I guess he is—a keen dick, but there's a big slice of ham in his make-up. He works up his effects and then leaves them hanging in the air to keep us all taut with suspense."

"You may be right, Sam, but 'I have a feelin'' that quite soon he will hold out his hand and magician-like pull the solution out of that same air."

"I doff my hat to your experience in working up and solving mysteries, Molly B. You, more than anyone present, know how it is done. I met Prexy today crossing the campus. The old boy has dropped ten years. He was skipping along like a young doe. Lander is off his neck and the job he loves is secure until retiring age. Great guns, why hasn't someone suggested that he had a motive for the shooting? It's a wonder The McGregor hasn't lined him up as a suspect."

"It would be as absurd as some of the other sus-picions." Sophy Brandt swallowed an hysterical giggle as Sam took a purposeful step toward her. "I'm all right, I'm steady now, really, Sam."

"Sure of that?"

"Cross my throat and hope to die." She imitated the voice of a child. Each person in the room drew a sigh of relief. Sophy was herself again. What was behind her hysterical breakdown, Tim wondered, where was his ivory-handled revolver? She knew.

"You didn't have to use your ammunition against the late lamented, did you, Tim?" Sam Farr's question switched his thoughts for the possible disposal of his gun.

"No. Let's get off the subject of the Judge and his—"

"Not yet."

Stella Dane followed her furious protest into the room. The bright green coat flung across her shoulders accentuated her pallor, the silver-gilt sheen of her hair. Her brother loomed behind her, his ruddy face marked with deep lines of worry.

"Sit down, Stella. A cup of hot, strong coffee will be good for us all." Molly B. looked past the girl to the butler lingering on the threshold. "Scragg, serve it here as soon as possible. Bring breakfast cups and plenty of heavy cream and sugar."

"Yes, Madam." He glanced at the two Danes and disappeared.

"I won't sit down," Stella declared as if the interlude between Molly B.'s suggestion and her refusal had been unnoticed by her. "Doubtless you have been told of Burke Romney's accusation that I was in Judge Lander's pay. I wasn't in the sense he implied. The Judge wanted papers belonging to Ingrid Johnson he was sure would be in your safe, Madam Stewart." She had the grace to color vividly. She drew a deep breath and hurried on:

"I knew they were there because once when I was alone, putting away the payroll, I looked through some of them. From curiosity, no other motive at the time, honestly. The Judge offered to hold off the foreclosure on our place indefinitely—solemnly promised he would give me a sworn statement to that effect—if I would get them."

"Did you know why he wanted them?" Tim inquired.

"No. I didn't want to know. Neither of my brothers knew of his offer. It was entirely my affair."

"Did you get the papers?" As Tim asked the question Ingrid Johnson put her hand to her face as if shielding it from the heat of the fire.

"No. One attempt was made to get into the room in the early morning of Ingrid's nightmare. After that, the Judge said we'd better wait, go slow, until that was forgotten and then—he was gone and I was free of the hateful compact, at least I thought I was."

"Did you make that early morning attempt to get the papers?"

"No, Tim."

"Who did? Come clean, Stella. Having told so much you've got to go on."

Her brilliant, hard eyes moved from face to face, lingered on Sophy Brandt who was counting stitches in her knitting, came back to Tim. She flexed her stiff lips before she opened them.

"It was—"

"Scragg," declared Burke Romney from the threshold behind her.

XIX

HAD Tim been looking at a television screen the picture couldn't have been clearer than the scene his memory projected. He saw the frightened group before Molly B.'s living room door in the early morning and he saw Burke Romney come down the stairs in his crimson corduroy robe which didn't quite cover the pants of his red and white pajamas, saw the wet tips of his black evening shoes.

"How did you know that Scragg tried to get Miss Johnson's papers that morning, Romney?" he asked.

"I didn't know then but I happened to see him gumshoe up the steps of Madam Stewart's balcony and wondered what he was doing there. Back in my room I heard the commotion in the hall and suspected that someone had heard him and given the alarm. It is easy after what I've learned tonight to put two and two together."

"Just why were you prowling round the place at that time in the morning?" Sam Farr demanded.

"I can answer that one," Stella Dane declared. "Earlier in the evening he saw me meet Mort at the game house, didn't recognize him and put me through the third degree as to who the man was, he pretended to be jealous. I didn't tell him. He must have seen me steal out with Scragg. He's either a spy for a gang of blackmailers or just a common little snooper like his pal, Clive Warner."

"Skip it, Stella. Sit down." Her brother pushed her into a chair. "Let Grant do the talking. You've said too much—"

"Here's the coffee and none too soon," Molly B. announced. "Scragg, set the table in front of Miss Johnson."

The butler snapped down the legs of the large tray. With a rustle of black taffeta Sarah Allen entered, a silver plate of sandwiches in each hand.

"When I heard you'd ordered coffee, Madam Stewart, I had a feelin' none of you folks would sleep a wink if you didn't have something solid and hearty to eat with it," she explained.

"It won't be coffee that will keep us awake, Sal," Deb declared, and placed a small table beside the large tray. "Park those luscious chicken salad sandwiches here."

"That will be all, Sarah, thank you."

It was a dismissal, there could be no doubt of that. Sarah jerked up her spectacles and glanced from face to face. "Yes, Madam Stewart," she said in a deflated voice, and departed.

"Stay here, Scragg," Molly B. directed as he prepared to follow the housekeeper. "Pass the coffee as Miss Johnson pours it."

"Yes, Madam."

Tim couldn't decide whether the man's face was a degree more pasty than usual. If he were perturbed it didn't show in his hands. They were steady as he passed the cups which gave forth the aromatic scent of Mocha.

"Scragg, there are a few questions Mr. Grant will ask that I would like you to answer," Molly Burton Stewart announced after all had been served. "Take over, Tim." The butler, who had started for the door, stopped, turned.

"Yes, Madam. I will be pleased to answer if I can. What do you want to know, Mr. Grant?"

"You were seen going up the balcony steps to Madam Stewart's living room in the early morning a few weeks ago. How come?"

"I think you already know, sir. I went to help Miss Stella get papers from the Madam's safe." A little wave of sound like exclamations of quickly repressed surprise followed the calm statement.

"How did you expect to get into it?"

"I found a paper on the stairs which gave the figures of a safe combination. I have seen them before. There was only one safe in the house, I knew where it was, I had seen it open. Getting into the room would be simple. I had a pass-key."

"If it was so *simple* why didn't you go ahead and get the papers?"

"You haven't forgotten Miss Johnson's scream, have you, Mr. Grant? I should have known when she took the second piece of lemon chiffon pie she'd have a nightmare. She has them quite often, I've heard the maids say, sir." Ingrid giggled, a choked hysterical giggle.

"Scragg, you are mag—magnificent."

"Thank you, Miss, though I would say that magnificent is hardly the word to describe me."

"Have you the slip of paper with the safe combination?"

"No, Mr. Grant. I must have dropped it on the balcony when Miss Johnson screamed. The sound startled me quite a little, sir."

Tim remembered the two terrified yells which had sent him catapulting down the stairs with his heart pounding like an Indian war drum. He caught his lips hard between his teeth to discipline a grin. They had been loud enough to rouse the old-time celebrities in the campus cemetery and they had startled Scragg "quite a little." Ingrid was right, he was magnificent.

"Was Miss Dane waiting for you when you ran down the steps?"

"No, sir. She told me later that at the first scream she ran into the house and up to her room."

That checked. Stella had come down the stairs after the others and the toes of her gold sandals had been wet.

"If you will excuse me for making the suggestion, Mr. Grant, you might ask Professor Romney what he was doing out at that hour, sir." Scragg's aggrieved voice broke the mental photographic negative Tim had been studying. Burke Romney, who had been leaning an elbow on top of the piano, straightened and caught up the butler's challenge.

"I wondered how soon I would again be asked the question Stella answered when Dean Farr asked it."

"Come clean, Romney. Give us the works. Why were you out at 4 A.M.?" Tim demanded.

"Often after a day of brain-teasing problems I can't sleep. It is not unusual for me to tramp around the grounds, take a swim in the pool. I've even paddled a canoe across to the island to tire myself physically so that when I went to bed figures and problems wouldn't be crowding and jiggling through my mind."

Fair enough, Tim thought, no one knew better than he the incessant activity of a tired brain.

"When you saw Scragg on the steps were you suspicious of his presence there?"

"I wouldn't say 'suspicious.' I had rather liked the man and—"

"That's very good of you, I am sure, sir." Except for the impatient thrust of fingers through his hair Romney ignored the butler's unctuous approval.

"I was puzzled to know why he was there in the early morning, remembered that the dog ran away nights, decided that the butler had gone up the steps to let the cocker into Madam Stewart's apartment, went to my room and prepared for bed. Even when I heard Miss Johnson's scream I didn't connect him with it. Dumb of me, perhaps, but I didn't."

"That was kind of you, sir. I—"

"That will be all for the present, Scragg. You may go." The man hesitated as if in protest. "We'll ring if we need you. *That's all*," Tim repeated. He waited till Scragg had left the room before he said:

"Suppose you explain why you declared that Miss Dane

was in Judge Lander's pay. That is a serious accusation, Romney."

"Right. I had been suspicious for some time that the Judge had some kind of a hold on her. When on our way home from the Country Club last evening I accused her of it she denied a deal with him so furiously that my suspicion crystallized into conviction. I don't yet know what it was about."

"Too bad you didn't arrive a few minutes earlier and you would have had the entire story, Mr. Romney."

Nine pairs of startled eyes regarded Sophy Brandt as she set her coffee cup and saucer carefully on the small table beside her chair. The tinkle of silver spoons against china ceased. She leaned a little forward.

"You told me I could tell my story later, Sam. Don't worry, I won't have hysterics. It is time to clear up part of the mystery into which we are getting bogged deeper and deeper. Molly Burton does not leave every clue to be tied up in the last chapter, she staggers them. Her technique is successful, I'll try it."

"For the love of Mike, if you have a contribution that will help clear up the mess, go to it," Sam Farr exploded. "I can't rid myself of the feeling that sooner or later I will be standing in the prisoner's dock to defend myself against the shooting of Henry Lander. That's the way The McGregor works. He doesn't cushion his shots."

"Don't be absurd, Sam, if Stella hadn't dragged you into it, telling of our quarrel—"

"Skip it, Til," he interrupted his wife's excited protest. "Go on with your story, Mrs. Sophy."

"What I tell you now antedates the tragedy in the game house. Henry Lander, who was attorney for my husband's creditors, found out a foolish thing I did just before his death and threatened me with publicity. He has been an evil shadow in my life ever since. Now, I know that what I did was not criminal, but I was too heartsick and terrified to question his word about it. Several times when he came here for week ends he proposed that I get Ingrid's papers out of the safe. Each time I refused. Remember the morning I met him at the island, Debby? It was his ultimatum. I was to produce the papers or else. Now I know that Stella had failed in the early morning and I was his last resort. I tried a little diplomacy. Asked for a chance to think it over and didn't tell him that the day before I had phoned Ingrid and in an assumed voice warned her to protect her property." She picked up her knitting.

With Mrs. Sophy in a confessional mood—could it be the effect of the powerful coffee?—it was the moment to find out what she knew about the tragedy in the game house and

140

the disappearance of his revolver. Tim placed his cup and saucer on the mantel, thrust his hands hard into the pockets of his coat and prepared to go all out for the information he was certain she could supply.

"Mrs. Sophy." He was aware that all eyes in the room turned to him. "I agree with you that Molly B.'s technique of staggering the disclosures in her stories is the touch of a master craftsman. Suppose you adopt it and come across with what you know of the shooting of Henry Lander. You do know something. Don't deny it. Make your contribution. Until the mystery is solved each person who was at Beechcroft that morning is under suspicion of having committed the crime."

The room was so quiet that the snap of a burned log in the fireplace had the effect of a miniature explosion. Everyone jumped. Sophy Brandt dropped her knitting and clenched her hands in her lap.

"I'll be glad to get it off mind and conscience, Tim. Mark, stand beside the door to make sure no one is listening. I should have told this to Sandy McGregor but I was terribly afraid if I did I might point suspicion at—at someone I love."

"I'll be damned, Sophy. If you really know anything that will help, spill it quick."

"How can I spill it, Sam, if you interrupt? Sit down. Stop prowling like a lion ready to spring. Tilly, make him sit beside you on the piano bench. Don't let him move till I finish my story."

In spite of the seriousness of the subject it was evident that Sophy Brandt was enjoying her front-page moment. Her cheeks were a lovely pink, her eyes as deeply, brilliantly blue as sapphires.

"You have stage-center and a breathless audience, Mrs. Sophy," Tim reminded. "Give."

"I'll be as brief as possible. It goes back to the afternoon in the Dean's Den when Henry Lander declared that he had discovered a complication at the Center which would ruin you if he disclosed it, remember, Tim?"

"Yes. Go on."

"You heard the threat too, Mr. Romney."

"Was that what the row was about? I heard Grant say, 'kick you out,' but I didn't hear what prefaced the threat."

"No? Remember that at the time your ivory-handled revolver was on the desk, Tim?"

"I remember that you were afraid of it."

"The evening of the party here in your honor I noticed your expression of repressed fury when Henry Lander ignored you. Later, I saw you going down the stairs dressed for walking. I asked where you were going, you evaded answering. I was frightened. I remembered your quarrel with the Judge, the fierceness of your eyes when he had ignored you, I was afraid that you intended to have it out with him."

"Do you mean you feared I would *shoot* the Judge, Mrs. Sophy?"

"Forgive me, Tim. I was afraid of what you might do in anger. You had been through a war where killing was an everyday affair."

"My God, not that kind of killing."

"I know, Tim. You have been so wonderful to me, you have given me a new life, that I was afraid of trouble for you; I would do anything to save you."

"Get on with your story, dear," Molly B. reminded tenderly. Sophy brushed her fingers across wet lashes and swallowed hard.

"Where was I?"

"You had just said you were afraid I had gone to find Lander."

"Oh, yes. After I spoke to you I went back to my room, I couldn't stay there. I remembered that I had left my bracelet on the piano while playing for dancing, and glad of something to do that would take up my time, hurried to the game house, thinking that if you had gone there to quarrel with Henry Lander I might be in time to prevent trouble. I went in. The lights were on. My bracelet was not on the piano. I heard a sound in the badminton court. Ran in. There was something—something terrible on the floor. I drew back the covering. I must have dropped the orchid then. Had Tim been ahead of me, I wondered. Had he done this frightful thing? My world went black."

"Sam, fill her cup with hot coffee, drink it, Sophy, quick."

"No, Molly B." She waved the cup aside. "I've had too much already. I can finish."

"Did you know at the time that you had dropped the orchid?"

"No, Tim, I knew only that I must get out of the place quickly, or I might be picked up in a dead faint. I returned to the house and waited in the dusk of the library until I heard you come in. What could I do to protect you, I asked myself. Then I thought of imitating Henry Lander's voice. Someone was bound to hear it and if Tim were suspected I would swear that he came in before Lander's voice was heard on the terrace. As I tell it, the story sounds terribly melodramatic and full of holes, but it was tragically real to me then."

"Sophy," Sam Farr's laugh held a suggestion of tears. "Sophy, my girl, you should be in Hollywood concocting super-thrillers instead of keeping house for a scientist in a prosy New England village. Chills are playing tag up and down my spinal column and Romney has gone a pale yellow-green from shock."

"I'm not the only one. You all look as if you were standing in a green floodlight."

"Mr. Romney is right, you all look ghastly. You too, are right, Sam. It is a fantastic yarn. Looking back on it I think my adoration of Tim must have driven me a little crazy."

"How could you adore me and think I would do a thing like that?"

"I don't wonder you are angry, Tim."

"I'll bet the only reason you are sure now I didn't do it is the fact that it was a snub-nosed gun that did the trick. Is that why you snitched my ivory-handled revolver the next morning, Mrs. Sophy?"

"Yes, I took it from your suitcase. I hid it two days later. You'll find it behind the books on the top shelf in Molly B.'s workshop on the island."

"Heavenly day, what a story. Is that *all* you contributed to the mystery that early morning, Sophy?"

"No, Molly B., it was I who tried Debby's door. I couldn't settle down. She is so cool and levelheaded I thought if I told her, she would suggest what next—"

"Why not finish this super-chiller?" Romney interrupted. "Give us the works, tell us that you saw the man who shot—"

"Hist." Mark Taylor's warning brought each person in the room up standing. He stepped away from the door to allow the chief of police and a man with a scarred right cheek to enter.

"What's the big idea, Miss Johnson, urging your brother to leave town?" The McGregor demanded. "Don't you know that every road has been patrolled since the Judge was washed out?"

XX

"EVEN after the startling disclosures in the library at Beech-croft last evening, we still haven't a thread of clue as to who did the shooting or a motive for it."

Standing before the fire in the Dean's Den, Sam Farr rapped his pipe on top of a tall brass andiron till the ashes were consumed in a dancing flame. Timothy Grant turned from the window through which he had been watching the lights of a motorboat move across the lake.

"The police boat is patrolling tonight, I wonder why. You've got the right idea, Sam." He dropped into the swivel chair and glanced at Mark Taylor perched on the corner of the flat desk. "You saw McGregor for me today, I couldn't fit him in between appointments. Did he have anything to add to yesterday's revelations?"

"Not much. Ballistic experts have left no doubt but that the gun Miss Dane picked up is the one used by the man or woman—"

"*Woman!*" Tim and Sam Farr exclaimed in unison. "I'll bet he suspects Stella Dane," Sam added.

"Man or woman who shot Lander," Mark Taylor repeated. "I'm quoting the chief. He has quashed his suspicion that the ex-wife may have been the gunwoman now that he knows that Ingrid Johnson is the ex. He declared that no one could convince him she had a hand in the murder."

"That's a feather for his common-sense cap. How about that brother of hers he held up on his getaway out of town last evening?" Sam tamped tobacco into his pipe.

"Boy, oh, boy." Tim flung an empty matchbox at the heart of the fire and hit the bull's-eye. "When she confirmed Mc-Gregor's announcement that the GI who had been living in the trailer was her brother, my mind, already stuffed to the brim with preceding revelations, squeezed in one more idea, that at long last we had our man, that Johnson had learned of Lander's treatment of his sister and avenged her. Did The McGregor think of that solution, Mark?"

"He told me this morning that for a red-hot moment he was sure he had his man and the motive. The certainty went cold when he discovered, first, that Johnson never had known of his sister's marriage to Henry Lander, second that the man came to this country with the name and papers of an American aviator who had died in an underground hide-out in Norway, that he had fled to the United States to escape reprisal at the hands of the enemies of his country, who, he suspected, were still in hiding there."

"Why did he come here?"

"His work had been chemistry. He knew of the Center through Ingrid, figured he could get a job and be safe here. He wants to become a citizen. The worst he is up against is squaring himself with Uncle Sam. It is a serious matter to enter this country under a false name. Ingrid has been racked with indecision, whether to tell all and betray her brother to the authorities and perhaps his enemies; not to tell, protect him and double-cross the government. That agony is over. The question has been decided for her. I hope Johnson won't be forced to leave the Center. He's good. The country needs scientific manpower in peace as well as war."

He opened the porch door, looked out, closed it, repeated the routine with the door that opened into the hall and returned to his perch on the desk.

"The McGregor warned me to keep alerted for trouble after I had given him a play-by-play account of Sophy's last evening confession. 'She shouldn't have told in public that she was in the game house after the shooting, she should have come straight to me,' he fumed. He fears that if her story gets to the person who shot Lander, he or she may suspect that she had seen the crime committed and try to silence her. Romney was working on the premise that she had seen more than she was telling when the chief walked in and gummed up the works. Where is she this evening?"

"Playing cards with her contract group at Beechcroft. I told her I would drive over and bring her home." Tim glanced at his wrist. "I didn't realize it was so late. Want a lift, Sam?"

"I'll go the whole way. Tilly is substituting for one of the regulars. I'll pick her up and take her home."

"Coming, Mark?"

"Sure. Now that the mystery is beginning to unravel something tells me the denouement will come fast. I don't want to miss a trick. Go ahead. I'll lock the porch door and join you in front of the house."

After what seemed an interminable wait Tim glanced at the clock on the instrument board of the maroon roadster. He cut out the engine which had been purring softly as a kitten with its stomach full of cream.

"Where the dickens is Mark? We have been waiting ten minutes. It couldn't take him all that time to put out the

145

lights and lock the door. I'm going in. Stay here, Sam. If funny-business is on foot someone might grab this car."

The lights were out in the Dean's Den when he opened the hall door. The smoldering fire cast an uncanny glow which colored everything blood-red within its radius. The room smelled of wood smoke and the scent of a gardenia plant in the window which Mrs. Sophy had coaxed into bloom. Only the creak of a tree in the garden and the drop of an ember broke the silence.

"I wonder if the person who got Lander is after me?"

Mark's whispered words over the phone flashed through Tim's mind and set ice cubes coasting down his spine. He snapped on the overhead light. Crossed to the desk and picked up the slip of paper spiked into the green blotter with the point of a letter opener.

Someone was spying while we talked. Go on. I'm off on the bike. Lock the porch door. Make up an excuse to Sam. Don't tell him why I'm not coming.

There was no signature but it was Mark's almost undecipherable scrawl. "Lock the porch door" meant that he had slipped out that way. Wherever he had gone he had ten-minutes-plus start of the roadster.

"Did the Colonel change his mind about coming?" Sam inquired as Tim slipped behind the wheel.

"Yes. He decided that as the servants were at the movies he'd better stick by the house. Charge that up to The Mc-Gregor's warning."

"He has the right idea. Can't be too careful at a time like this. Calamities, like puppies, sometimes arrive in litters. Corking weather we are having this autumn. Ever thought that the stars seem a little nearer and brighter here than anywhere else? This car moves as smoothly as butter over piping hot pancakes. Look at the lights in the dormitory windows. That means there's a lot of plugging going on for tomorrow's classes. The GIs we have here are earnest workers, almost to a man."

"Not all the students are plugging this fine eve. We've passed three couples who had forgotten there was anyone in the world besides themselves."

"That's what I like about this old campus, Tim. You see life in all its stages; even 'the infant mewling and puking in the mother's arms'—I've taken a liberty with the Bard and substituted 'mother's' for 'nurse's.' Not many of the latter these days. Sure, I'm a sentimental guy, I can see by your grin that's what you're thinking. I love this college and I don't care who knows it. How's your job coming along?"

146

"I'm still in the game and hitting hard. I have a secretary who is a secretary. Deb is substituting for a short time. Boy, the way things moved today made me realize what the word 'efficiency' means."

"I've heard she was good. I don't know why she is taking up with that heel Warner again, though, it doesn't say much for her intelligence."

"What do you mean, 'taking up'?"

"Keep your shirt on, Tim. Her time is her own after office hours, isn't it? They were faring forth for a dine and dance evening at the Country Club when I left Tilly at Beechcroft before dinner."

"I would have thought after her first day of work at the Center she would have been too exhausted to step out. On top of taking dictation, making appointments, she straightened out the files my predecessor had left in a mess."

"That gal exhausted? You don't know her. She has boundless energy, and except for the cold she brought home with her, superb health."

"Like her, don't you, Sam?"

"Sure, don't you? Besides the fact that she is family— we're a clannish lot—she is so straight, so honest. She came through the hard years in Washington without picking up the 'bracer' habit which pretty near spoiled a lot of girls who worked there. Her outlook broadened but as far as I can discover her ideals and purposes remained unchanged, and they are something to write home about. *L'Affaire Warner* was a stunning blow to her pride, I never believed that it really dented her heart. She's coming out from under fast. There are three unmarried instructors at the college, men of fine family background, who have gone all out for her. Weren't you on to them the night of your party?"

"To tell the truth, I was too busy saying, 'Thank you,' 'So glad you could come,' trying to fit faces and names so I would know the guests again when I met them crossing the campus, that I didn't notice Deb and her stag line." Which is an awful lie, he told himself.

In the silence that followed, Sam slumped low in his seat and sucked at his pipe, while Tim lived over the events of the day. Deb had appeared in his office promptly at nine, lovely as a cover girl in a tailored navy-blue frock with narrow white frills of something that had holes in it at throat and wrists. She had quickly established the pattern of office relations with her crisp:

"What first, Mr. Grant?"

Which pattern was all right with him. The higher the wall between them while at work the better. Concentration on his job was a must. He had yielded to temptation last evening

147

when he kissed her, if it happened again he would lose her. She believed he was engaged to another girl. The next time he might not be able to control the passionate desire to catch her in his arms and hold his lips on hers till she flamed response. Why was she going out again with that heel, Warner?

At sight of the airfield Deb did a fade-out and anxiety for Mark Taylor closed in. Why the jitters, he asked himself impatiently. The Colonel had been one of the higher-ups in the Pacific Intelligence Division, hadn't he come through that experience unscathed? Deb's reference to a "dick" had given him the idea of bringing Mark to the Center to watch for scouts from other countries, who perhaps had registered for the purpose of transmitting information of inventions and progress to home authorities. Canada had had them. Washington had warned him to be on the alert. Had Judge Lander been tipped off to a net of espionage when he had threatened:

"I've discovered a complication at the Center that won't reflect credit on the new Head. I'll wait till you are nicely installed, then I'll break the news and ruin you."

Mrs. Sophy had heard the threat. It had laid a trail of gunpowder which had led to the explosions last evening. Romney had heard only "kick you out," but—

"Hi, Tim. Asleep? You've passed the Beechcroft gate."

"Sorry. Here's where I make a U-turn without threat of a fine. Wonder what revelations this evening has up its sleeve."

"I hope not any, unless it is the knockout blow that will produce the gunman. My mind is frayed at the edges with the constant shocks. I wasn't joking when I said I feared The McGregor might land me in the dock. I've done some loud talking about the 'deceased,' not only for personal reasons but because I thought him a skunk for trying to oust Prexy. Sometimes in the night I go haywire when I remember my lurid language."

"What can't one think of during a wakeful night? It gets me why it is always of the things one shouldn't have done, rarely of things on the credit side of the ledger."

"You've said something. I've learned a lesson. Don't talk about a person, if you must talk, talk *pretty*. Looks as if Deb and her ex-beau had returned. The green contraption parked close to the shrubs is Warner's apology for a car. It doesn't suggest enough of the commodity commonly known as 'filthy lucre' to make tax evasion necessary."

"Never can tell. The Center salaries are high and he was in the service the last three years of the war only."

"Maybe, but between you and me I think The McGregor laid off that guy as a suspect too soon."

"Why so sure he has laid off? As he reminded us, he's no rookie at this business. It wouldn't surprise me if Warner had his alibi shot from under him and soon, but, I'm prejudiced. I don't like him."

Molly B. was holding a skein of white yarn which Sophy Brandt was winding into a ball when Tim and Sam entered the library. The flamingo lace and pale violet of their frocks made a lovely splash of color in contrast to Ingrid's midnight blue as she sat on a hassock near the fire, elbows on her knees, chin in her hands.

Scragg folded a card table, added it to two others and carried them into the hall. The contract regulars had departed. Tilly Farr, in a net frock as golden as her bangles, and Clive Warner were on the piano bench smoking. His eyes kept straying toward Deborah seated among the cushions at one end of the sofa, Tim noticed. No wonder. She was something to look at and love in a black velvet frock with a collar of old lace and a gardenia corsage. Had Warner presented the flowers or were they from one of the men of "fine family background" who were giving her a rush?

"Major Timothy Grant, I presume?" Molly B. laughed and dropped a loop of white yarn which Mrs. Sophy hurriedly replaced. "You are looking us over as if you never had seen us before and weren't particularly pleased with what you saw." The gaiety of her voice changed to gravity. "Has anything new developed that you look so grim?"

"You read my expression wrong, Molly B. It was admiration of this domestic scene. Sam and I came to take home our respective girls. Ready, Mrs. Sophy?"

"Give me five minutes till this wool is wound, Tim."

"Take all the time you want, I am in no hurry." Back to the fire he looked down at the girl on the sofa who appeared absorbed in the crownless arrangement of pink roses in her lap.

"How was the Country Club, Debby?"

"We didn't get there," Clive Warner answered. "Halfway we were stopped by one of McGregor's men who said it was out of bounds for the evening for anyone connected with the college. I wonder how far Romney got? He said he was taking Stella Dane there to smoke the pipe of peace."

"But—"

"For the love of Mike, what has the chief of police got on his mind now?" Sam Farr interrupted Molly B. In his excitement he dropped his pipe on the tiled hearth. The stem broke into three pieces.

"From what I know of his tactics I'd ask, 'Who has he got on his mind now?' or should it be 'whom,' Sam, I'm never sure. Why didn't the Colonel come with you? Sarah Allen has repacked a mold of mousse left from our party for 'the boys.' "

"Mark decided at the last minute he would guard the house, Molly B."

"Why? Has anything—" Mrs. Sophy demanded breathlessly.

Tim retrieved the ball of white wool from the hall into which it had rolled when she sprang to her feet.

"Nothing, Mrs. Sophy, nothing to make you or—Warner turn white."

"If I am white it is with anger," Clive Warner declared. "I'm furious at having my evening with Deb blocked. It is the first time she has consented to go out with me. Instead of taking her to a swell joint we had steak and French fries at the village Inn, chaperoned by one of McGregor's men in a car behind us, then to a movie." He stood up and glared at Tim.

"I don't know what the catch is, Grant, but you may be interested to learn that your pal, the Colonel, who you say is playing watchdog at home, whizzed by this gate on a bike just before we turned into the drive. I—and here he is."

Mark Taylor stumbled into the room. Caught at the back of a chair. Tim sprang to him.

"Hit and—run, driver— Understand—hit and—run—" He leaned forward in the chair into which Sam and Tim carefully lowered him. "Hit and—" His eyes closed. Opened. "I —I—got the number. It was—" His head rolled against the back of the chair. This time his eyes remained closed.

XXI

DEBORAH shut the door of the conference room at the Center, lingered in the corridor outside, while men and a few women hurried by. It had been a stiff assignment. She brushed back a dark curl which dangled on her forehead. It wouldn't be surprising if every hair on her head stood on end. The scientific terms the experts had used were so unfamiliar. No wonder Tim had said he wouldn't trust the job to a less experienced person. He might decide that she—

"Wait, Deb."

Burke Romney sent his voice ahead as he approached along the corridor. When he reached her he glanced at the door behind her and lowered his voice.

"You haven't given me a chance to explain why I brought your name into the showdown at headquarters the other night. When I've phoned for a date you have either been out or otherwise engaged and I must—"

"I am otherwise engaged now, Professor." She smothered a smile as she realized that she had rolled the title off her tongue with a hint of McGregor's suavity. "Business for business hours was the first rule I learned in the secretarial course. Good-by." He caught her arm.

"Just a minute. Will you dine with me this evening?"

"Sorry, no can do. I'm working nights to make good here and believe me, I mean working."

"Been taking notes?" He nodded toward the door behind her.

"Notes? Where did you get that zany idea? I've been picking violets." She touched the purple flowers at the belt of her dark blue frock. "Now, this really is good-by, Professor."

Even without eyes in the back of her head she knew that he watched her till she rounded a curve of the corridor. She locked the notebook in her desk, as a temporary precaution, picked up a sheaf of letters and opened the door between Tim Grant's office and her own.

"How did you get on?" he asked eagerly.

"I won't know till you pass on the result. I nearly lost my mind trying to take down correctly—'Neptunium' and 'isotopes of plutonium,' and so forth, and so forth. I don't know

now what they can do. 'Mine not to reason why, mine but to do or die,' adapted for the occasion from you know whom."

"You're on top of the wave, aren't you, this morning? Are the violets you're wearing responsible? I'll help you with the terms when you are ready to transcribe the notes. There is special information in them no one else must see. Were you seen going in or coming out of the conference room?"

"Seen? It seemed as if every worker in the building had business in that particular corridor at that particular moment. Burke Romney appeared from the everywhere as I lingered before the door to clear my dazed brain."

"Did you tell him what you had been doing?"

"I didn't keep my Washington position by telling each person who inquired my boss's business, Mr. Grant."

"Sorry, it was a fool question. Could be I'm developing nerves over this assignment, there is so much that is hush-hush about it. Are those letters ready for me to okay and sign?"

"Yes." She laid them on the desk. "I was going to the island, but if you want the notes transcribed I will stay this afternoon and do them."

"No. It is Saturday. You've earned time off and double. You have put in a tremendous week of work for the first one." He glanced at the window. "That black sky doesn't look as if you would get much out-of-door fun, though." She started for the door, hesitated, returned to the desk.

"I haven't even breathed his name to anyone, but, I would like to know if Colonel Taylor is better, Tim. Four days have passed since the night you and Sam carried him home from Beechcroft." She lowered her voice. "It wasn't an ordinary hit-and-run accident, was it?"

"You heard Mark say that was what happened."

"I have ears as well as eyes. I heard him try to give the number of the car."

"Forget it. Don't know, don't suspect anything, and for Pete's sake, whatever you think, *don't* say it—here. It isn't safe, Deb."

"Sorry. Something tells me that the 'accident' is tied up with the Beechcroft Mystery. I thought you and I were co-operatives in that."

"While in this office we are employer and employee only."

"That's telling me." The blood stinging her cheeks brought tears of fury to her eyes. "Please sign these letters. I'll come back for them. They should go out in the next mail."

In her small office she put her hand to her burning cheek. "As if I had to be reminded," she said under her breath. "Does he think because he kissed me the other night I have

152

forgotten the girl in the Pacific? I wish she were in the Pacific, deep in."

She slipped a sheet of paper into the typewriter. Work must go on even if she were too furious to think of what she would write. Didn't I accept Clive's invitation to the Country Club just to show Tim that his kiss meant nothing in my life? Haven't I been out each evening since with—

"Hey, what goes, Debby?" Sam Farr demanded from the corridor threshold. He entered and closed the door. "Gosh, but you were punishing that typewriter. I heard the thump-thump when I stepped from the elevator."

"It's supposed to be noiseless. Charge it up to the frenzy of composition, Sam. I was typing a letter which would tell a man where he gets off. What brings you to the Center at almost noon on Saturday? Thought this afternoon was sacred to golf."

"It is. Allow smoking in these sacred precincts?" At her affirmative nod he straddled a chair and produced a pouch of tobacco from the pocket of his brown sports coat.

"As to why I'm here, that's easy. One of the students whom I have been advising has the urge to transfer from the college to the Center, thinks he will get more out of it. The atomic bomb still looms large in the minds of the public. I suspect that this GI has a rosy dream of being in on further tests. I've just had a heart-to-heart with the man who is riding herd for the Colonel as dean of students here."

"Did he say 'Yes'?"

"He did, not that you give a darn, your voice implies. What's up, Deb? You appear to have lost your *joie de vivre*."

"Nothin's up. Don't you ever have that end-of-the-week feeling? I'm all in. My late job was a lot simpler. Give me a government position every time."

"Fed up so soon, are you? Going to quit?"

"Of course I'm not going to quit. Monday morning I'll be young and gay again. This afternoon before I go home I have shopping to do in our village. Later I'm going to the island—"

"To the island. With that sky? Gal, you're crazy."

"I shan't stay. The weatherman this morning prophesied three days of storm. That means that the lake gets pretty rough. I want to pick up a manuscript there and bring it home, then I can push it forward if genius burns. Let the storm rage. I'll be sitting pretty."

"Sounds as if you've picked up the writing bug. Following in Molly B.'s footsteps?"

"I couldn't follow in better."

"You said something then." He hitched his chair close to her typewriter desk. "I'm all for her even if I never could understand why she had Lander hanging round."

"She did not approve of his attempt to get the presidency of the college and let him know it. She told me that her husband trusted him, that he had been honest and competent as a business adviser, that she felt a certain loyalty because he was Roger Stewart's friend."

"I suppose that covers it, women fell for him, all right." Was he remembering Tilly's flirtation which had ended so tragically? Who knew what he was thinking when his blue eyes were half covered by the heavy lids?

"I didn't. I always cringed inside when he looked at me. Do you think Mark Taylor's accident the other night is tied up with the shooting in the game house?"

"From here on it's anybody's guess, Debby." He rose and emptied his pipe in the brass tray. "Just between you and me, lady, I think every one of us who was at Beechcroft that night better watch his step. That goes for Tim, especially."

"You don't mean you think the person who shot Lander will try to get *him?*"

"Sit down again, Deb. Whoever it was has two strikes already, Lander and the Colonel. I didn't mean to frighten you, thought perhaps you could get it across to your boss that it wouldn't do any harm to listen to The McGregor when he tells him *not* to drive around at night alone. I'll be seeing you."

"Sam, wait a minute, please. Does McGregor think Tim is in danger?"

"You'll have to ask him. I'm supposed not to talk. Passed a hint along to you thinking you might help. It proved to have a shock value." He stopped at the door. "Quite a successful morning for me. Now I know what the score is, in one matter at least. Be good." Outside in the corridor he began to whistle, "Wonderful feeling, wonderful day." She listened until the sound faded into silence.

Hands in her lap she sat looking at but not seeing the half-finished letter in the machine. Tim in danger. Why? How could he know who had shot Lander? He had been at the Center at the time, hadn't he? McGregor must have ferreted out something serious to warn him not to go about alone. Would he listen to her if she begged him to be careful?

"While we are in this office we are employer and employee, only."

There was the answer. She couldn't, she wouldn't speak to him about it here and he hadn't been to Beechcroft since the night of Mark Taylor's accident. Perhaps he would listen to Molly B. The thought that anything might happen to him was unbearable.

She rose and went to the window. No escaping her fear that way. It crowded close. Why? The answer was easy. You're

154

in love with him, Debby Randall, you suspected it the night he held your hand in that smoky police court, knew it later when he kissed you. What are you going to do about loving a man who loves someone else? You've been hurt before, but, not this way, oh, not this way. You've got to work here till he gets the Center running smoothly, you promised. Then back to Washington or somewhere else, pronto. No use staying with a knife turning in your heart. That's pure melodrama. If a knife is turning in your heart no need to advertise the fact. "God grant me Serenity to accept things I cannot change," Molly B. had said. She had had years and years in which to acquire that serenity. In the distant future would Deborah Randall look back serenely on this intolerable heartache?

At the typewriter she resumed work with half her mind on the letter, half on McGregor's warning. How could she influence Tim to be cautious? Perhaps— The chapel clock was intoning twelve. She must get the letters she had left for him to sign if they were to go out in the next mail.

Be cool, poised, remember you are an employee only, she reminded herself as she opened the door between the offices. For an instant she stood transfixed with terror. Tim's left cheek and shoulder were resting against the desk. His right arm, which she couldn't see, apparently sagged toward the floor. She forced her voice through stiff lips.

"Tim! Tim, darling." She caught his shoulders and tried to raise him. "Tim, dearest— Have they got you, too—" He flung off her hold and rose. A letter was in his right hand.

"What do you mean, *got* me? Has McGregor been frightening you? I dropped this on the floor and was bending over to pick it up. *Debby*, you said—"

She didn't wait for the rest of the husky sentence. Back in her office she locked the door between them. He rattled the knob. She held her breath for fear he would hear her hurried breathing. Silence. She waited with her heart throbbing in her throat until she heard him answering the phone. Someone was talking on his private line.

In the village she did a lot of unnecessary shopping, anything that would occupy her thoughts and keep that impassioned "Tim, dearest," from echoing through her memory. The sky was still black, but she must go to the island. Luckily Molly B. was having tea with Prexy's wife or she would protest her going.

In her Wedgwood blue and mayflower pink room she changed her navy business frock for a white blouse, dark brown skirt and matching cardigan, shut her ears to the sound of wind moaning among the treetops. Why worry? In this part of the country storms took a long time to work themselves up, they made a lot of preliminary fuss before they arrived.

All set? Except for the key to the cabin. In her turmoil of mind she had almost forgotten that. If she could get out of the house without being seen no one could tell Tim where she was. He might feel it was up to him after her frenzied outburst to explain about the other girl. She couldn't bear that. She never wanted to see him again, at least, not until she had forgotten her impassioned "Tim, darling, Tim dearest."

"Why are you tiptoein' round as if you'd been stealin', Debby?" Sarah Allen, dressed for her afternoon out, hailed her as she was slipping soundlessly by the door of Molly B.'s living room. "There ain't nobody in this house I know of who cares whether you're comin' or goin'."

"I wasn't tiptoeing, Sal, that is, not intentionally. I was practising being light on my toes. Observe the technique." She took a few ballet steps, whirled and curtsied. "How'm I doing?" Sarah sniffed.

"I have a feelin' you're starting out to do something you know you hadn't oughtta do, Debby. You look white and scared. My sakes, you're not elopin' with that Clive Warner again, are you?"

"Where do you get that 'again'? Did I ever elope with him?"

" 'Tisn't like you to be so snappish, Debby. Won't you tell me what you're up to? I can keep a secret."

"Oh, for crying out loud. I haven't a secret. I am going to the island to get a manuscript and I am coming directly back. If you can make a secret out of that go to it. I'll be seeing you."

"There's a storm comin' up fast, Deb—"

She lost the rest of Sarah Allen's warning as she ran through the lower hall. She snatched the boathouse key from its hook and dashed down the garden walk between flower beds which flaunted an occasional red, purple or yellow blossom. Snuffles behind her? She stopped. The spaniel leaped on her with a joyous bark.

"Go home, Cocky. Go home." He sat back on his haunches and regarded her with grieved eyes. "Go home," she said again and ran on. When she reached the boathouse she looked back. The dog was where she had left him, a black hump of dejection. Trees bent and swayed and creaked. Leaves blew off thick as outsize brown rain. The wind caught and banged the boathouse door when she opened it. The sky was black with racing clouds. It would take her ten minutes to reach the island, five to the cabin if she ran, five more to pick up the manuscript, and the same time in reverse. She could make it before the storm really arrived. The lake wasn't rough yet. If it were she wouldn't make the attempt. She wasn't that crazy if she was crazy enough to be in love with a man who loved someone else.

Was she in love, she turned over the question as she picked up the oars and sent the boat ahead. Perhaps—a curious sound behind her. She turned. The spaniel was following, his black ears floating on the surface of the water like fins. The lake was getting rougher each minute. He would drown.

"Cocky, Cocky, you—you pest. Come here, you darn little fool." She reached over and pulled the dog from the water. He curled against her feet with a whimper.

She picked up the oars and the train of thought the rescue had interrupted. She had liked Tim better than any man she had ever met, she had realized that the night they had crashed on the stairs, that was why she had felt the sense of excitement, of adventure coming up. When he had told her of the girl in the Pacific theater the bottom had dropped out of her world. Pretty stupid of her not to have known why at the time, she had thought only that his marriage would spoil what promised to be a fine friendship between them, that his wife wouldn't want her husband to like a girl as much as he seemed to like her. And she had thought, why worry? I am here and the girl is far away. Why not enjoy his companionship while I have it?

The boat bobbed and danced as if it had gone crazy when she tried to fasten it to the ring in the float. Cocky whined and whimpered an accompaniment. Her palms were raw and red when finally she succeeded in making the painter fast. When she released her hold it pulled away from the ring and the boat danced off. She waded into the lake to her waist to catch it, but already it was several feet away. Back on the float she watched it bob and whirl. Drops which had been splashing on her face turned to solid sheets of rain.

"Looks like the island all night for us, Cocky-me-lad." She picked up the dog. "We've got to run for the cabin."

Trees creaked, birches and maples bent almost double, rain beat fragrance from the balsams. She ran along the trail, her feet going squish—squish, in the soaked pine needles. A pistol crack in the distance.

"Golly, Cocky, that was thunder." The dog whined and licked her wet cheek. The storm closed about her, slowed her progress.

The cabin at last. Another rumble, not so distant this time. Was the flash on the window reflected lightning? Suppose she had to spend the night here? Safe enough. The island was posted "No Trespassing." The key turned in the lock easily. The door swung open. She stepped in and stopped. Who had been here? Books that had been pulled from the shelves lay on the floor. A pane of glass near the lock in a rear window had been broken. Through the opening came the sound of rolling, rumbling thunder.

A man whose clothing dripped water was bending in front of the broad fireplace trying to coax a few sticks into a blaze. Her heart stopped beating. The blood seemed to leave her brain, her head felt light and empty. Was this wild-looking creature the Jap-crazy husband who threatened his wife with a revolver? Evidently the sound of the opening door had been muffled by thunder. Perhaps she could back out before he saw her. Cocky growled. He turned. Stared at her.

"If that cur so much as yips again—" His hoarse voice broke. A leveled revolver finished the sentence.

XXII

TIMOTHY Grant released the knob of Deb's door. Was it possible she had called him "Tim, darling" in that agonized voice, or did he love her so much that he had imagined deep emotion where there had been only friendly anxiety?

It hadn't registered at first, he had been so amazed at her frantic, "Have they got you too?" Who had frightened her? She had been right about the hit-and-run accident, it had been intentional. Later Mark had told the number of the car which had knocked him out. It belonged to a suspect on McGregor's list, though it hadn't yet been proved that the owner had been at the wheel.

That was Deb's door being cautiously closed. She had gone. If he followed her his timing would be bad. She wouldn't listen now. The explanation he intended to have had better be postponed until she was through at the Center, which would be the moment the mystery of the tragedy in the game house was solved. The possibilities of that moment set his pulses hammering. He answered a buzz on the interoffice phone.

"Yes? Certainly. At once."

Molly B. here to see him. What did it mean? She was a trustee of the Science Center but this was the first time she had been to the building since his installation as Head. He opened the door in response to her light tattoo.

"Come in. It's grand to see you." Even as he welcomed her he wondered why more gray-haired women with brilliant dark eyes didn't wear small American beauty red hats with a mink sling cape. The combination was a knockout on her.

"I won't take but a few minutes of your precious time, Tim." She lingered at the window. "There is no more beautiful view in the world to me than this. The hazy hills, the blue lake, white Beechcroft, the campus which at this distance resembles nothing as much as a toy village of pinkish brick buildings set in emerald lawns, even those racing dark clouds add to the picture." She laughed. "Here I stand raving about the beauties of nature when I promised to take but a few minutes of your time."

"Sit here and tell me what's on your mind, Molly B."

159

When she was seated he returned to his chair across the desk. She drew off her beige gloves and clasped her hands, ringless except for a wedding band and a huge diamond solitaire, on the desk in front of her.

"You may be sure it is something important or I wouldn't come here to consult you."

"Take all the time you want. I have a hunch it has to do with the late unpleasantness at the game house. Right?"

"Right. I didn't dare talk from home for fear I might be overheard there or by a listener-in at this end. I've reached the stage where I suspect everyone. I don't like Scragg, Tim. I'm sure he knows more than he is telling. I hate having him in the house."

"Don't discharge him yet, Molly B. No harm can come to anyone at Beechcroft from him, he is being closely watched. Were you seen coming into this office?"

"Deb was waiting for an elevator when I stepped into the corridor. She had just time to tell me she would be late getting home before the down car arrived. Clive Warner was coming out of the building as I entered. But that isn't what I came to talk about. Now that my mind has cleared of the shock and daze which followed the shooting of Henry Lander, I've had to break in a new legal adviser, I am beginning to think constructively."

"Or creatively?"

"Go on, grin, I can take it. Perhaps my imagination has seized the bit in its teeth but it may get results. The other day I decided that my mind had been scuttling from possibility to probability long enough, that I would go to work on the solution of the mystery as I would on the plot of a novel." She doodled on the desk with the rosy nail of her forefinger.

"That sounds reasonable. Where did you start?"

"Remember that on that tragic Sunday when Sandy McGregor asked Burke Romney who had recommended him for the professorship in the cyclotron lab, he answered, 'Judge Lander'?"

"I do."

"Remember the chief's response, 'I guess that gives you the green light, the Judge didn't pick phonies'?"

"Correct, word for word."

"That was where I started to backtrack to the day Prexy asked me to take Romney in at Beechcroft till he could find a place to live. I remembered he had said that the professor had come to the Center highly recommended by a group of engineers to do scientific work of great importance, and I remembered that the first week end he was in the house I introduced him to Henry Lander."

"Sure of that? Later, when questioned, he said they had met several times in Washington and that when the Judge told him of the work a team from the Center had done for the government during the war, he jumped at a chance of a professorship here, he knew he would *learn* so much. Remember?"

"So well that yesterday, with the excuse of talking over the projected GI parties, I called on Prexy, really to ask, diplomatically, I hope, who had recommended Burke Romney for his job at the Center. He told me the name of the engineering concern. I said I thought he was a protégé of Judge Lander's. He scraped his hand across his chin till it sounded like a miniature buzz saw—it takes Sophy Brandt's imitation to do it justice—'Lander?' he repeated. 'You surprise me. When I told the Judge Professor Romney had been engaged he was quite annoyed that he had not been consulted about his appointment.'"

Good old Prexy, not to betray the fact that he had been asked those same questions four days before by Tim Grant. Molly B. rested an elbow on the desk, chin in her hand.

"Since then I have been asking myself why that day in the game house Burke Romney pretended that Henry Lander was his sponsor?"

"That's easy. To prevent a suspicion that he had shot the Judge. We were all potential suspects with Sam Farr in top place. Remember how easily Romney got off at the cross-examination? 'What time did you go to your room, Professor?' The McGregor asked. 'At the same time the others went up. I said 'good-night' to Warner and closed the door of my room. Remember, Clive?' Warner said, 'That's right,' and the chief switched the spotlight on him."

"Clive Warner, heavenly day, I've never been sure he hadn't a hand if not a gun in the shooting. From the moment I heard he had applied for his old position at the Center I have suspected that something besides love for his work was behind his return."

"Love for Deb?"

"No, I am sure that was not the compelling motive. Which brings me to my next point. Before Colonel Taylor staggered into the library the other evening Clive had volunteered the information that Romney had taken Stella to the Country Club. At that very moment she was in her room upstairs."

"McGregor has found out that."

"How? Do you suppose someone in the house is working with him? That possibility hasn't occurred to me before. If so, who is it?"

"You'll have to ask the chief, I don't know. He is busy

161

now following clues that point to the person who ran down Mark Taylor."

"I had my suspicions that the Colonel wasn't injured by a casual hit-and-run driver."

"He wasn't. An attempt had been made to put him out of the running once before. Add that fact to your plot scenario, but keep it under that extremely becoming hat."

"That's an unnecessary warning. I never talk of my plots or of what I am writing till the novel is in print. Having gone so far, Tim, tell me more. Who, in your opinion, hid the gun in the shrubs at the Dane place? Romney had the opportunity, so had Scragg."

"How about Dane himself? It could have been Stella. Don't run away with the idea that I am saying they did, they had opportunity and possibly a motive for getting Lander out of the way."

"I don't believe it of either of them. They have been wild but never vicious. If only we knew the motive for the killing. Was it money? A woman? Had Judge Lander discovered a crooked deal in which the murderer was involved?"

"Touch spurs to your creative imagination and work out the solution, Molly B. The members of the Beechcroft household are not the only suspects on McGregor's list. The students at the college have been screened. Only one had a revolver, he was a GI who had been in a Jap concentration camp. The chief took possession of the gun, had it checked by the ballistics expert. When the automatic that did the shooting was discovered at the Danes' it let out the GI. The tragedy in the game house belongs in a collection of your stories. Any news about Johnson?"

"Ingrid has gone to the town where he is in custody. She wrote that it looked as if he would be detained for some time by Uncle Sam. I want her to bring the wife and child to Beechcroft to stay until her brother is free."

"Ever been told that you are a pretty special person, Molly B.? No more appointments," he replied to a buzz on the interoffice phone. "I am calling it a day and a week in about ten minutes." He snapped off the connection. Molly Burton Stewart rose, fastened her mink cape and drew on her gloves.

"I have taken a lot of your valuable time, Tim, and for what? To confide suspicions which may come from nothing but what Deb calls my 'Plot complex' at work."

"On the other hand, they may amount to a great deal. Keep at it." He opened the door to the corridor. "You'd better hurry home. That sky looks as if it would burst into tears at any moment and whopping big tears at that. Deb said she was going to the island. Don't let her."

"If she gets home before I leave for tea with Mrs. Prexy I'll tell her you said she was not to go." She laughed. "Knowing my granddaughter as I do I would be willing to bet that if she has made up her mind to go to the island she will go, regardless of the weather or advice. Oh, I forgot to tell you, the game house has been unsealed. New York decorators will arrive Monday morning to transform it into a quite different-looking place. When the mystery of the shooting has been solved we'll have a celebration that will exorcise the ghost of tragedy. This time I'm really going. Good morning, Tim, and thanks for listening."

He took a key from a drawer, waited to hear the clang of the elevator, then entered Deb's room from the corridor. He drew the key from the door between her room and his, locked the corridor door and returned to his desk.

It was a long ten minutes before he closed his door from the outside with a bang which bounced and bounded along the concrete walls. That sound would broadcast his departure. He spoke to several employees on his way out of the building, stopped to exchange weather predictions with the guard at the entrance, drove his roadster to a side street. Parked it. Returned to the Center. The guard at the door had changed.

"Going back to work, Mr. Grant?" inquired the tall, stoop-shouldered man with S.C. on the sleeve of his brown uniform.

"Only for a moment, Gustin, to pick up a paper I forgot."

"Seems to be something in the air today makes folks forget. Captain Warner came back for the same reason just as I reported for duty."

"Don't tell anyone you saw me, or I won't get away again."

"I'll be dumb as an oyster, sir. I'll see you get your half day. All of us here think you'll be killing yourself with work."

"Work never killed anyone, Gustin, it's worry that gets them. My problems will iron out once I have the job under control."

He sprinted up a flight of spiral stairs. Lady Luck was with him. He met no one. In his office he slipped the catch which locked the door. Now, it could not be opened from outside.

What next? He couldn't smoke, the scent of tobacco would betray his presence; he couldn't read or write, even the faint crackle of paper would put a listening scout wise to the fact that he was inside. The sky was so dark that the room was dusky. A light might be seen from outside. He would have to sit here and wait. How long? For what? Was he crazy to suspect that some interested person would try to secure Deb's notebook on the chance that she had left it in her desk? She had said:

"It seemed as if every person in the building had business in that particular corridor at that particular moment."

If there were persons at the Center interested in its contents—where did he get that "if"? Hadn't the visiting Canadians tipped off Mark to watch three employees in high places, men who were suspected of having violated oaths of secrecy?

Two o'clock. Two-thirty. Three. Three-thirty. Time crawled forward as he relived the past; the tragedy, excitement, achievement of the war years, the fighting across the Pacific from one bloody, costly victory to another; the news of his mother's passing. It hadn't brought a sense of loss—through his youth he had been kept at school, then came M.I.T.; next an engineering assignment in the West. He had never really known or loved her, they hadn't been pals as were so many mothers and sons he had met. He thought of the pictures of Deb he had found in her diary and of how they had changed the world for him. "Tim, darling," he was back to that again. Did it mean—

A faint sound swept across his consciousness like a soft breeze and cleared it of retrospection. Someone had tried his office door. Another try. He watched the knob. It didn't turn. Would that satisfy the person outside that there was no one inside? He glanced at the wall clock. Better wait five minutes before he moved.

At last the long hand had crept around. He crossed to the door of Deb's office. Lucky that his predecessor had spent a couple of thousand bucks on the rug—an expenditure which had wrung tears from the majority of the trustees—it was so thick he could have stamped his way across without being heard. The knob of the door between the two offices was being tested. He restrained an impulse to jerk it open.

"Softly, softly, or you'll lose your man," he warned himself.

He rested his head against the door with his hand on the key for a quick turn and listened. Someone was inside, someone had used a passkey. A drawer squeaked. The sound gave the investigator pause. Silence.

Why the dickens did his private phone have to ring at this critical minute? Another ring. It had frightened off the person in Deb's office. A door closed. He sprinted to the corridor door. Softly opened it. No one in sight. Whoever it had been might be flattened out in a doorway—waiting—

The phone again. Three sharp rings. The signal he and

164

McGregor had agreed upon which meant haste. He closed the door. At his desk he answered the call in a whisper.

"Yes. Yes. My man? At once."

He cradled the telephone. The suspect McGregor had had watched since he had tipped him off to a few facts had started for the island in a college shell. The chief wanted him to follow. Sure he would follow. At last the mystery would be cleared—

For the island? Consternation followed jubilation. The *island!* Terror set his heart thumping. Suppose Deb was there waiting for the storm to let up. What might not happen to her with a desperate criminal in hiding? He took the stairs three at a leap. The guard at the entrance door touched his cap.

"Did the man who was looking for you find you, sir? I did my best to head him off, but when—"

"What man?"

"He said he was the butler at Madam Stewart's, sir, that he had an important message for you, so I let him through."

Scragg? Had it been Scragg in Deb's office? Why?

XXIII

"YOU heard me. If that dog so much as yelps—"

At the repetition of the ugly threat Deb grabbed the cocker's nose and smothered his bark. Her eyes widened in amazement, her blood surged back into normal channels, her heart resumed its steady rhythm. She laughed.

"You scared me stiff. Do you know who I thought you were? I—"

"Stop talking. Keep that dog quiet. Or else—"

She wasn't seeing the haggard face or the threatening gun, she was in the library at Beechcroft, seeing Mrs. Sophy's pink cheeks, her brilliant blue eyes, hearing her say:

"I took it from your suitcase, Tim. I hid it two days later. You'll find it behind the books on the top shelf in Molly B.'s work room on the island."

The man in dripping clothes in front of the fireplace had come here to get the ivory-handled revolver. The empty top shelf, the books scattered on the floor, betrayed him. Why did he want it? Did it mean that the gun found among the Dane shrubs was his? That having disposed of that he needed another? That he had shot—

"Come away from the door."

She made a valiant attempt to swallow her heart, which was obstructing her voice with its anvil beat. He must not suspect that she was desperately frightened and just as desperately determined to keep him here until someone came. Of course, someone would come. Didn't a rescuer always arrive at the crucial moment in Molly B.'s whodunits? Was it probable that Tim would leave his revolver here all this time unless he suspected that a person who had heard Mrs. Sophy tell where it was hidden might come for it?

That thunderous crash was a tree down. The wind, not a banshee, was wailing and moaning in the broad chimney. Would anyone think that even a hunted criminal would allow himself to be trapped on an island in this storm? Was this man a hunted criminal? Would he have threatened to shoot unless he were? Better give up all thought of help and rely on herself.

"Does anyone know you came here?"

166

Should she admit that Tim, Molly B. and Sarah Allen knew she was coming? No. Perhaps by this time the first two had decided she had stayed at the village, that even she wouldn't be silly enough to take out a boat in this blow. Sarah Allen had been dressed for her afternoon out, she wouldn't be there to tell them.

"If this is to be a quiz session—mind if I sit down, then you may—I was brought up that it is a breach of good manners to keep a gentleman standing unnecessarily." Her shaking knees gave way and lowered her suddenly into a reed chair cushioned in red and green near a window. She held the squirming dog close. The attempt at a fire blinked a couple of red eyes at her and went out.

"You really needn't keep that fiendish pistol aimed at me—"

"Don't mention my name."

"And why not? Who can hear? You don't think inhabitants of town or college are running round this island hunting flora and fauna specimens in this storm, or do you?"

"How did you get here?"

"By boat. Something tells me you swam from the campus boathouse."

"Never mind how I came, I'm leaving in your boat and taking you with me."

"In this storm? That's a joke. My boat—" Better not tell him that it was cavorting in the middle of the lake, possibly sunk by this time. "We'll capsize before we've rowed ten feet. The lake has gone crazy. It will be cold at the bottom. How about a cup of tea before we start?"

"What do you mean, 'tea'?"

"T-e-a, you've heard of it, the cup that cheers. Molly B. keeps a sterno and provisions of sorts in that cupboard. If you'll pocket that darn gun we'll have a party. The icy chill in this cabin is going creepy, creep, up and down my spinal column, my clothes are wet from the rain. Are you looking from the window in the hope that someone will come? Who but a neuropsychiatric would venture on the lake in this tornado?"

"You came, Deb—"

"*Don't* mention names. If I can't speak yours, I object to having mine used. Who knows, there may be a reporter concealed in the chimney on the lookout for a sensational episode at the college, and is this sensational! They did a fine publicity stunt on our murder. Is it to be tea first or a watery grave?"

"Why so sure the boat will capsize?" He cast a furtive glance at the rear window He was expecting someone. Who?

"Nothing is sure in this vale of tears. There goes another

tree. My word, what a crash. If you open the front door you can see the water whipped to whitecaps. I couldn't row the boat. You appear so attached to that gun you'd have but one hand." She glanced at the watch on her not too steady wrist. "Four o'clock. It's getting dark. I'll light the lamp."

"No light."

"The noes have it. Would you mind telling me why you are putting on this cockeyed act? Are you practicing for the college play or have you just gone haywire?"

"You think you know the answer. You're not fooling me for a minute, but you're on the wrong track." He shivered violently. "Start that tea. If you so much as make a move to signal—"

"Now really, signal whom? Put that pistol on the type-writer desk. You can grab it before I could reach it. See the pump in the corner? I need water for the tea. Get busy." She rose and dropped the spaniel into the chair. "Stay there, Cocky, and I'll give you a love-ly cookie."

She watched as he started for the typewriter desk, apparently changed his mind and slipped the revolver into the pocket of his trousers. They were dripping wet. Would the dampness affect the cartridges or bullets with which it was loaded? Her firearms education had been nil. If she were to continue her checkered career in the pursuit of crime she'd better major in the subject.

She unlocked the cupboard, produced a large sterno, a whistling teakettle, crackers, jam, and a package of paper napkins with not unseemly haste considering that she was functioning under the threat of shooting. This must be how a soldier felt when advancing under the guns of a fortress.

"Why are you rummaging in that closet?"

"Well, for crying out loud." This is the second time today you've used that expression you never used before, she reminded herself. "I'm looking for tea balls. I have them. Fill the kettle with water while I set up this for Operations Tea Party." She snapped down the legs of a card table.

"We might as well enjoy a touch of elegance with our last meal on earth." She spread a cloth gay with printed nasturtiums, placed cups and saucers, silver teaspoons, sugar, crackers, jam and cookies slowly, trying to think of some way to send a smoke signal up the chimney, alerting her ears for a human sound above the din of the storm. She set the filled kettle over the lighted sterno.

"Sorry, there is neither lemon nor cream for our party. Place those two straight-back chairs at the table. Why doesn't that pesky thing begin to boil? Don't remind me of that 'watched kettle' stuff."

Even as she babbled—it was the only word which fittingly

168

covered her remarks—she wondered if it would be possible to dump the box of paper napkins with a lighted match on top of the kindling already in the fireplace. They might make a little smoke that would be seen from the shore. With that rain beating on the roof? Now she was crazy.

"What was that?"

A tap on the front window. She wasn't fooling herself. Was it a friend or another heel like the man with the gun? Was he coming in? What would stop him? She had left the key in the outside lock.

"Sit in that chair and stay there. Don't move. If the dog barks—" The leveled revolver finished the threat.

"Come here, Cocky. Don't you hear the 'Master's voice'?" Deb realized that her whisper had more carrying power than spoken words. The dog jumped into her lap. "I suppose you'll shoot us on the principle that you might as well be hung for a sheep as a lamb, for two mur—"

"Ssh-sh." He listened. Came two quick taps, then a single. He opened the door a crack.

"Couldn't find the notebook." The harsh whisper which sifted into the cabin was punctuated by hard-drawn breaths as if the speaker had been running. "Nearly broke my back rowing from the Beechcroft pier. Come out. McGregor's on to us. I'll bet the guy who's been painting the college boathouse was his man. We've got to beat it. Remember, they swore they wouldn't help—"

"Don't move." The man holding the door flung the warning over his shoulder as Deb jumped to her feet. "What's that infernal noise?" The whistling kettle was putting on its act.

She sank back in the chair and abandoned the idea of hurling the lighted sterno wrapped in the tablecloth into the fireplace for a smoke signal. As if understanding her disappointment the cocker reached up and licked her cheek.

"Who've you got in there? Why don't you answer?" The voice seeped through the opening. "The key's in the lock. Is this a trap? I'm coming in."

The door was banged open with such violence that the man holding it dropped the revolver. As he stopped to pick it up Clive Warner brushed past him, kicked shut the door and stopped.

"Deb," he whispered. "*Deb*, what are you doing here alone with—"

A tree fell with a crash which shook the cabin. A shower of soot rained down the chimney. Cocky whined and snuggled closer in Deb's arms. The kettle kept up its shrill whistle. Her defiant eyes challenged the man staring at her as if

169

she were a visitor from a distant planet and a horrific one at that.

So, this is the setup, she thought, even as she finished his sentence in a tone she hoped was flippantly sophisticated:

"What am I doing *alone* here? Why not alone? Don't be old-fashioned, Clive. Can't you see? I'm having tea with your pal—Professor Romney."

"Did you drag her into this?" Clive Warner demanded furiously.

"Me? Drag her in? Ask her. Do you think I'm nuts to load myself up with a girl? She butted in, now she'll take her medicine. I'm off in her boat. She's coming with me."

"Oh, no, she isn't. You're going. I'm going. She stays here."

Deb drew the first long breath she had drawn since she stepped into the cabin, partly relief for herself, partly gratitude that Clive had the decency to protect her, if leaving her alone on the island in a hurricane were protection. Was that a shout? Every fiber in her body stiffened. If only her heart would stop pounding. If only the kettle would stop whistling so she could hear. Ears alert she listened. The sound again. Was it her imagination, or had a voice shouted, "Deb. Deb." Had the two men heard? Apparently not, they had forgotten caution and were arguing angrily.

"*I* said she was going. Better think that over, Warner." The threat in Romney's voice blanched Clive's face. "I can see that you have."

"I'm going, Deb, to look after you." His shamed voice hurt her. After all, she had believed in him once. "Come quietly and no harm will come to you, I swear."

"That's mighty good of you, Clive." She rose with the dog in her arms as if preparing to leave. Was she the only one who heard that shout? Perhaps it wasn't a shout. Perhaps she was imagining it. "I won't burden you with the care of a girl in your getaway. I haven't the slightest intention of going in that boat. Who's pounding on the door? . . .

"Don't come in," she shouted. "They have a gun—" A hand over her mouth reduced her warning to a gurgle, but she could still see. The door was flung open.

"Take it easy, Deb." It was Tim, Tim in glistening raincoat and dripping slouch hat on the threshold. "That gun won't help you, Romney. I don't leave a loaded revolver in a suitcase. Take your hand off her mouth, Warner, and take it off damn quick." The hand came off, but not before Deb had given it a vicious bite.

"Who do you think you are, giving orders here, Grant?" Romney had emerged from his coma of surprise. "This isn't the Center. Get busy, Warner, we'll tie him up before we leave with D—" A blow smashed the name back on his lips.

That does it, Deb thought, as the two men backed Tim into the corner. He pushed the table with a lamp behind him as he retreated. The cocker yelped and whined as he circled the struggling men, caught the leg of Warner's trousers and worried it. A kick sent him halfway across the room. He sat on his haunches, blinking as if wondering how he came there.

She must do something to help Tim. She was standing here like a dummy, her body shaken by the heavy thud of her heart. The men had forgotten she was in the world. Suppose they knocked out Tim, hurt him seriously? They would leave him here alone, perhaps to die. Between the noise of the storm outside, the queer sounds it was making in the chimney, the whistling kettle, Cocky's whine-bark, whine-bark, and the men's heavy breathing, any shout of hers would be unheard. Her eyes flashed around the cabin for inspiration, lingered on the great fireplace. Was her idea of a smoke signal the answer?

The lamp and table went over with a crash. With half her attention on the struggling men, she cautiously lifted the kettle and placed it on the chair behind her. Its whistle stopped. With her left hand she picked up the flaming sterno, with her right jerked the cloth from the table with a speed that sent china and silver crashing and tinkling to the floor, and flung both straight into the fireplace. The blaze lighted the room. She added the box of paper napkins. The kindling caught and flared. She must keep it going. Her manuscript would help feed— For the first time she noticed the brass Cape Cod lighter. It was full of kerosene oil. She seized it and recklessly poured its contents on the fire.

"Godamighty!"

The bellow in the chimney was followed by two dangling legs, a chubby body in a blackened uniform, topped by a soot-streaked face. McGregor jumped clear of the fire and dragged after him another begrimed figure. Tears streaming from their eyes had left white courses on their cheeks. Romney and Warner had stopped their furious attack on Tim to stare in open-mouthed unbelief. He was righting the table. Deb rigidly controlled an hysterical surge of laughter.

"Stop 'em, Sergeant. Don't let 'em get away," roared the chief of the county police as the two men bolted for the door. "Who thought up the dirty trick of lighting that fire?" he growled as he slapped out sparks on his clothing.

"I—I did. All by myself. It—it was supposed to be a smoke signal," Deb explained, even as she crushed back wave after wave of laughter interspersed with sobs of relief. Tim was safe. "Anything more Little Useful can do to help, Sandy?"

"You done plenty, Miss Deb, you almost put the sergeant and me out of business, lucky our clothes were wet."

McGregor slapped at a spark he had overlooked. The blaze in the fireplace had died to a heap of charred cloth with a glowing edge and a few blackened sticks of kindling. There was light enough in the cabin to make out the sergeant, hand on the holster at his hip, standing between Romney and Warner in front of the door. Tim touched a match to the lamp.

"That's the stuff," McGregor approved as light glowed. "Now we can see what we are doing."

"Sure you know what you are doing?" Romney demanded truculently. "Can't a man have a date with a girl on an island without calling out the police?"

"That's enough of that," Tim interrupted furiously.

"Suppose you start a real fire for us, Mr. Grant, and let me handle this," McGregor suggested. "Miss Randall is shivering." He doesn't know how right he is, Deb thought, now that the crisis is past my knees just aren't there.

"The storm seems to be blowing itself out," the chief went on. "We'll wait till the waves on the lake subside a little before we take these two men back in the police boat. It gave us an awful shaking up crossing from the college boathouse."

"Police boat!" Romney exclaimed. "You don't mean that you are arresting us?"

"Funny you guessed so quick." McGregor stepped into the middle of the room. Tim knelt in front of the fireplace and laid fresh kindling as Deb handed it to him.

Was this real or would she waken in her blue and pink room at home to find it a nightmare? McGregor was right, the storm was clearing. In the west the setting sun was coloring lingering clouds with splashes of red, scarlet, crimson, ruby and garnet with swirls of purple and violet.

Her eyes came back to the cabin. The stack of yellow paper beside the typewriter was real—thank heaven the police had appeared before she had added her precious manuscript as fuel to her smoke signal—as real as the slab of wood mounted with the stuffed skin of a bass, the largest fish her father had caught, which hung on the broad stone chimney above the granite slab which served as a mantel. The clutter of cups and saucers on the floor, with Cocky in the midst greedily devouring the spilled cookies, was real.

She wasn't dreaming. She was in the cabin on the island. Tim's fingers touched her hand as he reached for the pine stick she held. No doubt of the reality of the response of

172

her pulses. She was awake and terribly in love with a man who loved another girl.

"It won't be necessary to tell you that you don't have to talk without a lawyer present, Romney, I guess you know all the ropes."

McGregor's reminder recalled Deb's attention just as the kindling caught. It sent rosy shadows playing over log walls and bright-cushioned chairs, played fantastic tricks on the tear-furrowed soot of the chief's face as he backed up against an end of the broad mantel.

"That suits me." Romney took a step forward. The sergeant laid his hand on his arm and stopped him. "Take us back to the campus and I'll phone my lawyer."

"You've got the wrong slant and you know it, Romney. You haven't a lawyer, that was my little joke. The country that is paying you two guys to snoop for information at the Center pays big money, but, if you're caught, it will swear it never heard of you. Right?"

So, that was why these men were wanted? Not for the shooting of Henry Lander. Clive Warner's face was drained of color, Romney's was fiery red in contrast.

"Sit down, Deb." Tim drew forward a chair. "I'm sorry you've been let in for this, but it is safer to stay here till the wind goes down. That boat you came in is bottom-side up in the middle of the lake." He cleared his hoarse voice. "I—I almost lost my mind when I saw it."

Having devoured the last cookie crumb, Cocky jumped into her lap, circled and settled for a nap. She leaned forward to listen, aware that Tim was standing behind her.

"I don't know what you're talking about McGregor," Romney blustered. "I have an important assignment at the Center. Warner is an instructor there. Why should a country, beside this, pay us?"

"Perhaps you'll know what *I'm* talking about, Romney," Tim Grant answered for McGregor. "You are wanted in a country not far from here for violating oaths of allegiance and secrecy. Keen of you to be out with a cold the day the visitors from north of us came to look over the Center. You came recommended by men who had no suspicion that you are a traitor. It's amazing that you could find an American who fought in the war to agree to betray his country's scientific secrets. You drew Warner into it with the inducement of big pay. Too bad for him I didn't stop you before you shot—"

"I didn't shoot Lander," Romney's voice was loud, his face livid.

"How quick you are to fill in the name," McGregor took over. "I suspected you from the start, you were so free with information as to what everyone else was doing that night between the snack party and 1 A.M."

"Perhaps I was, but you can't prove by that I shot the Judge."

"Then you know it was your side-kick?"

"Who, *me?*" Clive Warner's voice was hoarse with fright. "I didn't see the Judge after he left for the game house."

"Hmm-m. But you did monkey with Colonel Taylor's plane so that he almost lost his life in a take-off, didn't you? What's that but premeditated murder?"

"Don't answer," Romney prompted. "He's trying to trap us into admitting we shot Lander."

"I haven't traveled as far back as that yet; don't be impatient, we'll get to it. You did run down the Colonel on his bike, didn't you, Professor?"

"Suppose I did, it wasn't very serious. I knew he was Intelligence. I might as well tell all. You're right about our reason for being here. We had most of the information we wanted. We were about to silently disappear."

"And the last bit was in the notebook of Miss Randall's you tried to get today, wasn't it, Warner?" Tim Grant suggested.

"How did you—"

"Shut up."

Romney's rough command snapped Clive Warner's jaws together. He glanced surreptitiously at Deb.

"Too bad you took all that trouble, Clive. I took the notebook to Beechcroft with me." He bit at the end of his mustache. Color flooded his white face at the contempt in her voice.

"Captain Warner was asking how we knew." McGregor ignored the interlude. "You should let him finish his sentence, Professor. We knew, the same way Henry Lander knew, of the espionage which had started at the Center. You killed him before he could betray you."

"I didn't kill him. I didn't kill him."

"Hmm-m. Don't shout. You're so excitable, Professor. I know who killed the Judge."

A spurt of flame from the blazing fire threw an uncanny light on the strained faces of the two men standing each side of the sergeant, on their wide, terrified eyes. McGregor fitted his fingers together.

"I know who killed the Judge," he repeated. In the silence which followed a log in the fire snapped with the suddenness of a pistol shot. Deb's throat was dry from suspense. *Why* didn't he say it? *Why* keep them on the rack?

"Scragg has confessed."

Fear died out of Romney's eyes, his body snapped out of

its rigidity like a stretched rubber band suddenly released.

"I thought you were bright enough to get your man, Chief." A hint of pomposity had returned to his voice.

"Scragg has confessed—" McGregor paused—"that he saw you shoot the Judge, Professor."

XXIV

"I'LL fasten your beads, Debby."

Sarah Allen's black taffeta rustled as with the pearls in her hand she approached the girl standing in front of the long mirror. She jerked her steel spectacles back to the bridge of her nose. "My sakes, you're pretty in that sparkly white dress. When you move the skirt floats out like an angel's wing."

"How come you know so much about angels' wings, Sal?"

"Seen 'em in my dreams." Sarah snapped the diamond clasp of the necklace at the nape of the tanned neck. She glanced at the window through which a large and beaming moon was visible. "Almost like spring outside, terrible unseasonable, though. This Thanksgiving Day was made to order for Madam Stewart's party to the college folks to celebrate the reopening of the game house."

"To celebrate also the clearing up of the mystery of the shooting of Judge Lander, plus the fact that a horrible cloud has been lifted from Beechcroft, don't forget that." Deb opened a cellophane box on the Wedgwood blue dresser. Gorgeous green orchids. No card.

"Lifted." Sarah Allen sniffed. "I'll say it's lifted, there ain't a wisp of it left. Even the stained badminton court floor has been replaced. Madam Stewart is thorough when she starts doing things. We've had some hustlin' times. You'd oughtta been here. I never did understand why you rushed off to Washington two days after Sandy McGregor caught the man who did the shooting."

Who did except herself, Deb thought. Who knew that Mc-Gregor had told her he had asked "the Head" to take her on at the Center for her protection for the duration of the man hunt? When she had asked Tim if it were true he had answered curtly, "Yes." Then and there she had resigned her position, then and there he had agreed, it was almost as if it were a relief to him to have her go. She had faked a summons from her Washington boss and had left Beechcroft the next day. She wouldn't be here now if Molly B.

hadn't made her promise that she would return for Thanksgiving.

She thought of the trip back from the island in the police boat, Tim at the wheel, the chief and sergeant with Romney and Clive Warner, their faces covered by their hands, crouching between them. In the car on the way to Beechcroft she had asked Tim how he had reached the island.

"In the police boat." A chuckle brought color to his white face. "It was The McGregor's idea for me to approach the front of the cabin while he and his man dropped down the chimney, he said he'd always wanted to try it. Sam was right, there is a slice of ham in the chief's make-up." Laughter gave way to gravity. "I've been sure for weeks that Romney was a dead duck."

"You said that you and I would work together," she had reminded. "Why didn't you tell me you suspected that Burke Romney had shot Henry Lander?"

"That 'together' arrangement was to follow up the mystery of the disappearance of Ingrid's papers. When it came to murder—you were out as my side-dick in detection." His curt declaration had ended conversation between them.

"Remember the first night you came back in September when we found the white pants in your bag, I told you I thought Professor Romney belonged in the movies?" Sarah's slightly muffled voice came from the closet where she was hanging the dark green gabardine suit in which Deb had arrived two hours before. She emerged and picked up russet shoes.

"Much as I despised that Warner fella for the way he treated you, I'm kind of glad 'twas proved he didn't know anything about the shooting. I suppose swearin' false oaths, trying to find out the secret inventions of your country to sell them is about as bad, though."

"Romney must have had a brain storm. Suppose the Judge had found out that he was at the Center as an observer for another country? Why didn't he make his getaway? Why commit murder? Why crawl out on that limb? He must have known he would be caught."

"It came out at the trial that he was wanted on another charge, I guess he figured that if he was caught spyin' this time he was down an' out for good, that he was in a country village and could get away with it. It came out he'd been promised big money by the folks who sent him here. I'm willin' to give the devil his due," sniff, "Scragg was the best butler we ever had here, I'm goin' to miss him something fierce, an'—"

"Miss him? Has he gone?"

"Sure, he's gone. You don't think Madam Stewart would

177

keep a man in her house who said he aimed to use a pass-key to get into her room, do you? She only kept him after he tried to get Ingrid Johnson's papers because Mr. Timothy told her to. Why didn't he come out right off quick and say he saw the professor shoot the Judge? He said he went to the Center the Saturday Romney was caught to tell Mr. Timothy the truth and couldn't find him."

"What is the truth? I haven't heard."

"You should have stayed here instead of runnin' off to Washington, Debby. The trial was terrible exciting. This county don't let cases drag on as some places do. Scragg testified that after the snack party he went to the game house to ask the Judge to let up on the Danes, to tell him he would make a payment on the mortgages, to beg him not to foreclose."

"Why was he so devoted to that family?"

"Their father took him in when he was down and out. I remember the talk at the time, we villagers figured he'd come from jail. The Danes was all the family he had. His story was that he went into the game house the back way, quiet like, and heard loud talking in the badminton court, saw Romney and the Judge standin' together. Then the Judge said something, sounded ugly, turned to go upstairs and the Professor shot him. Why didn't that butler tell right off what he'd seen and save these weeks of suspectin' everybody, himself included? What was he afraid of?"

"Perhaps of reprisals from the people who sent Romney to the Center, perhaps he figured on making the guilty man pay by the nose to keep him quiet. Did it come out at the trial who dropped the automatic among the shrubs at the Dane front door?"

"It was Professor Romney when he called to take Stella dancin'. They had him so twisted in his own lies that they got a full confession finally."

"I was sure it was Scragg."

"So was a lot of folks. Mr. Timothy suspected Professor Romney from the beginning, he tipped Sandy McGregor to watch him." Sniff. "He and I worked hard on this case."

"Sarah Allen, what did you have to do with it?"

"I was Sandy's inside helper. I kept him posted on who come here and whether you folks were in or out, and on Scragg's goin's and comin's. It was terrible exciting. I'm thinking of stealin' Molly Burton's thunder an' writin' a book about it. I think I could do real good."

"If you'll write as you talk you'll make the best-seller grade."

In front of the mirror she gazed critically at the dark-haired, gray-eyed looking-glass girl. Not too bad. The "spark-

178

ly white" skirt of sheer net floated and swirled with each movement of her body. The sleeveless silver jacket with its deep V made a perfect background for the orchids. The diamond bracelet on her left arm had been on the dresser when she arrived. There had been a card with it. "Love to my girl from Molly B."

"Think you'll do?"

She turned from the mirror to answer Sarah Allen's brusque question.

"Do you, Sal?"

"Sure, those flowers are awful pretty at your shoulder. Debby. You'll pass. Remember, handsome is as handsome does. I must hurry down. I don't know how that new butler will turn out, this is his first party here. I ought to have stayed at his elbow but I love to help you dress." She paused at the door.

"You'll turn a lot of heads tonight, child. Be sure you turn the right one."

"Which is the right one, Sal?" The quickly closed door was the only answer.

"Just as if you didn't know the right one for you," Deb reminded Deb. She picked up her white bag glistening with crystals, threw a soft-green satin stole over her left arm, and stepped into the gallery. She thought of the whispered threat she had heard coming from the bay weeks ago. She sat on the top step while in imagination she followed the trail of events from that moment, visualized the crash on the stairs with Tim. He had been such fun then.

From the moment she realized she loved him everything had gone haywire.

Right that it should go haywire, wasn't it? He loved another girl, didn't he? Would that make him treat her with such icy indifference on the return trip from the island in the police boat? Perhaps he thought she really had gone there to have tea with Romney or to meet Clive. He couldn't, he just couldn't be so dumb. Indignation brought her to her feet, sent her racing down the stairs into the library. A radioed voice was singing:

"Can't help lovin' that man."

"That's me," she thought bitterly.

"What's the matter, honey?" Molly B. exclaimed and snapped off the music. "You dashed in as if pursued by furies."

"Perhaps a guilty conscience was at my heels, though that usually does its stuff in wakeful night hours. There's something about this room in the soft fire and lamplight when I return after an absence that tightens my throat. Those tall floor vases filled with soft yellow mums are out of this

179

world. Isn't it time for the arrival of the family guests?"

"Yes. Tim phoned that his household would be a little late, the Farrs are dining with them and Tilly is never on time. Prexy slipped me the information that the Faculty had broken out their evening clothes and would appear in white tie and tails."

"They will be in character with the silver lace frock you're sporting. What genius thought up that shell-pink malines stole across your shoulders? It's dream-lovely. The diamonds and opals in your necklace and bracelets are perfect with it."

"I feel as if nothing could be too perfect for this occasion. Beechcroft was under a cloud for weeks, the neighbors, the students, spoke of it in hushed whispers. Now that we know the truth of what happened, let's forget it. Monday I start a new novel. Ingrid wants to take on the secretarial work."

"What happened to Stella Dane?"

"Resigned. She felt that after her attempt to get Ingrid's papers I wouldn't trust her."

"Would you?"

"I think she decided wisely."

"Perhaps she'll get the position at the Center I gave up."

"No. That place has been filled."

"By a girl?"

"You'll have to ask Tim. I've hardly seen him since you left for Washington. Romney and Warner were only part of a ring sent to the Center to report on its experiments and the results. The life of every worker there has been investigated from the cradle to the present. The Head has personally supervised the examinations to make sure that no injustice has been done, he shows the strain. Now he's up against a domestic complication. He is losing his homemaker."

"Losing Mrs. Sophy? What's happened?"

"Her bachelor son, Hugh Brandt, the career diplomat from Argentina, came to spend Thanksgiving with her. When he saw her presiding as hostess for Tim he decided she was what he needed in Buenos Aires. She is radiantly happy that he wants her."

"And she is leaving Tim? I call it darned ungrateful after he pulled her out of that old-age slump."

"He thinks she should go with her son. When she protested he confided that he had a substitute picked out and whispered, under her oath of secrecy, who it was. The servants are staying with him."

"That's a break. I suppose the girl in the Pacific is the new homemaker. Where's Ingrid?"

"Probably upstairs hovering over her brother's baby. He's a cute trick. I'm crazy about him myself. I wish you'd get married and have a baby, Debby, I'd adore it."

"Perhaps I will."

"Will what?" Tim Grant inquired from the threshold.

He looked sterner, taller than she remembered him, perhaps evening dress made him appear so. His eyes, which she had thought gray, were a burning black. Molly B. was right, his face did show the strain of heavy responsibility. Mrs. Sophy, in lavender lace, a tall, good-looking man with iron-gray hair and an air of worldly sophistication, Mark Taylor in uniform, and the Farrs entered the room at the same time. It needed but a fleeting glance at Sam's face tor Deb to realize that Tilly, in sleek yellow satin, had marked the new man for her own. It took an equally short time for her to decide that she would give the lady a run for her money.

"What were you saying you would do just as we came in, Deb?" Tim Grant persisted.

"Get married. It's being done. Mrs. Sophy, is this your son? Isn't he grand?" She held out her hand. "I'm Deborah Randall. Welcome to New England, Mr. Brandt. I so hope you'll like us." She experimented with an upward sweep of her lashes she hadn't tried out since her freshman year. It still worked.

"Like you. It isn't a hope, it's a certainty." His hold on her hand tightened. "Can't we get away from this crowd while I tell you that lightning has struck my seasoned heart at last? Will you excuse me, Mother?"

She liked his grin that showed how little stock he took in her fervent greeting, liked the voice in which he said "Mother." His "seasoned heart" was right. She would wager that he had loving and leaving reduced to a science.

"I am to be hostess at the game house, why not tell me on the way there?" she suggested, aware that Tim Grant was regarding her with frowning intentness.

"But, Hugh," Tilly's gold bangles clinked as she laid a detaining hand on the diplomat's sleeve. "Have you forgotten that *I* promised to show you this lovely place?" Her husband beside Tim was watching her. He needn't worry, Deb thought, the man from the Argentine was doubtless past master in extricating himself from a situation like this.

"You did, Mrs. Tilly, but I knew you were only taking pity on a strange guy, and would much rather be with your horde of followers. Now that Debby has taken me on, just drop me from your mind." He slipped his hand under Deb's arm.

"All right to call you Debby, isn't it? Mother's letters

have been so full of you, your charm and intelligence, that I feel as if we are old friends."

"Only friends?" She disciplined a laugh. They were playing stage center and the audience was stiff with amazement and disapproval.

"Come on and I'll tell you what you are already in my life."

"Curtain." This time Deb let the laugh come as they left the room together.

Except for its shape one wouldn't think of this great game room as being the same place in which Sandy McGregor had cross-examined the members of the Beechcroft household weeks ago, Deb thought as several hours later she stopped to draw a long breath. In between her duties as hostess she had danced incessantly with members of the Faculty and Hugh Brandt. Now the hangings were of rich yellow brocade, the banquettes were covered with a zebra stripe, the inlaid floor was a deep mahogany. A gleaming golden bowl on the piano was running over with tawny button chrysanthemums, two matching arrangements were on the high mantel.

"My dance," asserted a voice behind her. Tim Grant touched her shoulder lightly.

"Sorry. I've promised to dance the quadrille after this with Hugh Brandt."

"Like fun, you will. Come on, quick, unless you want an argument right here." A fanfare from the fiddlers on a raised platform was followed by the leader's call:

"Salute partners!"

"Just a minute." Deb played for time. "I'd like to watch this." He made no protest, just moved a step nearer.

"Forward and back!" shouted the leader. *"Swing your partner!"* The younger dancers laughed and romped through the figures, the elders sailed through with beautiful dignity. They "Balanced Corners," wound in and out of "Ladies' Chain," with gay abandon. Guests standing along the walls clapped their hands, stamped their feet to the rhythm of the music. One of them called:

"Change partners."

There was a mad scramble. The diplomat seized breathless, laughing Mrs. Sophy, who had been dancing with tall, unbending Prexy. Sam caught Tilly. The squares re-formed.

"This is our chance. Come on." Tim caught up the soft green stole that Deb had dropped on the banquette behind her. "This is yours, I know, you had it on your arm in the library. Quick." He drew her through the doorway to the colonnade. "You've done your duty for the present. I have a lot to say to you. First, glad to see that you are wearing my orchids."

182

He held her hand tight in his as if fearing she would make a break for freedom, till they reached the terrace. It was quite deserted. In the distance the lake lay wide and shining in the moonlight. The world was so still that the music from the game house drifted toward them through the open door, voices singing, *"O Susanna! O, don't you cry for me."*

"Great night, isn't it? Like spring."

Deb disengaged her hand. He might feel the throb of her heart in her finger tips.

"It is. 'Terrible unseasonable,' Sarah Allen speaking. Did you bring me here to talk about the weather?"

"No, about your behavior this evening. Snitched the diplomat right from under Tilly's nose, didn't you? Smart gal. Did you spot Sam's grin of appreciation? Do you like Hugh Brandt as much as you appeared to?"

"He's fascinating. Life in South America must be thrilling."

"Considering trying it?"

"I haven't been invited—yet. Having answered all these questions I will now return to the game house."

"No. You're staying here. I need your advice. I'm losing my homemaker. Mrs. Sophy is going to Argentina."

"Molly B. told me. This is where the girl in the Pacific theater should step into the picture."

"I'm goin' to Louisi-an-a my true love for to see"—the song came clearly through the soft air.

"Settle down. You act like a Marathon runner with one foot forward waiting for the start gun. You're not going." He swung her to the top of the terrace wall, threw the green stole across her shoulders. "Sit here and listen. That girl is here."

"Here? In this town?"

"Yes."

"Where is she?" Her breathless voice wasn't so good. She must steady it. "Why didn't you bring her to the party? You're not ashamed of her, I hope."

"Ashamed, where did you get that crazy idea? To me she is everything in the world and a bit of heaven." He coughed as if to clear his husky voice. "She's coming later. What do you think of presenting her as my fiancée when we go in to supper?"

"Perfect. What a sense of the dramatic you have. It would be worth a fortune on Broadway. Does Molly B. know of your plan?"

"I had to consult her. Want to see the picture of my true love—with a bow to 'O, Susanna'?"

"Can't wait."

"If you feel as bored as your voice sounds—"

"Don't be foolish. I'm not bored. I'm tremendously interested." From the game house floated the opening bars of "Pop Goes the Weasel." Then a voice, *Take partners for the Virginia Reel!"*

"Hurry, please, Tim. I must go back. This dance is promised." He slipped his hand inside the breast of his coat. "Do you carry her picture over your heart?"

"In it. Here she is." He held out a clipping from a magazine. "It doesn't do her justice but it will give you an idea."

It was a picture in color of a starry-eyed, dark-haired girl in white organza with a string of lustrous pearls about her lovely throat and a huge spray of white lilacs and freesias in her arms. Beneath was the caption:

"Miss Deborah Randall."

"Where did you get this?" Her steady voice was a triumph of will over emotion.

"Found it in Mother's diary months ago. Adorable, isn't she?"

"That was taken at the coming-out ball Molly B. gave for me in Washington the Christmas vacation of my freshman year. That girl looks too young, too glamorish, her eyes are full of star dust."

"I won't permit criticism of the girl I love." He slipped the clipping into his pocket. "The first time I saw the picture I knew what I wanted. From the moment I crashed into the original on the stairs I determined to have her for my wife." He swept her from the terrace wall to her feet and drew her close. "In words of one syllable, I love you, Deb. Look at me. You don't see a glint of gold in my eyes, do you?"

"Don't you ever forget the foolish things I say, Marine?"

"Once you called me 'Tim darling,' I haven't forgotten that." He kissed her. As if the touch of her lips had set his blood on fire he kissed her again, passionately, possessively. "Say you love me, Debby."

Head against his arm she laughed up at him through tears. "How can I? You don't give me a chance. I love you, Tim. Believe me?"

A prolonged fanfare cut off his whispered answer. Peals of laughter, a burst of clapping floated past on a balsam-scented breeze. *"Change partners,"* someone called. Tim's arms tightened around her.

"No 'change partners' for us, right, darling?"

She felt as if her heart welled up into her eyes as they met his, steady, demanding.

"Not so long as I live, Tim."

"Come on," he cleared his husky voice, "I don't want to, but we'd better go in. Shall we tell Molly B.?"

"You said she knew."

184

"I said she knew I loved you. She doesn't know that you —care."

"Oh, doesn't she? Something tells me that our internationally famous author had this finale plotted last September." She slipped her hand into his. "Let's ask her."